Little Village of Second Chances

Little Village of Second Chances

Gina Hollands

Where heroes are like chocolate – irresistible!

Published 2020 by Choc Lit Limited

Penrose House, Crawley Drive, Camberley, Surrey GU15 2AB, UK

www.choc-lit.com

A CIP catalogue record for this book is available
from the British Library

ISBN 978-1-78189-460-6

Printed and bound in Great Britain
by Clays Ltd, Elcograf S.p.A.

For my mum, Janet Harrison

Acknowledgements

A big thank you to my lovely, eagle-eyed friends, Sarah
Rhodes and Alfie Collens, who gave valuable feedback
on my manuscript in the early days. And special thanks
to Martin Taylor for the many conversations had
(mainly over cheese and wine), allowing me insight
into the fire service and what it feels like to get very,
very hot indeed – any errors are entirely my own.
Thank you to Juliet West, friend and author
extraordinaire, for her excellent proofreading
skills and all-round inspiration.

And where would I be without my wonderfully
efficient editor at Choc Lit, who helped me make
this book the best it could possibly be.

Buckets of gratitude also to the Choc Lit team, not to
mention the marvellous Tasting Panel, without whom
Sarah and Shay would never have materialised into
anything other than figments of my imagination: Michele
Rollins, Donna Morgan, Cordy Swinton, Vanessa
Wick, Bee Master, Alma Hough, Nikki Malam, Joy
Saunders, Rachel Masters, Janice Butler, Jo Osborne,
Jenny Mitchell, Hilary Brown, Luise Piri, Carol
Dutton, Wendy Stevens, Gill Leivers, Sharon Walsh.

And thank you to The Boys, Wayne and Rocco, who put
up with my incessant musings and relentless 'book talk'.

You are all fabulous.

Chapter One

Sarah stared down the black barrel of the gun, her feet rooted to the ground. *I could slam the door in his face. But what if he pulls the trigger before I get a chance? No. Stay put. Act calm.*

Slowly, she raised her hands. 'Wh-what do you want? There's nothing here of any worth. Just take whatever you want and leave me alone.'

The man frowned.

She lifted her gaze from the gun barrel to his face. He was craggy, scruffy even. Yes, definitely in need of a good brush-up. *I should get a good look at him in case I survive long enough to give the police a description.* The thought made her swallow hard and focus.

Mid-brown hair; unkempt. Brown eyes. Wait, not brown – blue, but so dark you could barely tell. Facial hair. Too much facial hair, come to think of it. Old sweater that had seen better days. Looked like he'd been rolling around in a field. Big, big guy. Head and shoulders above her five-foot-six frame. He was so tall that she had to tip her head up and squint against the yellow winter sun to get a good look at him.

Upon closer inspection he wasn't as old as she first thought. A decade older than her twenty-five years at most. Deep, angry lines slashed across his forehead giving the impression of a much older man, but the skin on his cheeks was smooth.

His face was tanned, even though it was January and freezing. White lines fanned out like sunrays from the corners of his eyes, suggesting at some point he must have laughed. By the mean look on his face, she couldn't imagine it. He sure wasn't laughing now.

'Take what I want? What are you talking about?'

He had a distinctive accent. What was it – Scottish? She searched her mind to place it. Irish – that was it. She must remember when giving evidence. *God, let me live to give evidence.*

She should have kept the door on the chain when she heard the knock rather than throw it open to welcome her new visitor. Hindsight was a wonderful thing.

Tentatively, she lowered her arms, clutched the edge of the door and took a step backwards. 'Well, if you're not here to steal from me, what *do* you want?' No sooner had she uttered the words than the answer hit her with a sickening thump. *He's going to attack me!*

With a sudden shove she swung the door with enough force to slam it shut. To her horror, the bottom of the door rebounded off something on the floor and sprang back. She put her hands out just in time to stop the heavy wood hitting her in the face, and looked down to see one of his huge, filthy boots over the threshold.

That was it. She was done for. She screamed.

'Calm down, will you?' His voice was low and gruff. He stretched out an arm towards her.

She flapped her arms in front of her to bat him away. 'No, no, get off me. Leave me alone!' Blood rushed through her head as newspaper headlines of a woman killed at her own front door flashed past her eyes. 'Don't shoot!'

'Shoot?' He raised his eyebrows and took a step backwards.

With his foot now out of the way of the door, she might just manage to close it. She lunged forward.

'It's not a gun – it's a speed detector,' he said, with a voice far too calm to come from a firearm-wielding perpetrator.

She paused, her hands poised above the door handle. 'What?'

He turned the black device around in his hand and jabbed his finger at the digital display. 'Thirty-five miles per hour.

The limit in the village is thirty. You were speeding. Breaking the law.'

She stared at him and blinked several times. Her heart was still beating like a jackhammer on overdrive. 'I'm sorry. Is this some kind of joke?'

He snarled and narrowed his eyes. 'There's nothing funny about endangering lives.'

She thrust her hands onto her hips. 'And there's nothing funny about scaring people half to death. I thought you were going to kill me!'

He lowered the gun to belt level and held it loosely in both hands. Even in his thick, woollen sweater she could see the outline of large, muscular arms. They weren't the kind of pumped-up muscles achieved from going to the gym, but rather from hard, physical labour.

'How do you propose I could kill someone with a Velocity Radar 360?' he said.

She closed her eyes and took a deep breath in, before releasing the air slowly to try to calm herself. She couldn't quite believe what she was hearing. 'Hang on. Let me get this right.' She pressed her fingers to her temples and released a humourless laugh. 'I move in here less than thirty minutes ago, and my first visitor is a man pointing a gun at me accusing me of speeding.'

'You *were* speeding.'

'What on earth has my driving got to do with you exactly?'

A shadow passed over his face. 'I'm trying to make this village a safer place to live.'

She gritted her teeth. 'I was only going thirty-five for goodness sake. It's not exactly Lewis Hamilton speed, is it?'

His eyes darkened. 'Yeah, well, it may not seem like a big deal to you, but maybe if you'd seen what I've seen, you'd realise that five miles per hour can make all the difference.' He tensed his jaw and appeared to look right through her.

The intensity of his expression shocked her and, as his words sank in, she held back from accusing him a second time of meddling. *What is he – a paramedic?* If that were the case, perhaps she had been a bit harsh. He must have seen more than his fair share of accidents. No wonder he was sensitive about speeding.

A paramedic though, really? Didn't you need a good bedside manner for that? She couldn't picture him sharing a sympathetic word with anyone. And – she ran her gaze down his bulk – you certainly didn't get a muscular body like that from driving an ambulance. His physique more resembled that of a builder who'd been wrestling a wheelbarrow through mud all morning.

'Okay, look, I'm sorry I was speeding. I really am. I'm normally very careful on the roads, I just—' She shut her mouth quickly. What was she about to tell him – she had a lot on her mind? That was an understatement. And like this do-gooder stranger would care what was going on in her life anyway.

She gave up trying to finish her sentence and sighed. This wasn't how she imagined her first day in the picturesque village of Wetherstone-on-Ouse would be. A friendly, elderly neighbour knocking on her door with a freshly baked cake as a welcome, perhaps, but not some oversized oaf criticising her driving.

Even though it was less than ten miles from her home city of York, Wetherstone, with its country lanes, chocolate-box cottages and mediaeval pub, felt like the back of beyond. Thank goodness. She'd needed to get away. She couldn't have carried on where she was for much longer. Not after everything that had happened.

'Fine.' His gruff voice reminded her he was still on her doorstep. 'Just make sure you're more careful next time.'

Honestly, the cheek of it! She'd already apologised, and now he thought he had the right to bark orders at her while standing on *her* property. 'Haven't you seen the signs all around the village?' she said. 'They're building a new bypass around here, and not before time if it means that people like you will stop terrorising single women by hiding in bushes and pointing your'—she gestured at his gun—'radar sixty-three, or whatever you call it, at them.'

He wiped the back of his arm roughly across his face. 'What this village needs isn't a new road where drivers can go even faster, it's a better awareness of what's safe. Not that the bypass proposal is even worth discussing. There's no way the people around here are going to stand back and let their homes and businesses be flattened so that some big conglomerate can shove three miles of tarmac in and make a few million quid in the process just because they're planning on building new homes on the outskirts.'

She shifted her gaze, hoping her eyes gave nothing away. 'Listen, Mister …?' She let her voice trail off, inviting him to fill the gap.

Without offering his name, he raised an eyebrow and continued to look at her.

'Well, whatever. This is my first day in my new home. I wasn't expecting a welcome committee, but nor was I expecting—' She held out her hand at him. 'This!'

He thrust a pointed finger at her. 'If you don't start watching your speed and treating this village with the respect it deserves, then I won't be the only one making you feel unwelcome.'

Her heart began to pound again. This time from anger. 'If you've got nothing pleasant to say, then you can take your speed gun and get off my property.'

He muttered something she couldn't make out, and started to walk away, his heavy boots crunching on the gravel drive. 'Slow down, Miss Pickering. Before you or someone else gets hurt.' He made his parting shot without bothering to turn back around to face her.

Unable to think of a suitable retort quickly enough, she stuck out her tongue at his retreating back. She went to close the door, but a thought occurred to her, and she leaned out to shout after him. 'Wait, how do you know my name?' But he was gone.

Shay shoved his bulk against the farmhouse door to force it open. He stepped inside the warm kitchen and was greeted by a pair of big, brown eyes. 'Sorry girl, didn't mean to scare you. Just more wound up than I should be by that woman who's moved into Ouseside Cottage.' He drove a hand through his wind-knotted hair, and winced when it snagged.

Tail wagging, his Border collie, Bess, bounded over to him and shoved her wet nose into his outheld palm. He gave her head a scratch, grateful, not for the first time, for her unconditional love.

He'd adopted Bess from the local animal shelter not long after he moved to Wetherstone. One of his first customers, Jane, who also happened to volunteer at the dogs' home, had practically begged him to foster a young Border collie for a few weeks, just while she waited for a new forever-home to present itself. Jane had thought McGillen's Farm would be the perfect place for a nervous dog, who had been terribly mistreated, to regain her confidence and rebuild her trust in humans.

Not wanting anyone – or anything – to shatter his isolated existence, Shay refused at first, but when Jane turned up unannounced at the farm with an undernourished, pathetic-looking Bess by her feet, there was no way he could turn the dog away. He could still remember her huge, terrified brown eyes looking up at him with a mixture of fear and hope. He'd reached out to stroke her, but she'd cowered away, her bony legs quivering despite the summer heat.

Jane warned him Bess might take a while to come to him, as whatever abuse she'd been subjected to had left her scared to death, especially when men were around. Jane had been right. In the beginning, Bess didn't trust him enough to go anywhere near him, let alone be stroked. He couldn't bear to think what horrors his poor girl had been through at the hands of a fellow human to make her so fearful.

As it turned out, the number of families in the market for a quivering wreck of a dog, who had no desire to be petted, was non-existent. When, after three months, no one wanting to give Bess a forever-home had come forward, Shay offered to keep her. Jane was ecstatic to have found the dog a good home, and Shay was, quietly, too. Although he thought he craved total isolation, the reality of rattling around the farmhouse by himself again, after getting used to Bess's nervy but reassuring company, wasn't a prospect he was looking forward to.

On the very same day he told Jane he'd keep Bess, the dog came up to him, nuzzled his leg and allowed him to stroke her. It was as if she knew she'd finally found someone who loved her. She'd been his best buddy ever since. His only buddy these days.

If only relationships with humans were as straightforward. The thought brought his mind back to Wetherstone's newest resident, and his heart plummeted to the tiled kitchen floor. With her big blue eyes, fair skin and spatter of freckles, Sarah Pickering was the picture of innocence. 'Straight in from the city no doubt, thinking country life's a bed of roses,' he said to himself. *How deceiving looks can be.* He shook his head, pushing away the image of her angelic features.

He sat on the floor, and leaned against the Aga. The heat from the metal door soaked into his back. He closed his eyes, allowing the tension between his shoulder blades to ease. 'Missed anything while I've been gone, Bess?' He stroked her velvety ears, and she yawned, then lay her head on his thigh. 'No, thought as much.'

His gaze fell on a brown parcel on the kitchen table.

'Urgh, forgot to take that with me to the cottage.' He gently nudged Bess out of the way, stood up and went over to the table. He read the typed black text on the parcel. 'Miss Sarah Pickering, Ouseside Cottage. I can hardly go around there again, can I, old girl? Not when I scared her half to death just now.'

He ran a hand over the coarse hair on his chin, realising just how in desperate need of taming it was. Vanity wasn't exactly his top priority these days. *I must have looked like a wild man turning up at her door.* Despite his annoyance at her irresponsible driving, guilt pricked at him. Through her eyes, he could have come across as menacing; an unkempt stranger chastising her on her own doorstep.

He looked over at Bess. Sometimes he wished she could talk back and tell him what to do. God knows, she probably thought straighter than he did most of the time. His black and white confidante sank down to her haunches.

'No, you're right. Why am I feeling bad when it was she who was in the wrong?'

The dog turned her head and licked her lips.

'It's okay, I understand. You're more concerned about your stomach than me improving relations with my new neighbour. Don't worry, I haven't forgotten your dinner. I'll get to it straight after I've been to the Post Office. I need to blow off the cobwebs after my first meeting with the less-than-charming Miss Pickering.'

He tucked the package under his arm and spotted a white envelope on the table that he hadn't noticed before. 'What's this?' It must have been caught up in the underside of the parcel. He placed the parcel back on the table, pulled out a chair and sat down. 'This had better not be another …' He picked up the envelope and turned it over. It was official-looking, just as the others had been, and had the same York City post mark. With one finger, he ripped it open and pulled out a single white sheet of paper.

He scanned the words and slammed his fist down on the table, making Bess jump. 'They think they can offer me more money and I'll give in. I've already refused four times!'

He stared at the figure printed in bold on the paper. It was almost double what the farm was worth. No wonder some of the locals were faltering, and how could he blame them? He didn't need the money but many of them did. So far, no one in the village had accepted the offers made by LJ Networks to buy their properties and enable the city-based conglomerate to build the bypass through the village where their homes and businesses lay, but now the offers were becoming more and more generous, he'd heard a few were having second thoughts.

When the first letter arrived all the locals had rallied together to oppose the plans for the new road. They were as adamant as him: no one was going to steamroller over their lives. But now the stakes were higher ...

A new start with an injection of cash could really help some of the villagers out. Not him. It had taken every ounce of what little strength he had left to drag himself from rock bottom and set up a new life for himself in Wetherstone. He couldn't survive being forced to uproot after everything he'd been through. He had to fight. If not for himself, then for Clodagh.

He squeezed his eyes shut and tried to picture Clodagh, but after five years the image was fading. Sometimes, as he was falling asleep, he thought he heard her voice call his name, as clear as if she were lying next to him. Other times, like today, when he tried to summon her in his memory, all he could manage was a blurred vision of her face. The vision would be mute, for he couldn't remember how her voice sounded. In his mind, her mouth mimed his name, but his ears were deaf to her words.

God knows things hadn't been perfect between them, far from it. For some reason that made what happened even harder to bear. If he'd have been a better husband; a kinder one, who was more understanding, more romantic, more … Just *more*, then perhaps none of it would have happened. Perhaps he'd still have his family, still be in touch with his in-laws, who had been like parents to him when his own had died, still live in Ireland. Perhaps he'd still have some damned self-respect.

'Clodagh,' he whispered. 'Give me the strength to carry on fighting this. For you. And Elsie.' At the sound of his own voice saying her name he snapped his eyes open. *No. Don't think about Elsie.* He didn't have the headspace for any more dark thoughts today.

He stood up, sending the wooden chair flying backwards. Without stopping to pick it up, he grabbed the parcel from the table and headed for the door.

Sarah closed the door and looked down at the cardboard box she'd been about to empty before the arrival of her unwelcome visitor. 'Aargh!' she cried out into the empty hallway.

Unpacking hadn't seemed such a daunting task before her run-in with the grumpy giant. Now, she felt exhausted. Their heated exchange had left her void of all energy. She couldn't get the image of him, all scowling and stormy-eyed, out of her head. There was something about the way he'd looked right through her when he'd talked about what he'd seen that sent a shiver down her spine.

She folded her arms across her chest and rubbed her upper arms. 'I'm probably just frozen to the core.' She hadn't had a chance yet to figure out how the gas heating worked in the new cottage, and the temperature couldn't be higher than three degrees – inside and out. The instructions she'd been left hadn't worked. She'd been about to look up a number for a plumber when she'd been so rudely interrupted by that awful man.

'Oh, hello, Clive. Managed to get your bearings yet?' She bent down and held out her hand. The ginger tom trotted over, his white-socked paws tapping on the wooden floor. He nuzzled his head into her arm, and purred as she stroked him.

'I'm glad I've got you to love me,' she said. Clive's soft fur against her skin instantly eased the throb of pain that had started to build in her temples. 'Hopefully we won't be seeing that horrible man again anytime soon.'

Clive cocked his head as if he were really listening to her. She laughed. 'You know, sometimes it feels like you're the only one who really gets me.'

He hooked a white paw over her arm.

'We'll have a cuddle in front of the telly later, I promise, but for now'—she looked over at the cardboard box—'I really need to do something useful.'

She freed her arm from Clive's paw, careful not to let his claws scratch her, and slid her hands into the holes on the sides of the cardboard. She grunted as she lifted the heavy load. 'Come on, Clive. Why don't you keep me company while I get this done?' He looked up at her and twitched his whiskers as if considering her offer, then darted off in the opposite direction.

'Well, at least I know where I stand.' Using her knee, she heaved the box up to chest height. 'Although you might do well to remember who feeds you!'

She struggled into the living room, which, apart from a single armchair, a chest of drawers and a TV, was bare. Not that it mattered. She'd only be here for a maximum of three months before her part in the new bypass was completed, and she'd move on to the next project.

She'd practically begged Duncan, her boss at LJ Networks, to send her on location. He'd been reluctant at first. After five years of having her based in the office he'd grown to rely on her to help him get organised, but she'd been adamant, and she could be very persuasive when something really mattered to her. And this job was going to require some serious persuasive skills.

The mediaeval buildings and narrow cobbled streets of York that she'd always loved, had started to close in on her, contracting tighter and tighter until she could no longer breathe. It wasn't the city itself, she knew that. It was what had happened there. What she'd *let* happen. All she had left to live for was her job, so she might as well throw herself into it with everything she had.

Arms shaking slightly with the weight, she lowered the box to the floor. She pulled open the folds of the lid, releasing the musty smell of cardboard, and peered inside. Seeing the contents, she swallowed hard and blinked rapidly. She was *not* going to cry. Moving to Wetherstone was meant to mark a fresh start, not just a new place to feel miserable. She'd had her fill of that recently.

Inside the box, the silver clasp on the lid of the vintage cream jewellery box glinted in the light. As she fingered it, a ribbon of bittersweet memories trailed behind her eyes. Her mum's beaming smile as Sarah unwrapped the beautiful gift on the morning of her sixteenth birthday ... the sound of the soft *swish* the lid made when she opened it and saw the awe in her own eyes reflected in the tiny mirror ... pieces of costume jewellery scattering across her bedroom carpet as the handle broke when she'd grabbed the box in haste ... her mum shouting, begging her not to leave.

She sniffed and blew out a stream of air. No tears, especially today. No tears.

Taking the jewellery box with both hands as she hadn't yet fixed the handle, she pulled it free from the cardboard container, and put it to one side. She saw what lay beneath and caught her breath. Carefully, she pulled out the object. It was a novelty fluffy purple frame, inside which was a photograph. It had stood on her dressing table for years, making her grin every time she looked at it, but this time, there was no grin on her face, only a quivering chin she couldn't still.

Two pairs of matching bright blue eyes shone back at her. She loved this photo. It made her realise how alike they both were. She hugged the frame tight to her chest, then released it, worrying she'd crease the picture inside. She hoped one day she could look at the photo and remember the good times, rather than focusing on how it had all ended, which is exactly what her counsellor had said she should try to do, and one of the reasons why this move to Wetherstone had come at exactly the right time.

Chapter Two

'Ah, now then, let me guess. You wouldn't be Sarah Pickering by any chance, would you?'

Sarah caught her breath as the middle-aged woman grinned at her from behind the Post Office counter. *How come everyone around here knows who I am?*

As if reading her mind, the woman laughed. Her appearance wasn't what Sarah would have expected of a village Post Office mistress. She had short white-blonde hair in a ruffled style, with dyed bright pink ends. She wore an oversized fluffy pink jumper in the same shade, embellished with sparkles, and a small diamond stud in her nose.

'Don't look so worried, love,' the post mistress said in a local accent. 'Everyone knows everyone in Wetherstone.' She laughed again, causing her long, dangly earrings to jangle. 'I'm Barb by the way.' She held out a hand adorned with large silver rings and tipped with bright pink nails as sparkly as her jumper.

Sarah shook her hand. 'Pleased to meet you. I'm Sarah Pickering.' She smiled. 'But you seem to know that already.'

'Ah, yes, my love. That's because I have *this* for you.' Barb's voice strained with effort as she reached over to a shelf behind the counter and pulled out a parcel wrapped in brown paper. She placed it down on the counter. 'See,' she said, pointing to the address label. 'Miss Sarah Pickering, Ouseside Cottage. That'll be you, presumably?'

'Yes, that's me.' Sarah relaxed her shoulders. She had started to wonder whether somehow the villagers had caught wind that a representative from LJ Networks had arrived on the scene. Duncan had warned her they might not be too welcoming if they realised early on in the project who she was. She'd brushed aside his concerns at the time. Once the locals learned how generous the offers to vacate their premises were, they'd be all for the bypass.

The thought of the grumpy giant from earlier and his hatred for the bypass made her heart race. Her reaction surprised her. She wasn't normally the type to dwell on things, but something about him sent her pulse into overdrive. Anger, she told herself. She should probably be relieved her emotions were starting to return. She hadn't felt anything for weeks, not since—

'Are you all right, my love?'

Barb's voice snapped her back to the present. The post mistress was leaning on the counter, a frown denting her forehead.

Sarah felt her cheeks grow hot. 'Oh, yes, I'm fine, perfectly fine. I just, um, wondered why the parcel wasn't delivered to my cottage. I've been in all day unpacking.'

Barb's bright smile returned. 'George Davenport has been delivering the post around here for over fifty years. We all love him to bits, but he's getting a bit doddery these days, bless him. He delivers more post to the wrong houses than he does the right ones.' She patted the top of the parcel. 'This one found its way to McGillen's Farm. You've got Shay to thank for making sure it got to you safely. He brought it down here not long since.'

'Shay?'

'Shay McGillen. Your new neighbour, well *closest* neighbour anyway. Your cottage is out on a limb there, tucked away on that lovely spot by the river but, technically speaking, Shay lives next door. He owns McGillen's Farm.'

McGillen's Farm. The top of LJ Network's target list – and therefore my target list. 'Oh. That was kind of him. I wonder why he brought it here rather than dropping it around to me at the cottage. It would have been closer for him.' She imagined an ageing farmer traipsing all the way down the hill with her parcel and felt heartened at his efforts. Perhaps there was only one unfriendly resident in the village after all.

'You can ask him yourself, love.' Barb looked over Sarah's shoulder and nodded. 'Here he comes now.'

The bell above the shop door chimed to mark the entrance of a new customer. Sarah turned and smiled, ready to meet old farmer McGillen – but as soon as she saw that messy brown hair, trademark scowl and beard-covered chin, her smile faded.

'Hi there, Shay, love. Back again? Forget something, did you? We were just talking about you. This is Sarah Pickering, the lady who's just moved into Ouseside Cottage. Your new neighbour by all accounts.'

Sarah's mouth dried instantly. Now she understood why he'd brought the parcel to the Post Office rather than her cottage. To avoid her, no doubt. Their first meeting had been fraught enough; he could hardly turn up again with a package in hand as if nothing had happened.

Shay walked over next to where Sarah stood and, without even glancing in her direction, swung a loaf of bread onto the counter and handed Barb a stack of coins. 'We've met.'

He doesn't reserve gruffness just for me then.

Barb continued to chat easily to him, seemingly unaware of any awkwardness. *Maybe the people around here are so used to him being rude, they don't think about it anymore.*

The shop aisle was narrow and there was barely enough space for two normal sized people to stand side by side, let alone one normal person and one who would give Goliath a run for his money. Jammed in next to him, she didn't have the room to get out of his way, so instead she squeezed her arms tightly to her sides and breathed in, trying to make herself as small as she could, just to get out of his way. Even then, his large arm pressed against hers. Despite the cold weather, he'd come out in just a T-shirt. No sign of the woollen jumper he'd been wearing earlier at her door. She found herself wondering what he'd been doing between his visit to her door and now, to make him take it off. Despite his lack of clothing, the heat from his body seeped into hers, all the way through her coat and three layers of clothes.

Barb's continuous friendly natter faded into the background as Sarah became lost in her own thoughts. It wasn't a great start, finding out her number one target was the same guy she'd had a run-in with. And that was putting it lightly. She'd have her work cut out if she was going to turn him around.

If anyone can do it, you can, Pickering. I'm counting on you. She could almost predict what Duncan's words would be when she checked in with him on their scheduled call later today. She was due to report on how the move was going, and her strategy for lobbying locals' support. A challenge which might be harder than she'd initially thought.

It wasn't Barb saying goodbye to Shay that made Sarah aware of him leaving, but the sudden coldness that enveloped her when he moved his body away. The bell over the door chimed once more as he closed it behind him.

'Man of few words, isn't he?'

'Oh, don't mind him, love. He hasn't always had it easy, poor lad, but he's got a good heart, which is the main thing. Oh damn, I forgot!' Barb clapped her hands to her cheeks.

'What's the matter?'

'The butcher closes at midday on Wednesdays.' She glanced at her wrist. 'That's in fifteen minutes and I can't leave the shop unattended.' She slid her hand down her face and fiddled with one of her dangly earrings. 'Oh well, never mind. I promised Mum I'd take her round a pound of mince tonight for shepherd's pie, but she'll have to make do with whatever she's got in the freezer.'

Barb's crestfallen look tugged on Sarah's heartstrings. She knew only too well what it was like trying to look after your mum, even though her own experiences of caring for her mother were more about her emotional needs than what she had for dinner. She cast a quick glance at her watch. She had time to help. Besides, it would be a good excuse to go and meet the butcher, whose business would also need to relocate once work started on the bypass.

'Or I could nip across to the butcher's for you now, before they close?'

'Oh no, I couldn't ask you to do that for me, love. I'm sure you've got a million and one things to be getting on with.'

'Honestly, I don't mind,' Sarah said. 'We can't have your mum disappointed. If the lady's got her heart set on shepherd's pie, then that's what she must have.'

Barb's laughter rang out. 'Well, if you're sure you don't mind?'

'Not at all. In fact, you'd be doing me a favour. I could do with a good reason to put off unpacking. It's so dull!'

'Fantastic. You're a diamond. Now, just let me get you some brass.' Barb pulled out her handbag from underneath the counter and started fishing around inside. 'Come on now, where's that bloody purse? I know it's in here somewhere.' She extracted a pack of tissues, two lipsticks, a pocket diary and a TV remote control.

'Um, how about we sort it out once I've got the mince?' Sarah suggested.

'Yes, yes, good idea.' Barb began cramming the miscellanea back in her bag. 'If that's all right with you. We might be here all day otherwise. I've got all manner of crap in here.'

'No problem,' said Sarah, spinning on her heel. There could only be ten minutes left. 'Where's the butcher's?'

'Oh, just a bit further along the road, on this side.' Barb pointed in the general direction. 'You can't miss it.'

Sarah spotted the butcher's almost immediately. The red and white striped canopy, under which crates of colourful vegetables stood, gave it away easily, as did the chalkboard advertising local Wetherstone bangers. As she drew closer, she realised that the butcher's shop took up only some of the space of what looked to have originally been one larger property. The other section, the one closest to her, was a tiny but gorgeous florist.

She slowed her pace as she reached the florist's shop. The sweet scent of freshly cut lilies and roses collided in her nostrils and for a fraction of a second took her back to a happy time back home in York. Her mum hadn't known her gerberas from her gardenias, but had loved having a vase of fresh flowers in the kitchen, and had treated herself to a bunch whenever she could afford to. When she was little, Sarah had spent ages marvelling at the petals' delicate veins, wondering how something so pretty and flimsy could create such a beautifully potent smell.

She admired the evergreens displayed out the front before her gaze travelled to the window display – an explosion of winter jasmine and snowdrops – and finally through the window into the shop where, who else but Shay McGillen should be stood at the counter talking to a young woman wearing a green apron. His bulky, masculine form looked slightly ridiculous in the quaint, pretty shop.

Does he actually have a wife, or a girlfriend? It was a surprise, considering the huge chip he seemed to have on his shoulder, but he must. Why else would he be in a florist's?

The woman in the apron laughed at something he said, then smoothed a finger down her fringe and adjusted the messy bun on top of her head.

Flirting with the florist when buying flowers for his other half. Classy. Very classy.

Sarah's presence must have caught the attention of the florist, because the young woman turned her head to the direction of the window. Before Sarah had time to move, Shay looked over too, meeting Sarah's eyes.

Oh, no. She managed a small smile and nodded, then scurried next door into the butcher's. In her haste, she tripped over a crate of cabbages, propelling herself into the door. The smell of raw meat that greeted her, mixed with the pain of her ankle, made her feel momentarily sick.

'Ouch.' She hooked her injured ankle behind her other leg and rubbed it up and down her calf to try to stem the pain.

'Steady there, Miss.'

'Are you all right?'

She looked up and saw two identical, concerned expressions behind the counter. Both belonged to long, slim faces that were topped with sandy blonde hair styled into fashionable crops.

Oh God, I must have hurt myself more than I thought. I'm seeing double.

'What can we get you?' said two voices in harmony.

Woah. This is too weird.

'Um, a pound of lamb mince, please.'

'Pound of mince coming up.' One of the figures reached down for the tray of mince behind the glass counter, while the other headed for the till.

Twins. She breathed out heavily. *Thank goodness. I thought I was having a funny turn.*

The twin at the till pressed a few buttons, then turned to her and smiled. 'Haven't seen you around here before, love. Are you new to the village?'

'That's right.' She was about to say more as a blonde woman in a fleece, jodhpurs and riding boots blustered in. 'Tim, Tom, help me please. I have an urgent need for sausages and yours are by far the best for miles around! Oh, sorry. Hi there. Didn't mean to butt in,' she said when she saw Sarah.

Sarah laughed. 'No problem. It sounds like your need is greater than mine.'

'Like you wouldn't believe,' said the woman. 'Got the mother-in-law coming over for tea tonight. She's always resented me for being an awful cook. Thought her Donny could have done so much better. In the kitchen stakes at least.' She laughed, making her rosy cheeks shine.

'So ...' The blonde lady clapped her hands together. 'I'm thinking I can't go wrong with sausages. The kids like them, the husband likes them, I like them. The mother-in-law won't like them because she never likes anything I cook, but she'll just have to ruddy well like them, 'cos that's what she's getting.'

'Got some lovely pork and apple bangers in today, Julie,' said one of the twins, pointing down to a tray of strung-together sausages. 'They should do the trick.'

'Good enough, Tim.' She rifled through her pocket and pulled out a teabag.

What was it with women in this village carrying around strange items?

Sarah pointed at Julie's other, bulging pocket. 'Um, I think it might be in that one.'

'Oh yes, silly me.' Julie tugged out a black purse, popped it open and pulled out a bank card.

'There you go, ladies.' One of the butchers handed Sarah and Julie a brown paper bag while the other dealt with their payments.

Julie tucked her paper bag under one arm, and held out her other hand for Sarah to shake. 'Julie Flynn, pleased to meet you. My husband Donny and I own the racehorse training place up Stable Street.'

'Sarah Pickering. Nice to meet you.'

'Sarah's new to the village,' said Tim and Tom in unison.

'Oh,' Julie drummed her fingers against her lower lip. 'You must be the lady with the red Mini.'

'That's me.'

'My youngest spotted your car this morning when I was taking the kids to school. Car-obsessed, that one. And he loves Minis.'

'He must have great taste,' Sarah said. She'd saved like mad to buy her Mini. It was her pride and joy.

'Well, it's lovely to meet you, Sarah. Come over for a cup of tea sometime if you like. It'd be good to have some human company. I love the horses, but they're not the greatest conversationalists.'

'Thanks. That's nice of you. I might just do that.'

'Good stuff. Bye Tim, bye Tom.' Julie waved at the butcher brothers, who bid them a harmonious farewell. One of them – Sarah still wasn't sure which was which – scooted around from behind the counter and held the door open for them. She wasn't used to this kind of service in the city. She said thank you as she followed Julie out.

'Good luck with your cooking tonight,' Sarah said when they were outside.

Julie sighed. 'I'm going to need it. I can't cook for toffee. Not that I care what the mother-in-law thinks, but I suppose it would be nice to have a bit more confidence in the kitchen. Give me a living, breathing horse, I'm an expert, but a joint of meat?' She sighed. 'I've not the faintest idea, unfortunately.'

Sarah could tell by the way Julie's shoulders slumped that her lack of confidence in the kitchen wasn't quite the joke she'd made it out to be a moment ago in the butcher's. Cooking had always brought Sarah so much joy. It might be fun to help Julie see it didn't have to be a chore.

'Actually,' said Sarah. 'I have a brilliant recipe for a sausage casserole, if you're interested? I'm sure I saw my recipe folder this morning when I was unpacking. It's dead easy. And quick. It was my Mum's own one. She was a really good cook.' A smile played on her lips as a short movie of her mum singing happily but tunelessly as she chopped, peeled and stirred, played behind her eyes.

'Are you kidding me?' Julie's voice cut into her memory. 'Of *course* I'm interested!' She grinned. 'It was the words *quick* and *easy* that sold it to me.'

'Tell you what,' Sarah said. 'I could get you started with the cooking if you like. It is easy, but only really if you know how and I've done it a million times before.' The offer had come out of her mouth before she'd had time to think it through. She hadn't cooked since losing her mum because she couldn't imagine it being enjoyable without company. She'd been so caught up with the idea of having a reason to get back into the kitchen again, that she had, for a second, completely forgotten why she'd been posted to Wetherstone.

What was she doing, making friends with the villagers like this? She needed to get them on-side, yes, but entering their homes and teaching them to cook was going a bit too far. She was desperately trying to think of a way to politely retract the offer when Julie's face lit up.

'Ooh, you're a darling,' Julie squealed. 'I'll get the kettle on ready. Do you know how to find us?'

Too late.

'Oh, erm, I'll look it up on my phone. Up by Stable Street you say?'

'That's right. See you shortly.' Julie half-walked and half-jogged away.

Sarah watched her go, picturing the map of the village she'd studied earlier. Stable Street wouldn't be directly affected by the bypass, so perhaps it wasn't such a big deal that she'd just agreed to show Julie how to make the recipe, and maybe she could use this afternoon as an opportunity to find out more about village culture. It could help with her work. She wouldn't tell Julie, of course, that she worked for LJ Networks – not yet, as it could scupper her plans. She hated being deceitful, but it would benefit the villagers more if she could collect some intel first. It was for the best, so she'd just have to cope with feeling uncomfortable about it for the time being.

Sarah did a one-eighty to head back in the direction of the Post Office ... just as Shay stepped out of the florist's.

Her heartbeat quickened. *Hardly surprising. A couple of hours ago I thought he was going to kill me!*

His eyes darted across to her, his expression gruff, but he said nothing.

'Hello,' she said. Even if he was going to be rude and ignore her, she didn't have to stoop to his level.

He didn't take his eyes off her, just continued to walk past. *Huh – doesn't even have the decency to look embarrassed about being so standoffish.*

Her pulse continued to tap out a rapid beat as she tramped down the hill. *Because he makes me angry*, she told herself. *Yes, we had cross words, but we're neighbours.* And more to the point, she needed to get in his good books if she was going to convince him to sell the farm. So far, Shay McGillen was the only person who hadn't welcomed her with open arms. Getting on with the other villagers she'd met hadn't been a problem – the opposite in fact. It had been a pleasure speaking to Barb and Julie, who were both lovely and such characters. Tom and Tim, whose likeness had freaked her out at first, were so polite, with a charm of their own. After just one afternoon in Wetherstone, she was already beginning to see why the people who lived here were so reluctant to move.

She'd almost reached the Post Office when the back of her head started to feel strangely warm despite the crispness of the day. She cast a glance behind her, and on the brow of the hill stood a sole figure. The sun, low in the sky, was behind him, making him nothing more than a black shape, but by his size there was no doubt it was Shay McGillen. He was still, and although she couldn't see any detail of his face, she knew those dark blue eyes were upon her. She could feel them.

She shivered. She didn't know whether it was their earlier encounter that had shaken her, or the way she caught him watching her, but something about that man made her feel decidedly unsteady on her feet.

Chapter Three

'Ah, you made it!' Barb's face lit up as Sarah swung open the door.

'Just in time,' Sarah said, holding up the brown bag.

'Ooh, you're a love.' Barb held up her purse. 'Found it. How much do I owe you?'

'Three-fifty.'

'I've only got a twenty-pound note, and there isn't enough small cash in the till – almost everyone has paid with card today. Do you have change?'

Sarah shook her head. 'No, but don't worry. I'll pop back in tomorrow. I expect I'll need some supplies by then, anyway.'

Barb smiled and lowered her purse. 'Okay, fine. I'm good for it.'

Sarah chuckled and slid the brown bag over to her. 'I'm sure you are. And it's not as if I don't know where to find you.' She grinned and began to turn away from the till. She'd better dig out that recipe and head over to Julie's as promised.

'Indeed! Better pop this in the fridge,' Barb said. 'I'll tell Mum she has you to thank for her tea. She hasn't been well recently, bless her. This will do her the world of good.'

Sarah stopped in her tracks. Thoughts of her own mum came rushing back. 'I'm sorry to hear that. Nothing serious, I hope.'

Barb's face fell. 'She's just not been herself, and her blood pressure's through the roof. She's nearly ninety, you know. I think the prospect of moving house at her age is all too much.'

'Oh?'

'Yeah.' Barb sighed. 'I don't know if you know, but there's

talk of them putting a new road through the village. It shouldn't affect you down at the cottage but everyone from McGillen's Farm to the far east side of the village has been asked to sell up. No one took it seriously at first – thought it was just some big company trying their luck – but now the planning's gone through despite our objections, the letters are coming in thick and fast and the tone of them has changed.' She sucked her teeth. 'It's a nightmare for people like my mum, who've lived in this village most of their lives. Goodness knows how they'll cope. It'll kill some of them.'

Sarah widened her eyes. 'Surely not. I would have thought we—um, the company, must be offering big sums to make it easier for people to move.'

Barb tangled one of her pink spikes around her finger. 'They're offering us money, all right, but what good is money if you haven't got your health?'

Sarah bit her bottom lip. If only she could make Barb see what a wonderful life her mother would have if she took the money. She knew the sums LJ Networks was talking about, and it would be more than enough for a beautiful cottage in another village. Plus it would cover all moving expenses. She'd have a hunt around on the internet tonight and maybe show Barb some options. That might make her realise how much better off her mum would be and then neither Barb or her mum would need to worry.

Shay smacked the steering wheel of the tractor. Damn thing never started in freezing weather like this, despite it supposedly being built for all seasons. He turned the key in the ignition and let the choking engine fall into silence. He could really do with things to go according to plan this afternoon. The shameless way that Pickering woman was strolling up and down the village, having friendly chats with the locals, left him reeling. Who did she think she was? First, tearing round the streets in her bright red Mini thinking she owned the place, then acting as if she, Miss Whiter than White, belonged here? The audacity of her.

He tried the engine again and was met with the struggling coughs of a motor that preferred a fair-weathered ride. He swore.

What was she doing here anyway?

It was slightly weird. Suspicious, even. A young, attractive woman on her own in a sleepy place like Wetherstone. Shouldn't she be out partying or something in nearby York?

Attractive? Had he really thought that? Yes, okay, he supposed she was in her own way. Curvy, he believed was the PC expression. With a pretty, somewhat cherubic face. And that long, wavy hair …

He shook his head as if doing so would force such thoughts away, and tried the engine one more time. It kick-started to life and his shoulders dropped a good three inches. *Finally.* He breathed a sigh of relief. At last he could do something productive today. He needed the distraction.

'Wow, that smells amazing.' Julie peered over Sarah's shoulder at the casserole pot she was stirring. 'You do realise I'm going to claim this as all my own work?'

Sarah poured red wine into the pot and breathed in the aroma. 'Absolutely. And don't worry, as soon as all the ingredients are in, I'll be out of your way, so no one will even know I was here. All you need to do is leave it to simmer until it thickens, et voilà, your mother-in-law will think her son's married Nigella Lawson.'

'Huh, in both their dreams,' Julie said as she laid plates on the table. 'It's so nice of you to do all this for me, Sarah.'

'That's okay. I actually really enjoy cooking.'

'I wish I did.'

'I just don't do it much now I'm living alone. There doesn't seem to be much point.'

'Well, you're very welcome to come here and cook any time you like.'

Sarah laughed.

'Seriously, though' said Julie, polishing a handful of knives and forks. 'We'd love to have you over for dinner one evening. The kids would be excited about having a guest and you can meet Donny. And I promise I won't really get you to cook. I'll do it, but it might have to be fish fingers.'

'Thanks,' said Sarah. 'That's sweet of you. I'd love to. And there's nothing wrong with fish fingers.' She washed her hands and dried them on a tea towel. 'I'd better be getting back now. I've got loads of unpacking to do.' *And some internet research for Barb.* 'Anyway, it must be close to school pickup now. I imagine you have to go and collect your kids.'

Julie threw a look to the clock on the kitchen wall. 'Shoot! You're right. I've got about ten minutes.'

'This'll be okay.' Sarah placed the lid on top of the casserole pot, untied her apron, and folded it up and left it on the side. 'Just turn the hob back on low when you're back and, like I said, leave it to simmer.'

'Wonderful. I don't know what I'd have done without you today.'

'It's really no problem. I've loved it.' And she really had.

'Hey,' said Julie. 'If you have time tomorrow, why don't we meet in the village tearoom for a cuppa? If we make it around half-three I'll bring the boys along for a treat after school.' She winked. 'I can tell you how dinner went down once they're busy chomping on their cookies.'

'Sounds good.'

'And maybe you'll get a chance to meet some of the other locals.'

'I've already met a couple.'

'Oh yes, Barb, you said. She's lovely.'

'Yes. And Shay McGillen.'

Julie raised an eyebrow.

'Why do you look like that?'

'Oh, nothing.'

'Julie?'

Julie looked down at the floor. 'No, really. I shouldn't say anything. I don't even know him that well. Probably just silly rumours, that's all.'

'Well, don't you think I should know? I *am* living next door to the man.'

Julie sighed. 'Okay, fine. I'll tell you what little I know, but I hate gossiping.'

'You're hardly gossiping. I'm having to prise it out of you, and I did ask, after all.'

'Okay, well, it's just that Donny was in the pub once, about this time last year, when Shay was in there. Apparently, he was fine one minute and the next he went berserk; shouting, swearing, barging people out of the way. Couldn't get out of there fast enough.'

Sarah's skin prickled with unease. 'Do you think someone said something to upset him?'

Julie shook her head. 'Couldn't have done. Donny said he was sat in the corner on his own, not talking to anyone.'

'What could it have been then?'

She shrugged. 'Maybe it was something to do with ...' Her voice trailed off.

'What?'

'Look, Sarah, it's all hearsay. Like I said, I don't really know Shay very well. We've passed the time of day and that's about it. Ask Barb, she knows him much better than—'

'Please, Julie. I'm living next door to the man. I really could do with knowing something about him.' *And it might help me appeal to his better nature.*

Julie zipped up her fleece and stuffed her hands in her pockets. 'All I was going to say was that his reaction in the pub might have been something to do with his past. I don't know what happened. I don't think anyone does. But I heard that something bad happened to him in Ireland, and that's why he came over here. To get away from it all.'

'I see.'

'That's all I know,' said Julie. 'You don't need to be frightened of him, though. He won't bother you. He seems to like his own company.'

'Oh, I'm not frightened.' She'd been through so much recently, that it would take more than a grumpy recluse to phase her.

'Good.' Julie smiled and patted her pockets. 'Got keys, got purse,' she murmured, then looked up at Sarah. 'And those who do know him better than me say he's got a heart of gold. Donates a lot of his profits to local charities and the village primary school, plus he dotes on that dog of his. And in my book, anyone who loves animals, must be a good sort. So, see you in the tearoom tomorrow?'

'Half-three,' confirmed Sarah. 'Looking forward to it.'

Although it took her only ten minutes to walk back to her cottage, Sarah barely remembered any of it. Her mind had been too caught up thinking about what Julie had said about Shay. *What could possibly have been so bad that he'd packed up his entire life and moved countries because of it?*

Chapter Four

'What's that?' Sarah asked, as Barb placed the tin along with a pile of coins on the shop counter in front of her.

'Money for the mince and my mum's date and walnut cake,' she said, her hot pink lips stretching across her face in a bright smile. 'I told her you'd run out to the butcher's for me yesterday and she was so grateful, she asked me to give you this.'

'That's so lovely of her,' Sarah said. She pocketed the change, peeled the lid off the tin and breathed in the sweet, buttery flavour of the fruit and nut. 'Mmm. Date and walnut is my absolute favourite. My mum used to make it all the time.' She replaced the lid. 'Please pass my thanks on to your mum for me.'

'Course, love,' said Barb whose choice of earrings today were large orange circles attached to sea-blue tassels.

'Actually, maybe she'd like to take a look at these.' Sarah drew a folder out of her shoulder bag and laid it next to the tin. 'I managed to get my printer working last night and ran off a few details of properties in nearby villages that might be suitable for your mum.' She flipped open the folder and pulled out the top sheet. 'This one especially looks lovely. It has a kitchen-diner and an en suite to the master bedroom. It's got a little garden too that would hardly need any maintenance. Look.' She pointed to the estate agent's photograph.

Barb lifted up a pair of spectacles that hung around her neck from a gold chain, and balanced them on her nose. She picked up the sheet to take a closer look. 'It *does* look lovely,' she agreed. 'Far nicer than the one she's in at the moment if truth be known.'

Sarah's spirits lifted. This is exactly why she'd wanted to do this job; to make people's lives better.

'Trouble is …' Barb placed her glasses back on her chest. 'Mum doesn't care all that much about the house. It's this village she loves. You could move her into a mansion and she wouldn't be happy. She loves Wetherstone. Always has done. Moving away would break her heart.' She gave a sad smile and handed the paper back to Sarah. 'You're a love for thinking of us though.'

'No worries.' Sarah's spirits sank down to the level of her thick socks, and she tucked the folder back into her bag.

'Goodness me. We don't normally see him twice in one week.'

Sarah looked up to see Barb's attention on something behind her. She turned around and out of the window saw a tall, broad figure with unkempt hair walking past. Once again, in her opinion, Shay McGillen was wearing far too few clothes for such a cold day.

Barb chuckled. 'Quiet lad. Lovely though, once you get to know him. He normally only comes down from the farm on Wednesdays for a few supplies. Wonder what's brought him out.' She gave a funny look that Sarah wasn't sure how to interpret, but she didn't spend too much time trying to fathom the meaning. If Shay only emerged from his farm occasionally, this could be a rare chance for her to do some important work.

She spun on her heel and darted out of the shop.

'Here, love, you've forgotten your cake!' Barb called.

'I'll be back in a sec.'

Once outside, she caught sight of Shay striding down the road. He was already at the tearoom, a hundred metres or so from the Post Office. Goodness knows how he'd got that far already. *Must be those long, toned legs.* Disappointed with herself for thinking of her number one target, and so far, number one enemy, in those terms, she pushed the thought out of her head, and jogged after him. 'Hey, Mr McGillen. Mr McGillen, wait!'

He's deliberately ignoring me, she thought, picking up speed. Finally, he turned around, sending her almost tumbling straight into him.

'I thought you were never going to stop.' She leaned forward, her hands on her knees as she panted to get her breath back. When she looked up from her bent position, she saw his face, as serious as ever, looming down at her. '*Whoo*, I'm more unfit than I thought.' She stood up and laughed, flicking her long fringe out of her eyes.

His frown didn't budge. 'What do you want?'

O-kay, you're going to be a tough nut to crack. There was no way she was going to give up, though. Now her job meant more to her than ever, she wasn't about to let a miserable man and his constantly bad mood get the better of her. She might be a huge failure when it came to her personal life, but at least she could draw confidence from being good at her job.

'Mr McGillen—'

'The name's Shay.'

'Right, yes, Shay. I wanted to say thank you for taking my parcel to the Post Office yesterday.'

'No problem.'

'I think we got off on the wrong foot earlier. I'm hoping we can start again. I'm Sarah. Sarah Pickering. How do you do?' She held out her hand.

'Nice to meet you.' Without meeting her eyes, he took her hand, gave it a cursory shake, and turned to walk away.

'Wait, wait, please.' She darted after him, taking two steps to match every one of his.

'I've got to get on,' he said, still walking, still looking straight ahead. 'I have a lot of work to do before the dark sets in.'

'Fine, but I wanted to ask you something.'

He stopped again and turned around. This time she couldn't react quickly enough to prevent herself from barging into him. His firm body felt like a brick wall against hers. 'Oops, sorry!' Despite the biting cold, she felt a flush creep up her neck. She smoothed her long, dark hair in front of her shoulders to try and conceal the blush, and looked up at him. At this close range she could see how full and even his lips were. *He'd be handsome if he didn't always look so mean.*

Yep, those deep blue eyes, hooded by dark eyebrows, flashed with irritation as he looked at her. A gust of freezing wind sent a ripple through his tousled hair. *Very handsome, in fact. Shame his face seemed to constantly be in disapproval mode. Every time I see him, he's frowning. No wonder he has a permanent deep groove in between those intense dark eyes.*

'What is it you want to ask me?' he barked. 'Be quick if you don't mind. Out here in midwinter there's only daylight till around four, and I've got a lot on my plate at the moment.'

'Would you like to come out for dinner with me tonight?' She could hardly believe how brazenly she blurted it out. She'd never asked a man out in her entire life, but then again she'd never had to convince someone to sell his farm to allow a bypass to be built. She had an important job to do and if that meant swallowing her shyness, then so be it. 'I mean, not in a *date* sort of way, of course.' She spoke quickly, remembering that he'd been buying flowers for someone yesterday. She didn't want him to think she was coming onto him. *God Forbid.* 'More in a getting-to-know-each-other-as-neighbours sort of way.'

He didn't answer, just continued to look at her, his expression unfaltering.

'To the local pub.' She pointed with her thumb up the road in the direction of The Plough with its stone frontage and gilded windows. 'Say, about seven?'

'Thanks,' he said, stuffing his hands in his jean pockets.

'But like I said, I've got a lot to do.' He turned and began once again to walk up the hill towards his farm.

She started after him, forced to break into a jog to keep up with his long strides. 'You'd be doing me a favour. The gas in the cottage isn't working properly, you see, and I haven't had time to get it sorted. I've heard the food's good in the pub, and I could really do with a hot meal in this weather.'

'The food *is* good. You'll enjoy it.'

'I'd feel a bit nervous about going on my own, especially when I'm new to the village. You know what it's like – woman on her own – people can stare sometimes.'

'You needn't worry about that. We're used to women here. They make up fifty percent of the population. And everyone in Wetherstone's perfectly friendly.'

Everyone but you, maybe. 'Please, Shay, let me buy you dinner as a way of apologising for what happened yesterday. I was stressed with the move, but there really isn't any excuse for speeding. I *am* sorry.' Her apology was genuine. She abhorred people who didn't respect the rules of the road and when she'd said she was normally such a careful driver, she'd meant it. Having a lot on her mind might be the reason for her failing to notice her speedometer creeping up but it wasn't an excuse.

Much to her relief, not least because she was starting to get out of breath again, he stopped and looked down at her. 'Okay.'

She hesitated, expecting him to say something else – such as a condition he'd accompany her as long as they didn't have to speak to one another. She blurted her words out quickly before he had a chance to change his mind. 'That's great, thank you. I'll meet you there, then.'

He narrowed his eyes. 'I thought you said you'd be nervous walking into the pub on your own.'

'Oh, yeah.' She hurriedly searched her mind for a way of covering up her faux pas. 'But I meant, if I were to *sit* on my own, which of course I won't be for long, because you'll be arriving shortly after me. Unless you get there before me of course, in which case—'

'I'll come by for you first. There are no streetlights in the village and the path's uneven. It can be dangerous walking around in the dark if you don't know the terrain.'

'That's very kind of you. If you're sure?'

'I have to pass your cottage to get to the pub,' he said, starting off up the hill once more. 'It wouldn't make sense not to stop by for you en route.'

Of course. For a moment there she'd thought he was doing something out of kindness, not logic. *How ridiculous of me!* But there was no point arguing. Not when she might actually be getting somewhere. 'Right-o. See you at seven,' she called, with a sunny voice, waving a mittened hand at his retreating back.

Sarah hugged her mug and gazed out of the tearoom window onto Wetherstone's high street. She didn't need to check the time on her phone to know it must be school pickup time judging by the number of parents bustling past with young children in tow.

Just as the stream of parents and children started to thin out, Julie, dressed in a different coloured fleece and jodhpurs to yesterday, came rushing around the corner. Two excited-looking young boys were at her sides, each clutching a hand. She spotted Sarah and grinned. Sarah grinned back and waved. Seconds later, the three Flynns bounded into the cafe, the boys clapping their hands at the sight of the treats behind the counter.

'Just let me get the boys sorted out,' Julie called over to Sarah. 'And I'll be over in a jiffy.'

'Right-o,' Sarah mouthed back. Unlike Julie, who didn't appear to mind everyone in the tearoom hearing her, she preferred to sit quietly and not be noticed.

Sarah smiled as Julie tried without much success to get a straight answer out of her boys as to whether they'd prefer milk or juice.

I wonder what kind of a mum I'd have been. She took a long gulp of her tea, swallowing the question along with the tepid liquid. She'd long since come to terms with the fact she'd never have children. Although it still hurt, it was a small price to pay for being alive and well. And it didn't stop her loving children, even if they would always belong to someone else.

Julie set an overcrowded tray down on the chequered tablecloth. 'This is Sarah,' she said to her boys. 'She's a lovely lady and a brilliant cook.' She winked at Sarah. 'And these two little monkeys,' she said, sitting down and unzipping her fleece, 'are Kenny and Jared. Say hello, boys.'

'Hi,' they said in turn, taking her in with big, hazel eyes.

'Hi there,' she said back. 'Those brownies look delicious.'

'Yeah, don't they just,' said Julie, flushed, despite the comfortable temperature in the tearoom. 'I'm sure letting them have them was a bad idea though. Their school shirts will be covered in chocolate within about ten seconds. But never mind—' She lifted a porcelain teapot off the tray and began to pour herself a cup. 'That's what washing machines are for.'

'How did it go last night?' Sarah asked once Kenny and Jared were tucking into their brownies.

Julie made an 'oo' shape with her lips and put a hand flat on the table. 'Like an absolute dream. You wouldn't believe it but—' She cast a sideways glance at her boys to check they weren't listening, then raised her hand and whispered to Sarah behind it. 'Christine actually believed I'd made the casserole myself.'

Sarah giggled. 'That's fantastic.'

'I know. She even paid me a compliment, well, if you can call it that. Said it was delicious and it was obvious I'd been listening to all the advice she'd been giving me over the years.'

Sarah covered her mouth to stifle an explosion of laughter.

'Can you believe it!' said Julie.

Kenny's chocolate-covered face looked up at his mother. 'Believe what, Mummy?'

'Never you mind, sweetheart,' said Julie.

'She's talking about Nana,' Jared advised his younger brother.

'Um, excuse me, boys,' she flicked a finger between her and Sarah. 'Grown-up conversation if you don't mind.'

'Mummy thinks Nana is annoying,' said Jared in a stage whisper.

Sarah battled to keep a straight face.

'I do not,' said Julie, pointing down to the boys' crumb-filled plates. 'Stop your ears flapping and eat your brownies.' She turned her attention back to Sarah. 'Did you manage to get more unpacking done?'

'Thankfully, yes. Making good progress now. More tea?'

'Please.' Julie nodded and slid her cup closer to Sarah.

'I need to do a supermarket shop but that can wait till tomorrow.'

'Well, if you need anything in the meantime, just let me know. We're usually pretty well stocked.'

'Thanks.' Sarah topped up both mugs then set the teapot back down on the table. 'I should be okay, though. I'm eating out at The Plough tonight.'

'Are you?' Julie added milk to her tea and took a sip. 'Who with? Got friends coming over for a visit?'

'Actually,' she began, stirring a sugar lump into her cup. 'I invited Shay McGillen to dinner.'

Julie's eyebrows shot up. 'Did you? Well, well, well. I know he's not someone you'd kick out of bed for eating biscuits, but that's pretty quick work as you only just moved in yesterday.' She raised her mug in a toast. 'I'm impressed.'

Sarah blushed furiously and quickly told Julie about her run-in with Shay and his speed gun, insisting that her invitation was nothing more than a friendly one aimed as an apology for righting her wrong. She was careful, of course, to leave out any mention of needing to get on his good side due to her involvement in the bypass. Julie was a lovely woman, and she'd tell her as soon as possible who she worked for, but it was important she didn't part with the news too soon. It could scupper her chances of winning the locals' trust.

'Good for you,' said Julie once Sarah had finished her explanation. 'It's not easy admitting you made a mistake. And it makes sense to be friends with your neighbours. Wetherstone is a lovely place, but it's small. It makes life easier if there's no awkwardness between villagers.

Sarah nodded. 'Exactly what I thought.' Guilt bit at her for not being entirely honest with Julie, but it was for the good of the villagers she was holding back the information, not because she wanted to be dishonest. As uncomfortable as it felt not being straight with her new friend, it was the first – and necessary – step to achieving what she'd come here to do. And she was nothing if not determined to make that happen.

Chapter Five

'Oh, thank you. That's just what I needed.' Sarah cupped her hands around the glass Shay placed in front of her, and breathed in the sweet and spicy aroma of cinnamon and nutmeg. She blew into the trail of steam billowing from her drink and took a tentative sip. 'I haven't had mulled wine for ages.'

He sat in the battered leather armchair opposite and took a sip from his pint of beer. White foam stuck to the dark hair gracing his upper lip.

She smiled and pointed. 'Saving that for later?'

'What? Oh.' He swiped the back of his arm across his face, removing the white moustache.

An awkward silence fell between them and she was relieved when the waitress came over to take their order. Once the waitress had left, the silence returned. Sarah made a show of looking around the pub, searching for something to comment on. Her gaze fell on a faded tapestry hung above the fireplace depicting mediaeval soldiers in battle. 'This place is ancient. It must be one of the oldest pubs in Yorkshire.'

He nodded. 'Dates back to the thirteenth century.'

'Wow. That *is* old.' She recalled Duncan mentioning the bypass would run along the front of the pub as the building couldn't be knocked down due to it being of historic interest.

He nodded again and took another sip of beer.

If I'm going to get Shay McGillen on side, I really need to get the conversation started, rather than stating the flipping obvious! 'So. How long have you lived in Wetherstone? Not since the thirteenth century, presumably.' She heard her synthetic laugh ring out, and cringed inside. Was that really the best she could do?

'Five years.'

'But you're from Ireland originally, I take it.'

'Yes.'

She bit her bottom lip and waited for him to elaborate. Instead, he looked down at the logs in the unlit fire beside them and fell silent.

'It's a bit chilly, isn't it?' It was cosy in the pub and she was a comfortable temperature, but she had to say *something*. Shay McGillen was hard work. 'Shall we ask them to put the fire on?'

'No!'

The vehemence of his reply stunned her. The people on the table next to them stopped talking and looked over, no doubt wondering what his sudden outburst was about.

'Okay, no problem,' she said in an extra soft voice, trying somehow to counteract his reaction.

She took another drink of her wine, swallowing so quickly the hot liquid scorched her throat, making her wince.

'So,' she said, smiling at him through the pain. 'You were saying?'

'Was I?' He ran a work-worn finger down a groove in the wooden table.

'Yes. About coming here from Ireland.'

'I said that already.'

'I just wondered ...' She took a deep breath in, searching her brain for a way to get the conversation flowing. So far it had been like getting blood out of a stone. 'Ireland's a long way from Yorkshire. What brought you here?'

'Just needed – wanted – to get away.'

'You must miss your family.'

He scratched hard at a patch on his head just above his ear. 'What are you, a journalist? You ask a lot of questions.'

A surge of frustration washed through her. Enough was enough. Shay McGillen was clearly out to make her evening as difficult as it could be. She placed both her palms on the table and stood up. 'Thanks for coming with me tonight, Shay, but I think I should probably go.'

He raised his eyebrows. 'But our food hasn't arrived yet.'

'All the same. I probably guilt-tripped you into accompanying me this evening. You clearly don't want to be here and I don't want to spend the next hour trying to make polite conversation with someone who looks like he'd rather be stabbing needles into his own eyes than being here with me. Let's call it a night, shall we?'

She bent down to retrieve her handbag from the patterned carpet when she felt a large, warm hand on hers. His heat shot up her arm, bathing her entire body in such a soothing glow she instantly relaxed.

'Please, Sarah, sit down.'

Something in his dark blue eyes implored her to do as he asked.

'I owe you an apology,' he said.

'Oh?'

'I probably shouldn't have come to your cottage yesterday all speed guns blazing, especially as you'd only just moved in. I can't have given you the best first impression.' He smiled, revealing an even row of teeth, which looked extra white against his tanned skin. It was the first time she'd seen him smile, and the effect was transformational. His eyes twinkled and creased at the corners, instantly changing his face from craggy and stern to breathtakingly gorgeous.

She was aware his hand was still on top of hers, and even more aware she didn't want him to move it. 'No. It's me who owes you the apology. I shouldn't have been speeding. It's really not something I usually do. I promise I'll be more careful from now on.'

He held up his glass. 'Truce?'

She sat back down. 'Truce.' She picked up her mulled wine with her free hand and clinked her glass against his.

He held her gaze – and his smile had her stomach

performing an involuntary somersault. *Oh, careful now, Sarah. Don't be like Mum – a sucker for a cute guy. Remember, he's your target number one. Target. Number. One.*

'One sausage and mash, and one chicken and leek pie.'

On the arrival of the waitress, Shay quickly pulled his hand away from hers. Sarah could have sworn she saw a blush creep up his neck, but couldn't be sure whether it was from embarrassment that he'd left his hand there too long, or from the heat emanating from their delicious-smelling food.

Once the waitress had gone, Sarah speared a corner of pastry and popped it into her mouth. 'Mmm, that's good.'

He smiled and picked up his fork. 'The food's great in here. Not that I come here much, but whenever I have done, it's always been well worth it.'

'You can't beat traditional pub grub,' she said, closing her eyes and savouring the taste. It was so long since she'd eaten a home-cooked dinner. Her mum would be furious with her. 'To have a happy soul, you need a happy tummy, Sarah Louise Pickering.' She could almost hear her saying it now, and see her wagging a wooden spoon in her direction.

Shay laughed. 'Like your food, do you?'

She opened her eyes and laughed, suddenly aware what her face must have looked like as she'd been blissfully eating. 'Oh yes.' She patted her tummy. It didn't exactly wobble, but it was hardly washboard either. 'I could never be a waif. I enjoy eating far too much!' She took after her mum in that respect. Cherrie Pickering always said men preferred to cuddle up to a woman with a few extra pounds than one who was all skin and bone. Not that Sarah tailored her diet around what the opposite sex found attractive. She couldn't imagine making that much of a sacrifice!

'Me too,' he said.

'Yes, but you have a manual job and can probably eat

43

what you like. I sit behind a desk most of the time, so could do to watch the calories a bit more.'

'Nonsense. You look great.'

His gaze ran down her body as far as the table would allow, and back up again. It was just a momentary flick of his eyes, but she noticed it nonetheless and grew hot under her jumper dress.

'Who's the cook up at the farm?' she asked, diverting his attention away from her body, even though being the object of his appreciative gaze – and she was sure it was appreciative – felt strangely pleasant.

His lips remained in an upward arc, but the twinkle in his eyes faded. 'I don't bother with cooking much.' He looked down at his plate and focused on slicing a piece of sausage. 'It seems a bit pointless when you live on your own.'

So there was no wife or girlfriend. Not living with him, anyway. In that case, who were the flowers for?

'Oh, I'm the same.' She sensed she'd touched a nerve. 'Cheese and crackers are all I have the energy for most nights.'

'Do you work long hours then? What is it you do?'

She chewed for longer than necessary while she thought how she should answer that one. It wasn't the time to tell him what she really did for a living. He'd find out soon enough, but hopefully not before she'd won him over. 'I work for a big company in York. The usual. Boardroom meetings, paperwork, pen-pushing, that kind of thing. You know how it is.'

He shrugged. 'Actually, I don't. I own a farm.'

'Oh yeah.' She laughed and put a hand in front of her mouth to spare him the sight of the forkful she hadn't quite swallowed. 'Of course, I forgot. What an idiot!'

He joined in her laughter, and she felt her shoulders relax. His laugh was *very* sexy. A husky baritone which matched his masculine appearance perfectly. Although she'd thought of this evening's dinner as the first step in completing her goals, she really was starting to enjoy Shay's company. A bit too much maybe, if she were honest with herself.

'What is it you farm?' she asked.

'Flowers.'

'Oh, I see. Do you supply the village florist?' She felt strangely relieved that he hadn't been in there with the sole purpose of flirting with the woman in the shop.

'I do,' he said. 'But the flowers I grow are edible, so florists aren't my usual market, just the local one. The villagers insist on it. They're pretty and grown locally. I think they like the exclusivity of being able to get hold of them.'

Shay's flowers, Tim and Tom's sausages. She was beginning to realise just how proud Wetherstone people were of their own.

'Edible flowers? I didn't know there was such a thing.'

'Yes, and they're more popular than ever. I generally sell to upmarket restaurants and hotels who want to impress their guests with something out of the ordinary.'

'That's really not what I was expecting you to say.'

The sparkle in his eyes returned. 'What were you expecting?'

She dabbed her lips with her napkin. 'Ooh, I don't know. You look more like you ride bulls around a field.'

'A rodeo cowboy? What – in the North Yorkshire countryside?'

He delivered the statement so deadpan, she burst out laughing. 'Well, probably not now you mention it, but what do I know about the countryside? I'm a city girl.'

'You don't say.' He was playing with her now, but from the smile that tugged at the corners of his mouth, she knew it was in good nature.

Maybe she was finally starting to break down his barriers. 'What gives it away?' she asked.

'Those shoes for a start.'

She looked down at her block heel suede boots. 'What's wrong with these? I bought them from a shop in *The Shambles*, I'll have you know.' She thought back to York's most famous and ancient shopping street. Its history and beauty were the things she missed most about the city.

'Wear those too much down Wetherstone's country lanes and you'll be the one who ends up in a shambles.'

She had to stop chewing to prevent herself from choking with laughter. 'That was a terrible joke and, by the way, this is the most sensible pair I own.'

'You might want to rethink your footwear collection then for your new life in the country. That's if you're planning on sticking around. What brings you to Wetherstone, anyway?'

'I just fancied getting out of the city. I've never lived anywhere but York and thought a change would do me good.' She hated lying. A quiver of shame crept over her and she battled for something else to say to take her mind off her deceit. 'What's the most important thing I need to know then, would you say, about living in the country?'

'Hmm, let me think.' He chewed thoughtfully. 'I know – always shut the gates.'

'What gates?'

'What gates?' That gorgeous smile, those crinkly eyes. 'Gates between fields, gates that lead to footpaths. There are gates everywhere in the country. Just remember to close them, otherwise animals can escape. Probably the worst crime you can commit in the country is leaving a gate open.'

She pulled a face. 'I hate gates in the country.'

'Why?'

'I never know how to open the bloody things, never mind shut them.'

'What do you mean you don't know how to open them? You just lift up the shutter.' He mimicked the movement with his hand.

46

'Yes, those ones are all right. It's the other ones. You know, the ones with the funny latch thing.'

He shook his head and covered his eyes with his hands, laughing. 'What an earth are you talking about?'

'You know those ...' She struggled to find the word and flicked a finger up and down to try to show him what she meant. The more she struggled, the more he laughed. 'Oh, come on, you know what I mean. The ones with the funny metal triangular things. I never know how to open them.'

'You just push them in,' he said.

'Yes but ...' She scrunched a handful of her hair and laughed, despite herself. She really hadn't set out to give him the impression she was so naïve to country life, but it was a relief to be honest about *something*. And, surprisingly, he didn't seem to be judging her for it. 'Well, let's just say I have bad memories of one of those awful contraptions.'

He leaned forward, eyes twinkling. 'What? You have bad memories of a country gate?'

'Yes!' She laughed. 'I know it sounds stupid but—'

'You've got to tell me now.'

'Okay, as long as you promise not to laugh.'

'Hmm. I'll give it a try. Depends really how this story unfolds.'

She took a deep breath in. 'It was during a school trip when I was about fourteen.'

'Tough age.'

'Yes. Especially when you make a complete idiot out of yourself.'

He swallowed a mouthful of food. 'I can't wait to hear this.'

'We were walking, on the Moors. It was chucking it down.'

'It's always chucking it down on the Moors,' he said, looking like he was enjoying this story far too much.

'And I, well, I—' She stopped talking as he began to laugh.

'Let me guess,' he said. 'You fell over the gate.'

'Oh God, it was so awful.' She started laughing too. 'It was one of the gates with the silly metal things we said about. I didn't know how to open it and thought you had to climb over, so I started climbing over and my cagoule got stuck. I ended up face first in a massive pile of cow pat.'

He was laughing so hard a tear ran down his cheek.

'Glad you find it so amusing,' she said. 'It was mortifying.'

'Sorry. I'm sorry.' But it took him a good few minutes before his laughter had subsided enough for him to resume eating.

Even though it had been highly embarrassing to recount her country fail from her teenage years, the conversation started to flow after that. He was, she thought, actually rather charming. She was beginning to see now why the florist had been so taken with him yesterday.

'Anyway, enough about me,' she said after he'd managed to prise out of her yet another embarrassing story from her youth, this time about how she'd auditioned for the lead role in the school musical *Flash Dance* only to split her trousers when she attempted a split jump. 'Tell me something about you. What inspired you to go into the edible flowers business?'

Despite not having yet finished his meal, he placed his knife and fork down on his plate as if he'd suddenly lost his appetite. 'It was actually my wife's dream originally.'

A heaviness thudded onto the pit of her stomach. 'Your wife? I thought you said you lived alone.'

'I do. Now.'

The heaviness inside her lifted. *Why am I relieved he's divorced? This is just business, nothing more.* 'Oh, I see. I'm sorry to hear that.'

She noticed a watery film had covered Shay's eyes, and that he'd screwed up his napkin tight in his hand. She hoped her probing questions about his personal life hadn't scuppered her progress. She considered what she should say next, but scared of saying the wrong thing and making it worse, she kept quiet. *What would I say anyway? I haven't got a clue about relationships!* Life at home hadn't been remotely conducive to having a boyfriend, not that she'd wanted one having seen the string of unsuitable men her mother brought home.

He picked up his pint glass and downed what remained.

She floundered for something else to say. It had been going so well until she'd managed to put her foot firmly in it. 'Do you have any children?' She kept her voice light, trying to get the conversation back on track.

He placed his glass back. 'It's getting late. Probably best we get going before the frost sets in.'

'Sure. I'll go settle up. My treat.'

He dug a hand into his pocket and produced a wad of crumpled notes.

'No, please. Let me.'

'Oh no, I invited you.'

'Please.' He peeled off several of the notes and pushed them towards her. 'By way of apology and as a welcome to the village.' He managed a weak smile. 'I'm aware I probably haven't been the best company tonight.'

For the second time in one evening, she found herself unable to refuse him. 'Okay, but I'll go up and pay. I want to introduce myself to the landlady. This is my local now, after all.'

He nodded, although she wasn't convinced he'd registered her words. His eyes were dull once again, but this time there was such a deep sadness behind them that the sight of them almost moved her to tears.

Sarah handed the money over to the glamorous, tanned-looking woman behind the bar who, according to the sign above the door, was Shareen Banks, the landlady. 'That was delicious, thank you. And please keep the change.'

'Thanks, darling.' Shareen smiled and winked a heavily made-up eye at Sarah. 'Hey, you've done well.'

Sarah cocked her head to the side. 'Have I? In what way?'

Shareen rested her arms on the bar, and leaned forward, conspiratorially. 'Getting Shay McGillen out. We don't get to see him much.'

'Don't you?'

Shareen propped her chin on a beautifully manicured hand. 'Only been in here a handful of times since he moved to Wetherstone.' She smiled, her eyes glazing over. 'Shame though. He's a lovely guy. Quiet, but lovely. And pretty easy on the eye too, wouldn't you say?'

Sarah felt her cheeks grow hot. She didn't think she was a good enough liar to rebuke that statement. She dipped her head, busying herself with pulling her mittens out of her pocket. She was glad that Shay had appeared to have gone to the loo, and wasn't still sat at the table, to possibly see her blush.

'I suppose so,' said Sarah. 'I haven't really noticed.'

Shareen threw her head back and laughed loudly. 'Aye, whatever. You'd be the first woman around here who hasn't. I'd have lit the fire for you to make things more atmospheric, but that chimney really needs a sweep. If sparks are going to fly in this pub, I'd rather they were of the romantic variety.' She laughed.

Sarah managed a watery smile, hoping her face wasn't giving her away.

'I've worked in pubs all my life,' Shareen continued. 'And, do you know what? It makes you an expert in not only pulling pints but also learning about folk. I could read your body language a mile away.' She pointed a finger at Sarah. 'I'd say that you, my love, are very sweet on our Mister McGillen. Hmm?' She waggled both eyebrows.

'Oh no, not at all. We've only just met. We're neighbours.'

'Okay, darling, whatever you say.' Shareen placed a hand

lightly around the handle of the beer pump. She looked so confident and at home, Sarah could imagine that was her usual stance. Despite her best efforts, there was no way she could fool this woman who'd probably seen it all.

'All right,' Sarah said in a low voice. She cast a quick glance behind her to check Shay hadn't returned. 'He's quite a dish, I admit.'

Shareen laughed again. 'I knew it!' she said, with a grin.

'Tell me …' Sarah leaned on the bar. 'Is there anyone in his life?' She was asking only for professional reasons, of course. Knowing more about Shay's personal circumstances would allow her to help him get the best possible package from LJ Networks when it came to him moving out of the farm.

'A woman, you mean? Nah. There've been plenty who've tried, mind you, but he doesn't seem interested. Like I said, keeps himself to himself most of the time. You've achieved where many have failed just by getting him out for a meal. And as for actually making him laugh …'

'Honestly, we're just here as friends, and new neighbours, that's all.'

A man approached the bar and Shareen flashed him a bright smile. 'Be right with you, Dave. The usual?' Shareen reached beneath the bar, pulled out a glass and started expertly pulling a pint. 'Whatever you say, love,' she said to Sarah over the top of the beer pump.

At the far end of the bar, the door to the gents' bathroom swung open and the toned, figure of Shay emerged. He began making his way across the pub to the bar to join her, keeping his head down to avoid the beams in the low ceiling.

Shareen lifted her gaze from the rapidly-filling pint long enough to clock Shay approaching. 'Well, all I can say from *his* body language, is that he's just as into you as you are him.'

Sarah was desperate to ask her how she'd come to that conclusion, but Shay reached them before she had the chance.

'Ready to go?' he asked. 'I'll walk you home.' He thanked Shareen for the meal and headed for the exit.

Sarah waved at Shareen who responded with a wink and a quick thumbs up. She didn't know how accurate the landlady's skills of perception were, but a part of her, a part she wished she had more control over, couldn't help hoping they were spot on.

Shay dug his torch out of his pocket and switched it on, illuminating the potholed tarmac sprawling out before them. During many of his sleepless nights he'd trod this road in the dark, and could have navigated it with his eyes closed. It was preferable to staring at the ceiling for hours or slipping into another terror-filled nightmare. He expected Sarah, however, being a city dweller, to be unaccustomed to the pitch darkness of country lanes at night, and so had pocketed his torch on his way out of the farmhouse. He was glad he had after learning about her hilarious antics during her school trip to the country. And seeing her footwear.

Despite the bright orange stream of light that led their way, she walked unsteadily, her body so close to his that her duffle coat brushed his arm with every step. An urge to lay an arm over her shoulder to offer reassurance overtook him, so much so he had to squeeze his arm to his side to stop himself. He'd enjoyed himself in the pub. He hadn't been looking forward to it, but Sarah had surprised him by being such good company. She'd put him at ease. It wasn't often he felt at ease these days. That was until he'd felt obliged to mention his wife. And she'd asked whether he had any children. That had been an innocent enough question. If only he knew how to control himself better rather than go into shutdown mode. Maybe it wasn't too late to pick the mood back up. It would be a shame to end the night on a downer when it had been so good earlier.

'Giving you the lowdown on all the locals, was she?'

he said, hoping sparking up conversation might do just that.

'Who?' Her voice was shaking with cold. The urge to put an arm around her and pull her into him grew stronger. His nature was to protect. At least, he'd always believed that, until he'd let down those who trusted him the most.

'Shareen.'

Sarah laughed, a sweet tinkle of a sound, which sent a flow of warmth through his chest.

'She seems like a nice lady.'

'Her heart's in the right place, but she does like to think she's the oracle on human behaviour.'

'I guess you see a lot of life from behind a pub bar.'

'Oh yeah? What did she have to say, then?' He battled to keep his tone light, and risked a quick glance down at her face to try to read her expression. He'd had one of his worst attacks in the pub a couple of years ago. Most people had put it down to him having one beer too many, and hadn't mentioned it since, although he'd actually been stone cold sober at the time.

Shareen, the responsible landlady she was, paid him a visit to the farm the next day to ask if he was all right. He'd apologised and claimed the drink had got to him, but she was perceptive and hadn't bought his explanation. At least she'd respected his wish not to push the matter.

Sarah looked up at him. Her pale blue eyes shone in the moonlight. 'She said you don't venture into the pub much. Why not? It's such a nice place.'

Shay wet his suddenly dry lips. *This is why I should have said no to coming out tonight. The questions. The blasted questions. Why can't people mind their own damned business?* Most people were curious, but never so bold as to ask, especially when they'd only just met him, but then again, he'd only spent one evening with Sarah Pickering and already he knew she wasn't like most people. She hadn't seemed fazed by him when he turned up at her door criticising her driving. *After* she'd realised he wasn't pointing an armed gun at her, that is. She'd argued her point and stood her ground. And her appetite this evening – so many women seemed obsessed with their weight, but she ate more than he did and looked to be savouring every last mouthful.

'I prefer my own company most of the time,' he answered. And that was enough. He wasn't going to burden her – or anyone else – in his messed-up past.

Suddenly, a high-pitched *yiiiip* pierced the air.

'What's that?' Sarah stopped abruptly and grabbed his arm.

This time, he didn't have time to think about putting an arm around her – he did it instinctively. 'It's okay. It's just a fox. They're harmless.'

She looked up at him. 'Oh really? I didn't know foxes made noises like that. It sounded like someone screaming.'

They were so close that his senses filled with the scent of her coconut shampoo. The wind stopped rustling the bushes and the foxes fell silent. It was just him and her. Even his better judgement had disappeared with the last gust of wind. Running on pure animal instinct, he bowed his head towards hers. The closer his mouth got to hers, the more his awareness began to creep back in. He needed to pull back, but all his instincts were screaming out at him to kiss her.

Sarah's face tipped up towards his, her cute sprinkling of freckles visible against the milky moonlight and her eyes filled with the same longing that burned inside him. Holding her in his arms was like nothing else. It stirred a feeling inside him that had lay dormant for so long he'd forgotten he'd ever possessed it. He closed his eyes and lowered his head the last inch. His lips were almost there when a woman's voice, loud and clear, even though it existed only in his head, caused him to freeze.

'What are you doing, Shay? What are you doing?'

Chapter Six

The smooth, painted tile was cold in Shay's palm. He traced his finger lightly around each tiny toe imprint, being careful not to scratch the little foot with his rough, calloused hands. He let out a sound halfway between a laugh and a cry. Who was he kidding? It was a ceramic tile, nothing more. Elsie couldn't feel the pad of his finger tickling her little foot now. Nor would she ever again.

To the best daddy in the world
I love you
Elsie 3 months

He read the inscription over and over again, the lump in his throat hardening every time he did. If he concentrated, really concentrated, he could just about recall the feel of Elsie's velvet-soft cheek against the back of his finger. When the bright red lump, screaming at the top of its voice, had been lain in his arms seconds after she'd come into the world, he'd stroked her cheek, and her chubby little legs and arms, in complete awe at how beautiful and precious she was. Love like he'd never felt before had burst out of his chest so fiercely he could barely breathe.

He'd made a silent vow to his daughter there and then that he'd do everything he could to give her the best life possible and would protect her with every fibre of his being. Some promise.

'I'm so sorry I let you and Mummy down, Elsie, so sorry.' He didn't know he was crying until a fat teardrop hit the tile, ran off its smooth surface and pooled above his watch strap. He pressed the heel of his hand into his eye sockets. No, not tears. He'd never let himself cry, not once since the accident.

He didn't deserve to have his pain relieved. Clodagh and Elsie had lost their lives and he'd stood and watched them die. The least he could do for them now was to experience just a fraction of the suffering they had. 'Stop feeling sorry for your pathetic self,' he murmured.

Bess, who was lying on the rug by the unlit fire, responded, as she always did to his voice. Her ears pricked up, then she stood up, came over to him where he sat in the well-worn armchair, and rested her soft, warm head in his lap.

He lay a hand gently over her head and gave her a scratch between the ears. 'You're my rock, Bess.' The dog licked his forearm with her rough tongue. He smiled and sniffed. 'You never even knew Clodagh and Elsie, and yet sometimes I think you miss them as much as I do.'

Bess whimpered, as if in agreement.

'So, tell me this, Bess. If after all these years it still hurts so much, why did I almost kiss Sarah tonight?' Bess released another whimper, softer this time. Her breathing grew heavier as she drifted to sleep.

Shay glanced up at the clock on the mantelpiece. Almost 4 a.m. No wonder the poor girl was tired. He'd kept her up half the night by pacing the living room, going over and over in his mind what had happened earlier that evening when he'd nearly kissed Sarah in the middle of the deserted country lane. He couldn't even say it was in response to her coming onto him. He'd started it, taken her in his arms, bowed his head and come so close to pressing his mouth against hers.

'Was it because the fox scared her, and I was trying to comfort her?' he said aloud. He pondered over his own explanation, then shook his head and laughed lamely at himself. 'As if that would ever be the right thing to do!' Even in the state he was in, he couldn't pretend he'd been moved to kiss Sarah Pickering for any reason other than he'd desperately and urgently wanted to.

He lay his head against the back of the armchair and closed his eyes. If he was going to be in any fit state to work tomorrow, he had to get some sleep. But when he blocked out the sight of his living room, all he saw was Sarah's face tipped up towards his in the moonlight. He couldn't wait a second more to indulge in the sweet, sweet taste of her mouth. Just before their lips met, she paused and knitted her brow. One by one her freckles began to fade away, like snowdrops melting. She screwed up her eyes and nose as if in pain and, like a scene from a horror film, her features began to contort. Her rounded cheeks slimmed down, her chin became pointier and her skin a few shades darker.

'What are you doing, Shay? What are you doing,' she said.

He tried to cry out, but his mouth was welded shut and all he could manage was a freakish growl.

'It's okay, Shay, darling. It's just me, Clodagh.'

He took a step back from her. Where Sarah had been, now Clodagh stood, one woman transformed into another.

'Shit!' His curse woke him up. He licked his lips and focused on breathing calmly to steady his thumping heart.

This is how it's always going to be now. The guilt he carried weighed so heavy on his conscience that he'd never be free – even when he slept. There hadn't been anyone since Clodagh. He hadn't the appetite for a relationship, and even if he had, it would never work. He didn't deserve to feel pleasure or happiness, especially not with another woman; especially not when his wife and child were dead. And their blood was on his hands.

Chapter Seven

Sarah cupped her hands over her mouth and nose, and breathed on them before refocusing her phone's torch back to the path in front. The warm air provided a few seconds of relief before the relentless cold bit at her once more. She could have driven the quarter of a mile to McGillen's Farm, but in between a few visits to villagers she'd been cooped up in her cottage for almost the entire week under a mountain of paperwork, and thought the exercise would do her good. 'Do me good if I manage to get there in one piece,' she muttered to herself as she dodged yet another patch of ice.

She couldn't pretend the will to stretch her legs was her main reason for venturing up to the farm. She'd neither heard from nor seen Shay for almost a week, not since the night of their dinner together.

It was obvious by the look of horror on his face when he jerked away from her that he regretted almost kissing her. They'd walked the rest of the way back to her cottage in mostly silence punctuated with occasional bouts of awkward small talk. When they'd finally reached her door, he bid her a hasty goodnight and couldn't get away fast enough. She'd sat in her living room in a state of shock for a good hour before taking herself up to bed. She'd been comfort eating a lot recently and had shadows under her eyes that weren't there a few months ago, but she didn't think she was repulsive enough to cause the kind of reaction Shay had shown.

She heard her own breathing as the hill steepened. She really needed to get a grip on her diet and fitness if she couldn't even walk a short distance without puffing and panting at her age. It was just so difficult trying to eat healthily when sugary foods made her feel better, if only for the time it took to devour them. Even her mother – the one person she was meant to be able to rely on – let her down. But cake never did.

The road bent around, and the rows of winter-barren soil and long greenhouses of McGillen's Farm came into view. Despite it already being dark, even though it could only be around 5 p.m., the farmhouse stood out against the winter evening sky with its painted white frontage. She stopped, re-tied her ponytail that had loosened after the walk and waited until her breathing steadied. 'Here it is, at last,' she said, trying to convince herself she was relieved to be here. If she were honest, she knew she'd been putting off this visit, hoping Shay might turn up at her door instead, take her in his arms and actually kiss her this time. Without regrets. She sighed, and trudged across the slippery, uneven ground to the farmhouse. That was never going to happen. It couldn't, however pleasant a thought it was. It would be too dangerous a territory. Convincing Shay McGillen to sell up to LJ Networks was the main reason she'd been posted here. Fraternising with the targets was a sackable offence. It didn't matter that being held by Shay had made her feel more wanted than she'd ever felt in her whole life. Nothing was going to get in the way of her achieving her career goals. She couldn't cope with losing her job on top of everything else.

She knocked on the farmhouse door which, after a few seconds, was swung open by a man so big he filled almost the entire frame.

'Sarah. What are you doing here?'

Her heart sank. Although she knew nothing could happen between her and Shay, she had hoped for a warmer reception. She plastered a smile on her face and held out the stack of letters addressed to him. 'George has been up to his old tricks again. These arrived at my cottage.'

'Oh, thanks.' A flicker of disappointment seemed to cross his face as he took them from her.

So much for her even daring to fantasise about him taking her in his arms again – if the sullen expression now on his face was anything to go by, she was the last person he'd hoped would show up unannounced.

'Did you walk all the way up here in the dark?'

'Well, yes,' she said. 'But I used the torch on my phone.' She'd soon realised after the embarrassing moment when she'd jumped a mile at the sound of the fox, that if she was going to manage life in the country, even if it was temporary, she'd have to be more prepared.

'You'd better come in.' His invitation was clearly delivered out of politeness alone, but she accepted it, nonetheless. She'd never manage to sway his opinion to sell up if she didn't get a chance to speak to him.

'Thanks.' She stepped inside the farmhouse kitchen, and was instantly enveloped in a homely warmth. 'Wow, this isn't what I expected,' she said, admiring the traditional oak kitchen and the matching table and chairs in the centre of the expansive room.

'What? Of a man living alone you mean?'

His tone was so flat, she wasn't sure how to read him. She smiled to diffuse any ill feeling. 'I guess that *is* what I mean. You surprised me with the edible flowers too, if you remember.'

He looked down at the floor, and she knew as well as he did, he was recalling how their night out together had ended.

'See you took my advice about getting some decent footwear.'

'What?' She followed his gaze down to where a pair of garishly coloured rubber boots covered her feet and lower legs. They'd been the only pair the local garden centre had left in her size. She laughed. 'Oh, yes, I figured you were right about that, so I invested in these.' She held onto her laugh a little too long. She stood, awkwardly by the door, her arms feeling long and gangly now her hands were empty of the letters. 'That smells good,' she said, not knowing what else to say.

'Just fish pie. Nothing fancy.'

Instantly she regretted her choice of conversation. It must have sounded like she was hinting at an invitation to stay for dinner. Silence fell once more. 'Right,' she said, unable to deal with the discomfort of the situation any longer. 'Well, enjoy.'

'Thanks.' He held up the letters. 'And thanks again for these.'

'No problem.' She turned to face the door. 'Well, see you around.' She pushed down on the handle and opened the door, allowing a blast of freezing air to force its way into the kitchen.

'Wait. Sarah.'

She turned back to face him.

'Forgive me,' he said, as he absentmindedly brushed the pile of letters backwards and forwards against his thigh. 'I'm being rude. Would you like to stay for something to eat? I'll walk you home later so you don't have to go back on your own in the dark.'

A surge of hope rose in her heart, and she forced it back down again. *Silly, silly girl, Sarah. It's just an empty invitation. He doesn't really want you to stay.* 'Oh, no, don't worry. I don't want to disturb your evening.'

'Have you managed to get your oven working yet?'

She smiled meekly and shook her head. She was hoping the plumber Julie recommended would be able to sort it when he came tomorrow. It was the earliest appointment she could get. She had, as a result, been making excellent use of the microwave.

'Then please stay. It's freezing tonight. You'll need some hot food inside you, and there's plenty.'

'Well, if you're sure you don't mind. It'd be lovely to have something more substantial than a microwave meal.'

'I'm sure. I can't promise a culinary masterpiece but as least it's home-cooked.' His face stretched into that gorgeous smile, the one she'd witnessed last week at the pub. Perhaps his offer was genuine. *He probably just wants the company,* she thought. *It must get lonely all the way out here.* But then, Julie had said he was pretty reclusive. Did hermits like him ever really want company?

She shut the door, forcing out the cold, sharp air. 'Then I'd love to.'

'You'd better take those monstrosities off.' He gestured towards her feet.

'Oh yes.' She laughed. 'Not the prettiest things, are they?' She tugged off her rubber boots and rested them against the door.

'Why don't you go through to the living room?' He held out his arm to a room across the corridor. You can meet Bess while I fix you a glass of wine. Is Rioja okay?'

'Lovely.' She rubbed her hands together, but it didn't stop the chill that ran down her spine. *Bess? I thought he lived alone.* She made her way over to the living room, ready to paste another fake smile onto her face. She suddenly realised that although she knew Shay was no longer married, she couldn't be sure there wasn't a woman in his life. Just because Shareen believed him to be single didn't mean he actually was – especially as, just like everyone said, he was a man who played his cards close to his chest. If this turned out to be a girlfriend who had called around for a visit, she'd have to do an Oscar-winning job of acting pleased to meet her.

'Oh, hello there.' Relief washed through her as she sank to her knees to pet the black and white sheepdog, who was enjoying a big yawn and stretch. 'I guess you must be Bess. Sorry to disturb you from your nap.'

The dog sat in front of Sarah and raised a paw. 'Pleased to meet you too.' Sarah laughed, and stroked her soft, wavy coat.

Shay walked in and handed her a glass of wine. He'd taken off the heavy sweater he'd had on and now wore a dark grey T-shirt over a pair of well-fitting, worn jeans. She thanked him for the drink and tried not to stare at the way the thin cotton clung to his firm torso and how the short sleeves stretched to accommodate his muscular upper arms.

'This is Bess, my best girl. I see you two have met.'

His best girl. Oh, to have him describe me like that. She gulped. She had thought it would be easy coming here to explain her part in the bypass and talk him into selling. She even thought the memory of their almost kiss wouldn't get in the way. Now it was all she could think about.

'She's beautiful,' Sarah said. Shay clearly loved his dog. If she kept on the subject, he might warm up to her and make it easier for her to lead on to what she'd come here to say.

Shay scratched Bess's ear, and the dog peered up at him with big, brown eyes, which shone in adoration. Sarah looked on, and couldn't help but wish Shay's big hand was stroking her instead – then shook her head at her own craziness. *Am I actually jealous of a dog?* Bess wagged her tail furiously. *Seems I'm not the only female around here to have fallen for the charms of the local flower farmer.*

'Beautiful *and* loyal,' Shay said. 'I know it sounds corny, but she's my closest friend. She always listens to me moaning on.'

'I get that completely. I feel the same about Clive.'

'Clive?' Shay stopped scratching Bess and turned to look at Sarah. Was it her imagination or did his smile fade momentarily?

'My cat.'

'Oh, I see.' His smile returned, wider this time. 'You're an animal person too, then?'

'Well, I'm not sure I'd go that far, but I am a cat person. They pretty much look after themselves. Independent. Like me.'

Shay nodded and sat down on an old fabric armchair. This time Sarah didn't even try to avert her gaze. His long, lean legs filled out his jeans in all the right places. She was so taken in with the sight of pure man in front of her she hadn't noticed the silence that had descended until he broke it.

'Sarah, about the other night—'

'Yes, thanks for that.'

His eyes widened.

'Coming out with me for dinner, I mean. I really enjoyed it. The food, that is,' she added quickly. 'I really enjoyed the food.' She laughed. A high-pitched sound, which set her teeth on edge.

'Yes, me too, but I meant—'

'How it ended?' She sighed, giving up on trying to gloss over it. 'I know. You wished it had never happened. Don't worry, I feel the same, so let's just forget it, shall we? Let's get on with being friendly neighbours.'

'Oh, okay. Deal.'

Deal? So that was it, done and dusted, as if it had never happened. That's what she'd wanted, wasn't it? To get it out in the open and pave the way for the more serious business she'd come here for. Rather than feeling glad, though, she felt unwanted. Is this how life was for her mother? Is that why she did what she did?

'Super.' Sarah stretched her face into the brightest smile she could manage and threw a gulp of wine down her throat. It was too big a mouthful, and it scratched its way down to her stomach, adding to the rawness that had begun to fester in her gut.

He slapped his hands onto his thighs and stood up. 'Dinner should be ready by now. Why don't you make yourself at home while I serve up? Is crusty bread okay to go with it?'

'Sounds like a dream,' she said, and placed her glass on the mantelpiece.

He left the room, with Bess trotting loyally after him.

If she was going to have to cope with being brushed off by man *and* dog, carbohydrates should definitely be on the menu.

She looked around the room. No television, no magazines. She turned, noticing a tall wooden bookshelf behind her. Scanning the spines of the books, she soon realised they were all botanical textbooks. 'Shay McGillen,' she said quietly. 'You certainly are a man with one thing on his mind, I'll give you that. Unfortunately for us womenfolk, that thing seems to be flowers.'

With her head tipped at an angle to allow her to read the titles, she reached over, without looking, to retrieve her wine glass from the mantel. As she curled her hand around the stem, her finger knocked a thick piece of card onto the rug beneath. She bent down to pick it up, turned it over and saw it was a frame, which held a photo of an attractive red-headed woman wearing an off-the-shoulder floral dress and a straw hat. The woman was smiling broadly at the camera, leaving Sarah in no doubt that, whoever the photographer was, she was madly in love with him.

Who was she – Shay's ex-wife? Why would he have a photo of his former lover on his mantelpiece, and why had it been facing the wall? She'd have noticed it before had it been on display the right way round.

She was so lost in thought, the soft thud to the back of her calf almost made her jump out of her skin. 'Bess, you startled me!' The dog's tail pounded rhythmically against her leg as she looked up at Sarah, with hope in her eyes for a stroke. She bent down to pat the dog's head.

'Food's ready.'

Sarah shot a glance behind her to see Shay standing at the doorway, a bowl in each hand.

'What are you doing with that?' He frowned, nodding towards the frame still in her hand. His expression suggested he'd caught her stealing the family silver rather than looking at a photograph.

'Oh, sorry. I didn't mean to pry. I knocked it off by accident.' She placed the frame back on the mantelpiece, and turned around to smile at him. 'There. No harm done.'

His eyebrows hooded over darkened eyes. 'The other way around!'

Quickly, she fumbled with the picture, turning it over so the redhead faced the wall. Almost scared to risk a glance at him in case the pain that had been etched all over his face was still there, she looked up at him through her lashes. 'I didn't mean to cause you any upset. Is that …? Is that your ex-wife?' She hated herself for asking, but something inside her needed to know.

Shay placed the bowls down on the coffee table and lowered himself into the armchair. He rested his elbows on his knees, and fixed his gaze down at his hands. 'No. I don't have an ex-wife. The woman in the picture – that's Clodagh – my *dead* wife.'

Sarah swallowed. What to say to that one? She walked over to the sofa and sat down in the corner nearest to his armchair. 'I'm so sorry, Shay. I had no idea.'

He sniffed and ran an arm across his face. 'Look, don't worry about it. I get it must look weird, having a photo of my dead wife facing the wall.' He bared his teeth, but it wasn't a smile – more of a grimace.

Instinctively, she reached out for his hand. He froze as soon as she touched him, but didn't look at her, just continued to stare into his lap as if he wasn't really seeing it.

'It's not weird,' she said. 'I get it.'

He let out a humourless laugh. 'You're not going to tell me you're widowed too, are you?'

'Not widowed, no, but I lost my mum three months ago.' The confession slipped out so easily, even though half the reason she'd been desperate to move away from home was so she wouldn't have to talk about the tragedy that had turned her life upside down.

He turned his head to look at her. The darkness in his eyes had lifted slightly and his expression was softer. 'I'm sorry to hear that.'

'I've got a photo of her I keep hidden in a drawer in my living room because I can't yet face seeing it every day.'

'Really?'

She nodded and looked down at her hand on top of his. He followed her gaze, and for a moment they sat in silence. She should pull her arm away, but his big, rough hand felt so good under hers that, for the first time since her mum's death, the edges of her grief seemed to smoothen.

'How did she …?' His voice trailed off.

'How did she die? She took her own life.'

He squeezed her hand. 'Oh God, Sarah. That must have been awful for you.' His soft Irish lilt soothed the pieces of her heart that her mum's suicide had caused, giving her the strength to want to talk about it. Something she hadn't managed to do so far except out of necessity.

She nodded. 'It was. She was only forty-six. She was young when she had me.'

Shay shook his head. 'That's no age to die.'

'She hanged herself. I found her, hanging there, over the stairs. The paramedics said she'd been there for at least a week.' She surprised herself that she managed to tell him that – her deepest, most shameful confession – without her voice cracking.

He stared at her, open-mouthed. 'You must have been beside yourself.'

She recalled how she'd stood on the stair. It had been the third one up from the bottom, the one with the small dark red stain where she'd spilled blackcurrant juice as a child. She looked up at the blue face and bulging eyes and wondered who on earth that woman was, hanging from her mother's landing light, and why she'd chosen their modest terrace house to kill herself in.

Despite the horror, she'd continued to look, trying to make sense of the scene. How uncanny that this woman wore the same silver chain and glittery pendant around her neck as the one she'd bought her mum for Mother's Day when she was eleven. That's when reality dawned. The dead woman wasn't a stranger; it *was* her mother.

She'd screamed, and hadn't stopped screaming until the emergency services arrived. She didn't remember them cutting her mum down, or even how they did it. The next thing she remembered was being in the police station answering questions.

When did you last see your mother alive?

Three weeks ago.

Do you know why she might want to end her life?

Yes. Yes, I know.

Shay turned over his large hand and closed it around hers, shaking her from her memories. 'It's okay. You don't have to talk about it if you don't want to.'

She ran her top teeth over her bottom lip, snagging the dry skin. 'Sorry. I didn't come here to offload all my problems onto you.'

He ran the pad of his thumb over her wrist. 'If you want to get anything off your chest, go right ahead. The fish pie is boiling. We won't be able to eat it for a while anyway and I'm sure Bess is grateful to hear someone else's voice for a change.'

At the mention of her name, Bess's ears pricked up. She gave them a cursory glance before realising a walk wasn't on the agenda, and settled back down to her snooze on the rug by Shay's feet.

Sarah smiled at the dog's reaction, and turned her head back to Shay. He was smiling back. Not for the first time, her stomach flipped when she took in those twinkly eyes that made his skin crinkle at the corners. Only this time she was closer to him than she had been at the pub. If it hadn't been for the arm of his chair, their legs and shoulders would be touching.

'In that case,' she said, her voice husky with emotion. 'I'll bore you with it. The counsellor did say it could help.' *Why did I just say that? I'm a professional. He's my target! I shouldn't be telling him my darkest secret.* Despite the logical part of her brain imploring her to stop, her heart begged her to carry on, to ease herself of the burden, so this gentle giant of a man could make it all better.

He reached over and stroked a hand lightly over her hair. 'You won't bore me, I promise.'

Her resolve melted under his touch, along with her body from the chest down. She closed her eyes and felt the warmth from him seep into her, heating her through, easing her pain. *Don't stop*, she begged him silently. *Don't ever stop.*

His hand slid down to the side of her face, and she tipped her head, so her cheek touched his palm. It was so good having him beside her. So comforting, and *right*. There was no denying it. This strange hermit of a man, who was bullish one minute and so tender the next, entranced her.

Without moving her head, without opening her eyes, she began to talk. 'It was just me and Mum when I was growing up. I don't remember my dad. He left when I was a baby. I adored Mum. She was glamorous, and funny, and a lot of fun. Like a kid herself sometimes.' She laughed at the memory. 'And maybe because of that, she always doubted herself. She used to say she could never give me everything she wanted me to have until she found me a dad. I'd tell her that was rubbish, that she was all I needed, but she wouldn't have it.'

Still cupping her face, he traced his thumb over her cheek. 'She must have loved you very much if all she wanted was for you to be happy.'

Sarah nodded, her hair brushing his palm. She sniffed back a trail of snot, which threatened to escape. The last thing she needed was to end up a blubbering mess. 'I know she loved me, I know. And I loved her so, so much. I've got some wonderful memories of the times we spent together. Unfortunately, as her obsession to find a man grew, those times became few and far between. I still have them though, right here.' She placed her free hand on her chest, and Shay nodded. There was an understanding in his dark eyes she hadn't expected.

'I had cancer, you see. I was only five, but I think that's what made Mum so determined to give me the best life she could. I think she was always scared of losing me.'

'Cancer? It must have been terrifying for your mother to watch you go through all that so young.'

She licked her lips. 'Yes, I'm sure it was. I barely remember it. I was so little. The operation I needed left me unable to have kids, but apart from that I've been clear ever since. I guess you could say it was a small price to pay if it meant I got to live.' She tried not to think of her barren womb, but now she'd unlocked the sorrow deep within her that she'd never have a family of her own, a sob rose to the surface.

'It's okay. It's okay.' He took his hand away from her face and stroked her arm. For a man so big and strong, his voice was calm and soft, giving her the reassurance she needed to carry on.

'Mum's dream was to find a man and get married so we could all be one happy family. She thought finding her a husband and me a new dad was the answer to everything.'

'Did she ever get her dream?'

A single tear spilled over her eyelids onto her cheek. 'No. She auditioned plenty though.' She laughed and sniffed as another tear tickled its way down her face.

'She just became so, so ...' She searched for the right word. 'Desperate. Bad men sniff out desperate women a mile away. Even when I reached adulthood, she was still going out with a series of men. I told her I was too old to need a father figure, but she just laughed and said every girl needs a daddy to walk her down the aisle. I think she needed to prove to me – and herself – she was worthy of being loved.'

'But you loved her.'

'Yes. With all my heart. I even stayed living at home with her until recently. I told her she was doing me a favour having me there because property in the city is so expensive, but really I stayed to make sure she was okay. You should have seen some of the guys she brought home. I didn't like the idea of her being alone with them.'

He stopped stroking her, pausing his hand at her wrist. 'Really? That bad?'

'Well, maybe I'm exaggerating.' She attempted a small laugh to throw him off the scent, but knew it sounded fake.

His expression turned stony.

'Did someone hurt her?' he said.

She shook her head.

He narrowed his eyes. 'What then?'

'Oh, it doesn't matter.' She took a sip of wine.

'Holding things in can make things worse.'

Don't I know it.

'You don't have to tell me though,' he said. 'Not if you'd rather not. I'd understand—'

'Oh, it's not that. It's just … I'm just ashamed of it.'

'I've done a whole load of things I'm ashamed of, let me tell you. So, whatever it is, I promise, I'm in no position to judge you for it.'

'No, honestly,' she said, pulling her hand from under his and giving a dismissive wave. 'You don't need to hear all my problems.' Her hollow laugh fell flat. His expression remained serious.

'Whatever you want.' He gave a slight smile and leaned forward to pick up the bowls from the table.

'It wasn't my mum he hurt.' She couldn't believe she was about to tell him this, but he had a way about him. A wonderful way that drew all the badness out of her, making her feel better as soon as it had escaped her lips and met his ears. 'It was me.'

He dropped the bowls back down onto the table with a clatter and shot her a look. 'What did he do?'

She hesitated. It wasn't too late to change her mind about telling him. She could change her story; make something up that wasn't as bad as it had really been. She barely knew the man and yet here she was, on the verge of sharing with him her darkest secret. What had got into her?

'Seriously, Sarah, if he hurt you …' He clenched his hand into a fist and his jaw tightened.

'Honestly, Shay, don't worry about it. Let's just enjoy a nice dinner and not bother ourselves with miserable stuff. We've both had plenty of that to contend with.'

He continued to stare at her. His jaw was still clenched and he didn't move at all, other than the flare of his nostrils.

She'd come too far. She had to tell him. And deep down inside, she wanted to. She sighed. 'It was one night, not long before my mum died. Her latest boyfriend was staying over. I didn't even know his name – how crazy is that!'

'Go on,' he prompted. She didn't need to look at him to know his eyes were boring into her. She tipped her head back to look at the ceiling, blinking furiously to stop the tears. 'He came into my room in the middle of the night and tried to … He tried to touch me. I told him to get out, but he wouldn't budge. He had his filthy hands all over me, telling me to be quiet and enjoy it. I screamed, and screamed, and eventually, thank God, he left me alone. Mum ran into my room to see what all the noise was about. He laughed it off, saying he'd got lost in the dark and must have come into the wrong room, but she didn't believe him. She threw him out there and then.'

She brought her head back level to see that Shay had his hand over his face, his fingers pressed against his forehead.

I've gone too far. Whatever he said, no one really wants to hear the gory details. 'Sorry. I've said too much.'

'No.' He shook his head.

'You must think I'm disgusting. I'm clean, though – I checked. I got tested for STDs afterwards. Not that he went that far, but I felt dirty, just knowing he was in the same bed as me. I needed some sort of verification that I wasn't, I don't know – contaminated.'

He raised his head and she saw the deep lines etched into his forehead. 'Of course I don't think you're disgusting. *He's* disgusting for forcing himself on a woman like that. If I ever met him, I'd—' He didn't finish his sentence, just bunched his hands into fists and turned a furious shade of red. 'I'm sorry you had to go through that,' he said, eventually, the calmness of his voice belying the stormy look on his face.

'Not as sorry as I am. It's the reason Mum's dead.'

He raised his eyebrows. 'What do you mean?'

'The next day, Mum and I had a massive argument. She blamed herself for the attack, and if I'm honest, I blamed her too. I told her enough was enough. She had to stop it with all the men. I didn't need a dad, I just needed her to have some damned self-respect. She wouldn't listen, though, and for the first time in my life I had to get away from her. I thought if we both had a break from one another it might do us good. Maybe she'd see how independent I was and finally realise I didn't need a father figure.'

She was rushing her words, trying to reach the conclusion of her story before she lost her composure completely. Trouble was, she knew how it ended, knew she could never express what happened next without breaking down.

Thankfully, she didn't need to. He leaned over to her, stretched out his arm and stroked her cheek with the back of his finger. 'That was the last time you saw her, wasn't it?'

She nodded and failed to control her lower lip from wobbling.

'It's okay,' he whispered. 'It's okay.'

It wasn't okay, but just hearing him say it in his masculine baritone helped soften the blow of the guilt as it crashed over her.

'Thank you, Sarah.' His head was so close to hers she could feel his warm breath on her forehead.

She raised her eyes and regarded him through tear-glistened lashes. 'Thank you? What for? I've just indulged in a pity party for one when it's you who was widowed so young.'

The corners of his mouth turned up into a slight smile. 'Thank you for sharing that with me. I know how hard it must have been for you. Trust me, I really do. I don't have exclusive rights to sadness. It probably does me good to realise that from time to time.'

She took hold of his wrist and tipped her face into his palm. 'It's you I should be thanking. For listening. You're the only person I've spoken to about my mum's death, apart from my counsellor and some people at work of course, who I *had* to tell to explain the days I had to take absent.'

She pursed her lips and blew out a stream of air, which seemed to take with it any last hint of tension. 'I probably needed to share it with someone, and maybe it helps that we don't know each other that well.'

His intense dark blue eyes bore into hers. He didn't speak. He slid his hand down to her chin and tipped her face up so it was in line with his.

Yes, please Shay, kiss me properly this time.

To hell with professionalism, with goals and manipulating her targets. All she cared about right now was this very moment, and finding sweet oblivion in his kiss.

He pulled away a fraction and paused. He lowered his

gaze to her mouth and ran his thumb lightly, so torturously lightly, over her lips. Then he pulled away from her completely, and placed his hands on his thighs.

No, no, no, come back. I need you, Shay McGillen and, God, do I want you.

She was a millisecond away from throwing her arms around his neck and begging him to kiss her when he broke into an anguished expression and rubbed his forehead with the heel of his hand.

'Sorry,' he said, with such a sexy laugh, she wished his hand was on her thigh rather than his own. 'There I go again, wanting to kiss you. I *will* keep my hands to myself this evening, I promise. Shall we eat?'

He handed her a bowl, which she took from him. Her heart lifted, and it wasn't just the prospect of fish pie. Had she misunderstood or had he really just admitted to wanting to kiss her without a trace of shame or a mention of an apology? So, what was stopping him? Her mind raced with confusion and questions.

They fell into a companionable silence, the only sound: the ticking of the clock on the mantelpiece and the occasional clatter of cutlery against porcelain. With food in her stomach and the new knowledge that he really had wanted to kiss her, the intensity of the atmosphere lifted. 'Wow, that tastes incredible,' she said between mouthfuls.

He laughed, that sexy, hearty laugh again, and ripped off a corner of bread. 'Don't sound so surprised.'

She giggled. 'With your edible flowers and culinary talent, you're the one who's full of surprises.' His home-made food coated her belly with a comforting layer of warmth. She didn't know whether it was the supper or opening up to him that gave her a sense of wellbeing she hadn't felt for ... well, forever. Either way, for the first time since her mum's death, she detected a glimmer of hope that she wasn't destined to always feel so wretched.

'Anyway,' she continued. 'You told me you didn't cook. No point, you said, living on your own.'

'I don't cook *much*. I thought I'd treat myself tonight, seeing as it's so cold outside. You were lucky. On any other night, you'd have found me making a sandwich if you were lucky.'

'I guess you don't have a lot of time, with the flower farm and all. Although I suppose it is freezing at the moment. I can't imagine there's much in the way of growth during the English winter.'

'There wouldn't be normally, but with the greenhouses I can keep production going. Besides, I don't need to produce vast quantities. I'm fortunate enough that my trademark flower commands such a high price. It means I don't need to hire anyone to help me. It's called The Elsie.'

At the mention of the name, Bess stood up and came over to her master, settling at his feet.

'The Elsie? I've never heard of that.'

'That's because I created it. I'm the only grower in the world who knows how.'

'Really? I didn't know you could create a flower.'

'It's a matter of mixing the pollen, until you come up with a new species. I do grow others, but The Elsie is my most popular variety. The petals are bright yellow and delicate but the flavour ...' He touched his finger to his thumb and kissed them. 'It's out of this world.' He pointed to the corner of the room. She followed the direction of his finger to the top of the bookshelf and her gaze settled on a single flower standing proudly in a glass vase. She couldn't believe she hadn't noticed it before when she'd been looking through the books, but the shelf was tall and she would have had to crane her neck to see it. Now, from her position on the sofa, she had an ideal view. The flower's petals were bright, sunshine yellow, beaming off from a rusty red centre and tapering into perfect points.

'It's beautiful,' she murmured. .'

'She's done more for me than I ever could for her,' he said.

Sarah raised an eyebrow. It was endearing he talked about a flower as if she were a real person. 'What's that then?'

'Financially-wise, she sustains me. A luxury hotel in London started using her in their exclusive restaurant. A food critic gave a review commenting on the uniqueness of the flower, and that was it – orders for The Elsie went crazy. They were coming in from New York, London, Japan – I could hardly keep up. I could build more greenhouses, take more orders, hire staff, but I prefer working alone and earn more money than I spend, so what's the point? Money doesn't always make you happy.'

'No, true.' Sadly, she'd never had enough to know, but wasn't under any illusion a huge bank account would take away the pain of losing her mum. Just as long as she had enough to look after herself. That's all she cared about now.

She savoured the last mouthful of creamy potato. 'Money might not make you happy, but food certainly can. Thank you for letting me stay for dinner.'

'You're welcome.' He smiled, and a bright twinkle danced in his eye. 'I'll get us some coffee.' He reached over to take her bowl and his hand brushed hers, sending a delicious shiver up her spine.

This is getting far too cosy, she thought, and sat up straight. *I really must bring up the subject of the bypass. I don't want him to think I'm pretending to enjoy his company for my own gain.*

Nothing could be further from the truth. The man she'd believed to be a grumpy recluse was intelligent, funny and creative. And he seemed genuinely interested in what she had to say. She wasn't an expert in men by any stretch of the imagination, but in her experience, the traits Shay possessed were pleasantly unusual. 'I'll talk business once he gets back with the coffee,' she told herself – hoping that saying it out loud would make her do it.

A few seconds later, Shay appeared in the doorway, closely followed by Bess. 'I think we have a problem.'

'What's that? Are you out of milk, because if you are I'm fine with black.'

He walked to the far side of the room and pulled the curtain aside to reveal the view from the window. 'Take a look at this.'

She stood up, crossed the room to reach his side by the window, and gasped when she saw the view outside. For as far as the eye could see, the land was covered in a sheet of pure white, like a layer of thick royal icing on a cake. The roofs of the outbuildings were also covered – bright white against the cloudy night sky – creating a Christmas-card picture, prettier than anything she'd ever seen before in real life. 'It's so beautiful,' she whispered, worried that speaking too loudly might ruin the tranquillity of the scene.

'Beautiful it may be,' he said, and sucked air in between his teeth. 'But there's no way you're getting home tonight. It's far too dangerous.'

She waved a hand. 'Oh, I'll be fine. I can look after myself. It seems to have stopped now, anyway.'

He drummed his fingers against the windowpane, and furrowed his brow. 'It'll be ages before it melts, even if it doesn't start snowing again. There's no way I'm letting you risk walking home in this – even if I walked with you. It's not safe for either of us. I'd drive you but the bloody Land Rover's in for repairs and the tractor's playing silly buggers again. I've got a new part I need to install but we've had a couple of drinks and it really needs a steady hand.'

His concern made something inside her belly tingle.

'No, you'll have to stay here with me tonight, I'm afraid.'

Torn between finding his masterfulness exciting, and a hatred of being told what to do, she pursed her lips and folded her arms across her chest. 'I don't think that's your decision to make.'

He stretched an arm around the back of the sofa, retrieved black overalls and began pulling them over his clothes. 'Oh yeah?' He looked up at her as he pushed his long arms into the sleeves. 'Well, I don't see an alternative, unless you plan to summon a pack of huskies and sledge home.'

'Well, no.' Panic rose in her throat. If there really was no way she could get back to her cottage tonight—*Oh God!* She inwardly groaned at what had just dawned. *I can hardly reveal my part in the bypass now!* Not when he was letting her stay in the farmhouse. If she couldn't convince him of the advantages of selling up straight away, then it could be a very long and awkward evening. She'd no choice but to save the news for tomorrow morning, when the snow had cleared and she could make a swift exit if necessary. 'Do you have somewhere I could sleep?' she asked.

'There's a spare room upstairs. It's basic, but clean and comfortable.'

'Oh, okay. Thank you.' The thought of staying the night under the same roof as Shay filled her with a pleasant trepidation. He'd be in a different room of course, but just knowing he'd be there, metres away, was both reassuring and, for reasons she couldn't fathom, exhilarating.

The sound of him zipping up his overalls caught her attention. She scanned his body. Even under the heavy fabric she could make out the tight curves of his muscles. He caught her looking, and she quickly averted her gaze.

'What are you doing?' she asked, hoping he couldn't detect the embarrassment in her voice.

'I'm going to start shovelling the driveway so I can run you home after I've fixed the tractor tomorrow. If I don't make a start now it'll be a nightmare in the morning and neither of us will be able to go anywhere until God knows when.'

He held her gaze a beat too long, and heat prickled her cheeks. *More than one night snowed in with him at the top of the hill?* The prospect should have terrified her, but instead it left her hoping for the longest winter in history. *Do not fall for him. That would be bad. Very bad indeed.*

'Sure,' she said, battling to keep her voice light. 'Shovel away!' She forced out a laugh. 'Gotta get going tomorrow. Back to—Oh my God!' She clamped her hands over her mouth. 'Clive! What if I can't get home tomorrow? He'll need feeding and it's not like he can go out and catch a mouse or anything – he hasn't been in the cottage long enough for me to let him out yet.'

'I'll get you home to Clive tomorrow, I promise.'

His voice sounded so certain. So reassuring. She met his dark blue eyes, and they held hers. It was those pained but understanding eyes that had made it far too easy for her to tell him all about what happened with her mum. She believed his words. Totally and utterly believed them.

She could feel herself relaxing. 'I know you will.'

'Let me sort out the driveway,' he said. 'Then I'll fix us that coffee.'

She smiled and nodded. Why did he have to be so damned nice? If he were the miserable grump he'd been at their first meeting, telling him she planned to flatten his farm and build a new road over it would be a whole lot easier.

Chapter Eight

'I didn't realise it was so late. We should probably turn in for the night.' Shay couldn't believe how quickly the evening with Sarah had flown by. It was like he'd been in some sort of time warp. Conversation with her had been so easy, and he found himself telling her more about himself than he'd told anyone in the five years he'd lived in Wetherstone. He'd even told her about his decade working in the Fire Service – with one omission, of course, that he'd never tell anyone.

She stretched her arms over her head and yawned. 'Two in the morning? How on earth did that happen?'

He flicked aside the blanket that had covered their legs, stood up from the sofa and crossed the room to flick off the single lit lamp. It was a chilly night, and he'd considered lighting the fire, but he couldn't risk an attack – not with Sarah in the room. She'd think him a mad man if he lost it. Instead, he'd brought a blanket to lay over their knees while they drank coffee and talked. The mood had been more upbeat than during their conversation earlier, mainly about everyday topics from favourite films to how they liked to spend sleepy, sunny afternoons. And, of course, tales of Bess and Clive whose mischievous antics had them in stitches. He'd sensed she'd needed some light relief after everything she'd told him earlier, and so he'd steered the conversation – something he was out of practice at, considering how few non-essential human interactions he had these days.

'I've obviously been talking too much,' he said, with a sudden bout of self-consciousness. 'I hope I didn't bore you senseless.'

'Quite the opposite.' She smiled, and the light streaming in from the hallway caught her cheekbone, making her fair skin shimmer. 'I've had a lovely evening.'

He led the way up the stairs and along the corridor to the spare room. He bent his arm around the door to flick the switch, bathing the small but comfortable room in light. 'Is there anything you need?' he asked, suddenly aware how close he was standing to her in the entrance to the bedroom. Her thick, dark ponytail had loosened from where she'd been lounging on the sofa, and strands of hair framed both sides of her round face. He desperately wanted to reach out and touch them as he had earlier, but it somehow didn't seem right now.

'Do you have anything I could wear for bed?'

'What?' He was so mesmerised with the feminine image before him that he'd forgotten his question.

She laughed, an angelic tinkling sound, which stirred deep in his core. 'You asked if I needed anything.'

'Yeah, that's right I did. Is, um, a T-shirt okay?'

'Mmm-hmm.' She nodded and bit her bottom lip.

'Right. I'll fetch you one. Go in and make yourself comfortable.'

When he returned to her room, rolled-up T-shirt in hand, the scene before him made him pause in the doorway. She'd switched off the light, presumably so she could admire the scene outside better, and was stood by the window of the bedroom, looking out, her fingers touching the glass. She was smiling but there was the unmistakable glint of a tear in the corner of her eye.

The moonlight reflected the bright white of the snow on the ground of his land, and highlighted her face, giving her a beautiful, ghost-like quality. He didn't know why this voluptuous brunette made his insides turn to jelly, but he needed to curb his reactions to her. He'd had love once. *And look at the mess you made of that. You don't deserve to find it twice in a lifetime, so don't even go there.* Blocking out the thoughts, he called over to her. 'Is everything all right?'

She quickly wiped away the tear before turning to him.

'Yes, fine. I don't know what's wrong with me tonight. I'm not normally a crybaby, really I'm not. The beauty of it all just got to me I suppose, or maybe I'm missing Clive, I don't know.'

He joined her at the window and looked over her head at the sheet-white fields. 'It's a gorgeous spot, that's for sure.'

'It really is. You're so lucky to live here.'

'Hmm,' he replied. 'But for how long will it remain this beautiful?'

'What do you mean?' she asked, quickly.

'If that infrastructure company gets their way and builds the bypass, it won't just be my land that gets demolished. Not only will they slice through this hill and cover it in concrete – they'll also pave over part of the high street, all the way across to the far easterly side of the village.' He pressed his fingers against the glass. 'All to serve the thousands of new houses they want to build in surrounding villages. They want to change this place beyond recognition. Over my dead body.'

He heard her catch her breath and realised he might have come on too strong. The bypass wasn't her doing, after all. It was just difficult to keep his feelings in check when he felt so strongly about it.

'Is this okay?' He'd deliberately softened his voice. He held out the T-shirt, and she turned her body around to face him. They were so close they were almost touching, and he found himself breathing harder.

'Perfect. Thanks.' She took the shirt and looked up at him. Her lips seemed darker red in the faded light, and he couldn't wrench his eyes away from them. They were so luscious and kissable that he wanted nothing more than to taste them for himself.

'No problem.' His voice rasped, and he coughed. 'Goodnight then.' He forced himself to walk away before he lost himself in her completely.

'Goodnight Shay. And thanks again for tonight.'

He nodded his acknowledgement and closed the bedroom door behind him.

Shay stared, wide-eyed, at the ceiling, just as he had for the last two hours. How could he possibly relax when Sarah was in another room, just metres away? Perhaps making her stay was a mistake. Maybe he should have tried to fix the tractor, steady hand or not. Or had he really wanted her to stay? Was that the real reason he'd been so adamant she didn't go home tonight? He groaned with the confusion whirring around his head.

He imagined Sarah, lying in his spare bed, bare apart from his T-shirt that would be far too big for her. A wave of arousal washed over him. *What is wrong with you, man?* Why couldn't he get a handle on his emotions when she was anywhere near? He slapped both cheeks with his hands as if attempting to slap some sense into his being. It had been a long time since he'd been in close proximity to a woman. 'That's all it is,' he told himself in the emptiness of his room. 'Pure animal instinct. Nothing more. A result of being alone for so long.'

Half an hour later, when the digital display on his bedside clock told him it was 6 a.m., he gave up completely on the hope of getting any sleep. He kicked off the covers, pulled on a T-shirt and a pair of boxers, and went out into the hallway, careful to avoid the floorboard that always creaked. He was walking past the bathroom just as the door flew open, and only just managed to jump out of the way before it hit him.

Sarah emerged, her long, dark hair loose and tousled. 'Oh, I'm sorry. I hope I didn't wake you. I couldn't sleep.'

Her bare legs all the way up to the top of her thigh were visible beneath his white T-shirt, and he could tell, by the way the cotton hung from her breasts, she was naked beneath. He so wanted to take her by the waist and pull her soft body to him, but he clenched his jaw and held back. 'No, I couldn't sleep either.'

She closed the bathroom door behind her, and her body brushed against his in the narrow corridor. There it was again – that animal instinct. He averted his gaze in the interest of decency and flattened his back against the wall, allowing her the space to pass. *That's all it is*, he repeated in his head. *A pure human need. Ignore it. It'll go away.* He cleared his throat. 'Coffee?'

She turned around. With her dishevelled locks she looked wild and untamed. 'Just what the doctor ordered. Then I'll get out of your hair, I promise, just as soon as I'm dressed.'

The thought of her leaving made him inexplicably cold. 'No rush. Take your time.'

She flashed him a grin. Her face free of make-up shone with natural radiance, and for a moment he froze, unable to do or say anything other than to take in the picture of beauty before him.

'You've been very kind, Shay, letting me stay overnight. I don't want to outstay my welcome, though. And I've got to get back to feed Clive.'

'Do you think Clive could hold on till you've had a bacon sandwich? I made some fresh bread yesterday. It won't be nearly as good tomorrow. Care to help me out?'

'You bake bread? You're a man after my own heart.' She laughed, an early-morning throaty laugh that threatened to undo him completely.

'Well, I've got a machine that does the hard work.'

'Even so,' she said. 'I'm impressed. I reckon Clive would probably forgive you the delay if you're feeding and watering his human.'

'Great. And I'll go out and assess the damage – check it's safe for you to get out. I haven't even looked out of the window yet this morning to see whether the snow's melted or if more has fallen.'

Her smile faded. 'Come to think of it, Shay, I've been meaning to talk to you about something. Perhaps we can chat about it after breakfast.'

'Oh? Sounds ominous.'

Her lips curled back into a smile that didn't quite reach her eyes. 'Not at all. I think I could do you a favour actually.'

'O-kay. Well, I'll get cooking, then you can tell me all about it.'

'Sure. Thanks.'

He was about to ask her how she liked her bacon, but she disappeared quickly into her room. He had no idea what she wanted to talk about, but from the way her expression changed so suddenly from relaxed to anxious, he wasn't convinced he wanted to know.

Chapter Nine

Shay squinted. Was it the driving snow playing tricks on him or was there something ahead of him in the road? *It couldn't be.* From here it looked like two figures, the smaller one giving the larger one a – *was that a piggyback? Must be a couple of kids*. But if that were the case, the one being carried was a very large kid.

There was something about the pair that bothered him. The smaller figure, who was doing the carrying, looked to be struggling. He wouldn't normally interfere in people's business, but this weather was treacherous. He couldn't just drive on past if these two needed help. He slowed the tractor until he was as close behind them as he could safely be, then jumped down from the cabin.

'Hey,' he called. 'Hey!'

The smaller person heard him, and turned around, albeit very slowly so as not to lose his cargo, which Shay could now make out to be a woman.

'George! What are you—?'

Shay dashed over to the elderly man, and helped him to ease his female, and decidedly larger, companion off his back.

'Oh, thank you, son. Thank you,' blustered an exhausted-looking George once he'd got his breath back.

'What are you two doing out here in this weather?' Shay asked, shielding his eyes from the relentless snow.

'Just helping Doris home. She'd been over to visit me, you see.' George pulled a handkerchief out of his coat pocket and blew his bright red nose loudly. 'She's got bad ankles. I didn't want her getting a chill.'

'I see,' said Shay. 'Allow me?' He held out his arms to the old lady. As soon as she nodded he scooped her up into a cradle hold. She wrapped her arms around his neck and smiled up at him. He tried to smile back without wincing. He knew where George lived and was amazed the slight man had already carried her this far. 'It'd be too much of a squeeze trying to get us all in the tractor, and I'm not leaving either of you out here on your own. I'll carry you from here. Where do you live, Mrs, um …?' He thought he'd seen the lady before in the Post Office but didn't feel comfortable addressing her by her first name, not until invited to, anyway. He always felt he should be more respectful than that to the older generation.

'Mrs Grey,' she said, taking one arm away from his neck momentarily to adjust her woollen hat over a platinum curl. 'Just at the end of this road here.'

Shay began to stomp his way through the snow with George bustling alongside.

'If you don't mind me asking, Mrs Grey,' said Shay. 'What were you doing walking over to George's house in the first place. In this weather? You really need to be careful, especially if you have bad ankles.'

'That was last night,' cut in Doris. '*Before* it started to snow. My grandson was spending the night at a friend's house, so I thought I'd take the opportunity to cook George a slap-up dinner. At his house.'

Shay looked down to his side and saw George's wrinkled face beaming up at him.

'Grand cook is our Doris,' he said. 'And then she stayed over, you see.'

'Oh, I *see*,' said Shay, suppressing a smile.

Doris shot the old man a look. 'Yes, George. I'm sure this young man can work that one out for himself.'

Shay blinked away a snowflake that had landed on his lashes. 'So, what's the rush to get home now?'

'Jude will be home soon,' said Doris.

'Jude?' said Shay. *Surely not her husband?*

'My grandson. I mean, I know anything goes these days, but one does like to set a good example, you know, especially as Jude is so very impressionable.'

Shay grinned. 'I understand, Mrs Grey. Don't you worry – your secret's safe with me.'

Doris pursed her lips. 'Oh, it's not a secret, young man. I just want to exemplify proper behaviour, that's all.'

'Good for you.'

'It's just this one here, son.' George pointed to a semi-detached bungalow with a red front door.

'Don't be silly, George, it's three doors down from here,' said Doris. She hugged Shay tighter around the neck and moved closer to his ear. 'Good job he knows his way around a woman's body better than he does the village,' she whispered.

Shay quickened his pace. 'Err, yes, right.'

'There we go,' Shay said, gently lowering Doris to her feet once they'd stepped inside the semi. He straightened up slowly, ironing out the crick in his back.

George patted him on the shoulder. 'Thank you, son. You saved me a job there. My back's not what it used to be.'

Neither is mine, thought Shay.

'Now, you will stop for a cup of tea, I presume?' said Doris, already filling the kettle.

'That's very kind of you, Mrs Grey, but I'd better be getting back. I've got a cat to pick up.'

'A cat?'

'That's right. Sarah Pickering's pet – the lady who's just moved into the village.'

'Ah, yes.' A wide smile appeared on Doris' face. 'She came to see me just a couple of days ago. Lovely young thing, she is. And very pretty, don't you think?'

Shay scratched his beard. 'Um, yes. I suppose so.'

'Well, I'm sure the cat can wait a few minutes longer. You must be parched. Go through to the kitchen and sit yourself down.'

Shay, not feeling that Doris was a woman you argued with, joined her and George in taking off their snow-covered boots and coats and did as he was told.

'Where are you taking Sarah's cat?' asked George, settling in the chair beside him and blowing his nose once again.

'Not at the table, George!' Doris set two steaming cups in front of them and gave the old man a swipe on the back.

'Sorry, my love,' he said, grinning as Doris turned around to fetch a tin of biscuits.

Shay told them both about Sarah not having any central heating and that he'd suggested she and Clive stay with him until the worst of the weather was over. He left out the part about their intimate chat and how he'd been so tempted to kiss her.

'You could do worse than having a sturdy girl like Sarah around,' said Doris, resting her cup back onto the saucer. 'Lovely strong figure on her. And so helpful she was when she came here.'

'Oh?' Shay raised his eyebrows. Most people were a lot more sociable than he was, but he couldn't imagine what reason Sarah would have for visiting Mrs Grey in her first week of being in Wetherstone.

'Yes,' continued Doris. 'And very friendly she is too. I was telling her all about our plight to stop this blasted road being built and how worried I was about the effect it could have on Jude.'

George leaned forward. 'Aye. He's been a rum'n, you know, that Jude.'

'George!' Doris glared at him.

'Sorry, dear. Just saying.'

Doris looked back at Shay. 'Jude's not a bad lad. He just fell in with the wrong crowd, that's all. His father, my son, said he thought it would be a good idea if he could get away from the city for a bit – come out here to Wetherstone and spend some time with me. Parents are too soft on him,' she added.

'Doris has done wonders with him,' said George.

Doris looked down at the table and smiled. 'Well, a bit of old-fashioned discipline never did anyone any harm.'

'He loves his gran,' said George.

'And I love him.' Doris looked up and Shay could see tears in her eyes. 'That's what I was saying to Sarah. If we have to move now it could set him back to square one. He's done so well since he's been here. I don't want anything to upset him. He's such a sensitive lad.'

'So, what did Sarah say?' asked Shay.

The old woman's face brightened and she jumped up from her chair. 'She had these delivered to me.' She picked up a small pile of brochures from a shelf on the wall and brought them back to the table with her. 'Jude had to miss a year of education because of his difficulties, but he's recently started saying he wants to start college. He's planning to do bricklaying and Redman College offers it as a course. I don't drive, so that would have been perfect because Jude could have cycled there.'

Shay knew that Redman College was only about two miles out of Wetherstone. There was a French restaurant not far away that he supplied with flowers.

'Trouble is,' said Doris. 'As you well know, if they go ahead and bulldoze over our houses, we'll have to move, and the chances of getting a place anywhere near here are slim, what with the whole village looking for new homes. Even the new ones they want to build aren't close enough to Redman College to allow Jude to cycle there.'

'It won't get to that,' said Shay, his chest tightening. Even thinking about those cold-hearted creatures at LJ Networks chilled him to the core.

'Let's hope not,' said Doris. 'But have you read their latest letters? They're becoming more and more—'

'Frightening,' offered George.

Doris nodded. 'I'm praying it won't come to that either,

but if it does, I need to be prepared. Not just for me, but for Jude too. My grandson's future's at stake and I'm not taking any chances. So …' She laid out the brochures on the table. 'That lovely girl said she'd do some research for me and find out which colleges offered bricklaying courses that were in cycling distance of places with affordable properties. And this is what she came up with.'

Shay glanced down at the array of prospectuses in front of him. 'Wow. That's some serious research.'

'Isn't it?' agreed Doris. 'Such a helpful young woman. And Jude's found quite a few he likes the sound of. So, you see, even if we are forced out of here, I know things will be all right.'

Shay drained the last of his tea. He felt even worse now than he had before about the way he'd gone steamrolling in, accusing Sarah of speeding, especially after everything he'd learned last night that she'd been through. Maybe he just needed to calm the hell down.

Sarah hugged her mug of tea and darted her eyes towards the clock above the kitchen door. 'Where's your daddy, Bess?' At the mention of her name, the collie came over and sniffed her legs. Absentmindedly, Sarah stroked the dog's soft head. 'He's been gone for hours, and he only went to fetch Clive from the cottage.'

As soon as she'd got dressed this morning, the blizzard had begun, covering Wetherstone in a fresh blanket of white. Unlike yesterday, the snow was relentless, billowing from every direction. Just as Shay had been about to give her a lift back to her cottage in the tractor, she'd got a call from the plumber who had been due to fix her central heating, hot water and oven today – to say he couldn't get out to the village because of the snow. Shay told her in no uncertain terms that he wasn't going to let her go back to a cold house. She'd told him she'd be fine, but didn't resist too much; the thought of huddling next to her only heat source all day – the open fire in her living room – and having to boil the kettle ten times if she wanted a bath like she had been doing all week, was not appealing in the slightest.

Then there was Clive. Shay had offered to go and lay some food out for him but as the heavy snow was forecast to last at least until tomorrow, they'd decided the best option was to bring Clive to the farmhouse rather than have to make a trip out every time he needed feeding. She sipped her tea and pulled a face at the tepid, milky liquid. 'I hope they're both okay.'

Bess looked up at her with her gorgeous big, brown eyes, and Sarah knew she wasn't the only one worried about Shay.

'And I hope you're going to be kind to my cat,' she said. 'Your daddy tells me you're the most laid-back collie there ever was, and I hope he's right because my Clive's sure seen some changes recently.' She chewed on her thumbnail. Poor Clive wouldn't know whether he was coming or going, being brought here so soon after moving into the cottage but at least she'd be able to keep an eye on him. The tom wasn't getting any younger and she worried about him.

With every hour that passed, Sarah became more and more anxious about Shay's whereabouts.

What's wrong with me? Why am I getting myself so uptight? She wasn't normally such a worry wart and Shay was a mountain of a man and if anyone could navigate a blizzard in the hilly Yorkshire countryside, he could. But ever since her mum's death, her anxiety levels had been heightened. Her counsellor had said that was completely normal, but it wasn't normal for her, and she didn't like it at all. It didn't feel like her.

'I knew I should have gone with him,' she said to Bess. But Shay had insisted there was no point them both getting frozen when he was perfectly capable of fetching Clive himself while she stayed in the warm and had a proper hot bath for a change.

She walked over to the sink and tipped the remnants of her tea down the plughole, forcing her thoughts onto a more practical topic: the pressing subject of her job. Already a week into Project Wetherstone, and she still hadn't managed to bring up the subject of the bypass with her key target – the one person she needed to convince more than any other to sell up to LJ Networks. She had intended to confess her involvement in the project this morning. She'd been in Wetherstone a week now and was starting to make headway with the residents. It was time she came clean, but she could hardly bring it up now she'd be staying with Shay for another day at least.

The brightness of the white-out glared at her from the kitchen window. Everywhere she looked, all she could see was wave after wave of snowdrift, blowing from every direction. So intense was it, she couldn't even make out the edges of the greenhouses that housed Shay's flowers.

'Oh God, Shay. Where *are* you?' Was he deliberately taking his time? He'd been quiet over breakfast – a far cry from the easy closeness of the previous evening. It was her fault. She'd over-burdened him, she knew she had. Julie had made it clear he practically lived like a hermit. Having a woman in his house sobbing over her dead mother must have put him right out of his comfort zone. And yet, he'd been so understanding.

A rush of cold air blew in from behind her and halted her thoughts. She spun around. There, with ice hanging off his hair and beard, was Shay, looking like a Scandinavian wild man. A bedraggled and shivering ginger tom was cradled in his arms.

'Thank goodness you're back. I was so worried!' She launched herself at Shay and threw her arms around his neck at the same time Bess thundered over and jumped up, her front paws on her master's legs and her long nose sniffing at a wide-eyed Clive.

'Down, Bess!'

Obedient as she was, Bess landed all four paws on the floor, but didn't take her eyes off Clive.

'Careful now,' he said to Sarah, who was still hugging him. 'You'll squash your cat.'

'You got him. Thank you so much. You're my hero!' Clive was a big cat, but he looked small and vulnerable in Shay's muscular arms. She scooped up the hairy bundle and held him against her neck. His fur stood on end and he hissed down at Bess.

'Why isn't he in the cat carrier?' she asked. 'Wasn't it where I said it would be?'

Shay stamped his huge, booted feet on the doormat, leaving a pile of snow. 'Yep. On top of the washing machine, like you said. I was surprised how easy it was to get him in it. Trouble is, turns out Clive is something of a Houdini. Just as I was getting out of the tractor, he managed to escape and darted up the nearest tree. I had to climb the bloody thing like a schoolboy to get him down. That's why he's all wet.'

She chuckled. 'No worries. I'll take him into the living room and get him dried off. I was so worried about you both. You've been out nearly all morning. I was having all sorts of visions of you being stuck in a ditch somewhere.'

'I bumped into George and Mrs Grey and helped them get home.'

She smiled and touched his arm, still dusted with snowflakes. 'Not just *my* hero then.'

He shrugged. 'No biggie. George was trying to give her a piggyback down the street to save her ankles getting cold.'

'Bless his heart,' said Sarah. 'Are they okay?'

Shay nodded. 'They are now. Safe and warm.'

'That's good.'

'Mrs Grey said you'd helped find courses for her grandson. That was a nice thing to do.'

'Oh, that? Yes.' She shook her head so a strand of her hair

fell in front of her face. It was true that she had sent off for the brochures to help Mrs Grey and Jude, but if she could get them on side and stop them objecting to the bypass, it would help her do her job too. It was a win-win situation, but she wasn't sure Shay would see it like that, not before she'd had chance to explain things properly.

Shay reached out to stroke Clive's head as the cat glared down at Bess. 'Relax, buddy,' he said. 'She won't hurt you. You're safe and warm now.'

Something inside Sarah melted as Shay spoke to the cat in his gentle tone. She wished he knew the truth about her, then she could work to get him the best package for his farm. It would work out for the best. She was sure of it.

Chapter Ten

Sarah lay on the sofa stroking a purring, and much warmer, Clive while Bess, who had been mesmerised all afternoon by the new feline houseguest, had at last settled down onto the rug and drifted off into a snooze. Clive, on the other hand, was still eyeing the dog with suspicion, although his breathing had calmed and his hiss whenever Bess came too close had downgraded to an objectionable *meow*.

Bess, Clive and Sarah looked up as Shay entered the room, his overalls hanging down at his waist. 'This weather's showing no signs of letting up. The blizzard's calmed down but the snow's still falling. Five in the afternoon and it's pitch black already.'

He sat on the edge of his armchair, knees apart. 'It's the worst weather in over a decade apparently. I'm surprised we still have electricity. I thought the power would have been affected by now. It's not particularly reliable at the best of times up here, but I've got a generator I can use for the greenhouses if the power does go out.'

She smiled at him. 'People will start talking. They might think you're using the weather as an excuse to get me to stay longer.'

He finally met her eyes. 'Let them talk. I don't care what people think. Anyway, presumably you'll have to get home as soon as the weather lets up. You must have work to do.'

Her heart sank. *Work to do?* Was that really his concern? 'I do, of course, but I'm working from home now and put in extra hours last week, so I'm well ahead.'

He stood up from his chair. 'Well, you can tell me all about it tonight. I just need to check the flowers in the greenhouse, then I'll be back.'

'Great,' she said, and mustered as genuine a smile as she could.

'Didn't you say this morning there was something you wanted to talk to me about?'

She shot him a look. 'Did I?'

He raised an eyebrow. 'Something about doing me a favour?'

'Oh yes, I remember now.'

He headed for the door. 'I won't be long, then I'm all yours.'

If only you were, she thought, as she watched him, tight bottomed and strong thighed, leave the room. Immediately she chastised herself for thinking of him like that. *Why am I making this more complicated than it needs to be?* Deep down, she knew why. She'd let herself be drawn to the grumpy, reclusive and impossible Shay McGillen more than she had been to any man before and now she was suffering the consequences.

'There's no use putting it off anymore, Clive.' She rubbed her cheek against the cat's silky ear. 'I've got to tell him the truth about why I'm here.'

The wall light flickered several times before it went off completely. 'Looks like Shay was right about the electricity.'

The only light in the room now came through the window from the rising moon edging its way between the clouds. She looked around for her phone. If she could locate it, she could use its torch. Then she remembered she'd left it upstairs. She sat up, and hugged Clive to her. 'There's no way I'm going clambering around in the dark up there. I don't know this house well enough.' Her gaze fell on the inglenook fireplace across the room, highlighted by the moon's faint light. She could just about make out two baskets next to it.

She placed Clive onto the sofa, where he instantly curled into a ball and closed his eyes, and made her way over to the fireplace, kneeling down beside it. 'Ah, perfect. Everything's here.' One of the baskets contained piles of old newspapers and a large matchbox, and the other, kindling.

'Good job I googled how to light a fire,' she said to herself. Funny, before this week she'd never lit a real fire in her life. This week, she'd had to do it every single day. She was no expert but at least she'd proven she could get one going. And it would be good to show Shay she wasn't the ignorant city girl she might have portrayed herself to be in the pub.

She scrunched several sheets of paper and lay them on the grate. She added kindling and struck a match.

'There you go, Clive. Look at that. Not bad for a city slicker, wouldn't you say?' She sat back on her heels and admired her handiwork, enjoying the warmth of the flames as they lent a cosy glow to the otherwise dark room.

'No, no, get away from there! For Christ's sake, Sarah, I said get away!'

Shay thundered into the room, shouting at the top of his voice.

'Wh-what's the matter?'

He raced towards her, grabbed her waist and swung her onto the sofa. 'Stay there!' he ordered, then rushed back to the glowing open fire and began pushing his booted foot into it, over and over, like a madman unleashed.

She jumped up and went over to him, placing a hand on his back. 'Shay, what are you doing? What's wrong?'

He flicked his head back to face her. 'Get back, I said. Now!'

He delivered the demand with so much force, she automatically took several steps backwards. 'Please, Shay,' she begged. 'Please stop. You'll burn yourself.'

Ignoring her pleas, he continued quelling the flames with his foot. Only when the last ember had died down, did he stand back from the fireplace. He still had his back to her as he stood, fists clenched, staring at the black pit where the fire had burned. His back rose and fell as he panted.

She took a step forward, arms held out ready to comfort him, then stopped herself. What had she just witnessed? Was it safe to be here? Cut off from civilisation, with a virtual stranger, who had acted like a man possessed, stamping out a fire that burned in his living room fireplace? She watched him, stock-still, breathing heavily, staring straight ahead, and her intuition told her Shay McGillen might be a man with a past that haunted him, but he was not a man to fear.

'Shay.' She whispered his name as she reached out and lay her hands on his upper arms. 'Shay, what just happened?'

He hung his head and drove his fingers into his hair. 'Damn it.'

She could barely make out his words, they were so muffled under his breath.

'It's okay. You're fine. Just calm down.'

'I'm so sorry you had to see that. I hoped that wouldn't happen while you were around.'

'Come sit down.'

To her relief, he allowed her to guide him to the sofa. She sat beside him and clutched his hand, slotting her fingers between his. She half expected him to push her hand away, but to her surprise, he grasped it, and squeezed it gently, as if she was providing a lifeline he didn't want to let go of.

'I'm sorry,' he repeated. 'It's the fire. I don't—I can't bear it.'

'I don't understand. I thought you were a firefighter.'

He sniffed out a sardonic laugh. 'I know. Stupid isn't it? A fireman frightened of fire. It would be funny if it weren't so pathetic.'

She didn't laugh. There was nothing funny about the way his ruggedly handsome face creased with shame. 'What is it, Shay? Did something happen?'

He nodded slowly. 'You could say that, but trust me, you don't want to know.'

'Maybe not,' she said. 'But it might help to talk about it. Talking to my counsellor and sharing my story with you didn't undo all the pain, but they were important steps forward.'

He put his head down into his free hand and squeezed his temple. 'If I tell you, I can pretty much guarantee that you won't want to even look at me again. I'm the lowest of the low, Sarah.' His voice cracked with emotion, and she desperately wanted to throw her arms around him and pull him to her, but she held back, scared if she pushed him too hard, he'd clam up.

She rounded her back to get low enough to meet his eyes beneath his bowed head. 'Are you kidding? Not twenty-four hours ago I told you how I walked away from my mother when she was at her lowest, and left her to kill herself. I don't know what you did, Shay, but it can't be worse than that.'

He lifted his head back up and met her eyes. Swirls of moisture swam in his dark blue pupils. 'You wanna bet?'

'Try me.'

He took a deep breath in, as if resigning himself that he had no other choice but to tell her. 'My wife, Clodagh, said she was leaving me. I wasn't fun to live with, I get that. I was self-obsessed, as well as down most of the time. I'd been in the Brigade for almost a decade, seen too much. Death, destruction, dismembered remnants of what used to be human beings. There's only so much a man can take, you know?' A single tear slid down his wind-burned cheek, but he made no attempt to wipe it away.

She nodded and reached up to his face, removing the tear with a gentle swipe of her finger. He didn't react. It was like he was so immersed in the past, he didn't even notice.

'She took Elsie.'

'Elsie? Your flowers?' She knitted her brow, confused.

'Elsie was our six-month-old daughter.'

Sarah stifled a gasp. The past tense he used sent her heart beating double time. She hadn't even known he had a daughter. She held her breath, fearing his story was worse than she could have anticipated.

'I knew things between me and Clodagh hadn't been right

for a while, even before Elsie came along, but we'd loved each other once and I couldn't bear for our family to split up. I begged her to stay, promised I'd change, but she had put up with my moods for too long. She'd had enough. I was out of chances.'

Sarah closed her other hand around the one that already held his. 'Go on.'

He chewed his thumbnail. 'That night I was working the late shift. We got called out to a car accident. Nothing unusual there. We did a lot of that in the Brigade – cutting people out of vehicles, cleaning up, that sort of thing.'

She winced, trying not to imagine the carnage he must have witnessed.

'Only when I got there, I realised it wasn't just another job. I recognised the license plate of one of the cars before I even got out of the truck. It was Clodagh's. I remember shouting at the boys, ordering them to get the cutter before the car went up in flames. I'd been to similar smashes before. I knew how they ended. What could happen if you couldn't cut the driver and passengers out quickly enough.'

'Oh, Shay.' She bit hard on her bottom lip, stemming her own tears. Not that it mattered; he seemed unaware she was there. By the vacant look in his eyes, he was deep in that moment years ago, reliving every horrendous detail.

'Everything seemed to go in slow motion. Like a bad dream. All I did was stand and stare at her through the window. She was stuck in her seatbelt and screamed at me to help her. It was then I realised she wasn't the only one in the car. Elsie was in her baby seat in the back.'

Sarah gave up trying to keep her tears in and squeezed his hand. He didn't respond, just continued to stare blankly into the distance.

'Thank God our baby was unconscious. The impact must have knocked her out. I couldn't bear the thought she could feel the flames burning.'

Sarah flung a hand to her mouth. 'Oh God, Shay, please, no!'

His Adam's apple bobbed as he swallowed hard. 'The boys were running over with the cutting machine when the explosion happened. It knocked me flying. I got up and tried to run back to Clodagh's car, but the boys held me back. I wished they hadn't. I didn't care if I burned alive, I was just desperate to get her and Elsie out. They should have let me die with my family. I didn't deserve to be the one who lived. It should have been me, not them. I was the one who drove them away in the first place.'

'You can't blame yourself for the accident, Shay. You didn't know what was going to happen. Besides, it sounds like you were suffering from post-traumatic stress from everything you'd seen over the years.'

He seemed not to hear, and carried on regardless, as if she weren't there. 'I kicked, punched, screamed at the guys in my watch. Anything to get them to let me go to Clodagh and Elsie. They formed a human barricade in front of the burning car so I couldn't get through. They risked their lives to save mine.'

She looked at him through cloudy eyes. 'And the other car?'

'What?' He blinked and seemed to register her presence for the first time since he'd started recounting the past.

'You said cars plural, like there was someone else involved. What happened to them?'

'The driver who caused the accident, you mean?' He clenched his jaw. 'She was only eighteen, just a kid.' His hand began to tighten around hers. 'The inquiry found she'd been travelling at almost twice the speed limit, had traces of alcohol *and* drugs in her blood.'

'Did she ... did she ...?'

Before she could bring herself to say the word *die*, his mouth turned down at the corners. 'She was trapped in her car too. It was rammed up against Clodagh's from the impact. It only took seconds for the girl's to blow too.'

So, it wasn't just Clodagh and Elsie who'd died in the accident; it was the young girl too. She may have been responsible for the collision, but being unable to rescue her as well must have made Shay feel even worse. If that were at all possible.

She took one of her hands away from his and rubbed his back. Everything started to make sense. The speed gun and the comments about having seen what speed can do. Shame washed over her for thinking him a miserable grump when he'd complained about her driving. He had every reason to hate her for it.

'There was nothing you could have done.'

He lowered his gaze to where their hands were clasped on his thigh. 'I really don't know, Sarah. I've been over that night so many times in my head. I ask myself the same questions every time – why didn't I fight harder to get Clodagh to stay? Why didn't I insist she leave Elsie with me? What could I have done to get to them both before the flames took hold?'

'You've got to stop all that. Beating yourself up over it isn't going to change anything.'

He turned his head to look at her. 'It's better than the alternative.'

She stroked the soft, wavy hair at the nape of his neck. 'What alternative?'

'That I somehow learn how to move on.'

'What's so bad about that? Surely that's what you need to do.'

He pressed his lips into a thin line and clenched his jaw. 'No. That's where you're wrong. How can I move on after what I did? I don't deserve to. And as for ever being a father again – I could never be a father again ...'

Her heart cracked as, overwhelmed with emotion, he broke off. 'Did you ever get help?'

'Help?'

'Yes, you know, professional help. A grief counsellor. I did – still am – and it's making all the difference.'

He shook his head. 'The Brigade offered it to me, but I turned it down; chose to get away instead. I don't see how anyone, even someone with fancy letters after their name, could do or say anything to make the whole thing any less terrible.'

'It's not an instant thing. It's more about learning how to handle your feelings. You really should give it a try.'

'There's no point.' The searing anguish in his eyes burned so fiercely she had to force herself to hold his gaze. Looking away would have been the far easier option, for in his eyes, all she could see was a mirror image of her own pain. The circumstances were different, but the grief and guilt were the same.

'Having an edible flower farm was Clodagh's dream really. I thought by realising it, I'd at least be doing something good for her. As it turned out, moving here and starting the business saved me. If I hadn't come to Wetherstone, found my own oasis on this farm, found escape in my flowers, I honestly don't think I'd have survived. But even this piece of paradise can't take away the horrors. This place allows me to carry on, but it can't make everything right. I don't deserve to be happy ever again, not after what I did to Clodagh and Elsie.'

A bucketload of sorrow swept through her. She shook her head. 'That's not true, Shay. God knows, it's tempting to believe that. I walked out on my mum when she needed me most. But if I chose to live a life of misery, I'd be soiling her memory when she spent her whole life trying to make mine happy. She didn't do it the right way, of course, but it's the only way she knew. The best thing I can do for her now is to be the best I can. We're the ones still alive, Shay, you and I. You owe it to Clodagh and Elsie to live the happiest, fullest life you can. For them, if not for you.'

Silence fell. The only sound was the clock ticking and Bess's tail whacking rhythmically against the carpet.

'I felt it last night.' His deep voice came out as a croak. 'Contentment, I mean, or at least, I think that's what it was. It's been so long, it took me a while to recognise the feeling.'

'When we stayed up half the night talking,' she whispered. She didn't phrase it as a question – didn't need to. His emotions were hers. United in their grief, she didn't need to second guess what he meant.

He nodded and repositioned his hand to hold hers tighter. 'Until then, the only time my head isn't filled with flashbacks is when I'm tending to my flowers, but even that wasn't the same as I experienced when I was with—when we—'

'And you felt guilty about that?'

He rubbed his hand down his bristled chin. 'Yep. Guilty as sin.'

'If it's any consolation, so did I.'

'So, what are we, Sarah? Two lost souls destined for a life of misery and guilt?'

'That all sounds far too self-indulgent.' She rested her head on his shoulder. Her forehead brushed his short beard, which was much softer than it looked, and sent a shockwave of desire and comfort running through her. She shouldn't think of him in that way, not when he'd opened up his heart about his dead wife and daughter. *Shame on you, Sarah Pickering.*

'So, what do you suggest?' He moved his head, and where his beard had rested against her forehead, it was replaced by something much softer. His lips. The single, firm kiss he planted there awoke a sleeping butterfly in her stomach that spread its wings and tickled her insides the moment his mouth pressed against her skin. She tipped her face up and was met with those deep blue eyes, hooded by dark brows. His expression was intensely serious, as if he was about to embark on a dangerous journey, one he wasn't sure it was safe to make, but he had to, because the destination was far too beautiful a place to miss out on.

'You have a way of making me feel better,' she said. 'At a time when I never thought I'd find anyone who understood.'

He bowed his head towards hers, just as he had done several nights before when they'd so nearly kissed in the deserted country lane. He came so slowly towards her she thought she must be imagining it. She reached up and put her hands on either side of his face, guiding him towards her.

His lips were almost on hers when he spoke. He was so close his breath warmed her skin, and she could smell fire smoke on him from his battle with the small blaze earlier.

'You can do a lot better than a guy like me, Sarah.' As big and powerful as he was, he wasn't capable of a whisper. Instead, his voice rasped, as if he was waking from a hundred-year sleep.

She raised her head and gently kissed the corner of his mouth. 'What's so wrong with a guy like you?'

'I'm, I don't know, damaged. You don't want me, trust me. I can't give you what you want. What you deserve.'

'Perhaps, right now, all we both need is comfort from one another.'

He wrapped his arms around her back and pulled her to him. 'Comfort. Is that what this is?'

'I ... I don't know, but if it is, is that really so bad?' Her head told her yes, that's exactly what this was. Her need for Shay to take her in his arms was about being offered solace and compassion. So why was her heart going crazy in her chest like she'd just found her soulmate?

Barely had she processed her thoughts when his mouth fell on hers. She should pull away. This wasn't right. He was hurting, and so was she. And that was without considering she was only here to buy his beloved farm from him. Once he discovered her part in the bypass project, he'd hate her. That was for sure. But for now, just for tonight, she wanted to selfishly languish in his arms. His kiss was so anguished, yet so painfully sweet that every one of her senses ganged up on her, preventing her from pulling away.

In that one, beautiful kiss, she was lost in him; in his smokey scent, his taste of faint roasted coffee, and the softness of his shirt against her skin. She was his. And there wasn't the slightest thing she could do about it. By the time her whirling mind caught up, they were lying side by side on the sofa, clinging to each other as if they'd been starved of human contact for a lifetime.

She melted against him, and with every second their mouths pressed together, a tiny bit of the hurt she'd carried around for the last three months lifted. She didn't know how long the kiss lasted, but by the time it ended and he pulled away breathing hard, her head was filled with him. No hurt, no pain. Just him.

'Sorry if I was squeezing you,' he said. 'I just don't want to ever let you go.'

Her belly flipped. No one had ever said anything like that to her before. Especially not laden with so much heartfelt sentiment as his gruff voice conveyed. 'Then don't.' She nuzzled into his neck and kissed the area where his facial hair petered out to smooth, tanned skin. 'I don't want you to let me go. In fact ...' She paused, deliberating whether the words on the tip of her tongue were really about to come out of her mouth. Her mother was the man-chaser, not her, not timid little Sarah Pickering. She breathed in the masculine scent of him. The earthy aroma swirled down her arms and chest and made her mind up for her. 'In fact, what I think I need now more than anything, is for you to make love to me.'

His silence made her heart plummet. *Did I really just say that? Here, on the sofa? Why?* The one time she'd had sex had been with a man she'd met at work. They'd only been out a handful of times, and she should never have let it happen so quickly. But she did, maybe because she got so few chances to go out, or maybe because she just wanted to see what all the fuss was about. It had been such a disappointing experience it turned her stomach to think of it. *What was she trying to do – replace a bad memory with a good?* Shay doesn't love you though, she tried to drum into her head. *It would just be sex, and that's not the answer.*

She tried to tell herself her hormones were obstructing her judgement, but the way her limbs wrapped around him, as if magnetised to his body, told her something different. Shay McGillen wasn't just any random man who happened to be offering her solace with his brawny and rugged body; he was a gentleman, whose embrace soothed her very soul. And she needed to know that her past experience with men wasn't how it was meant to be. She bit her lip, waiting for him to tell her that sleeping together was a very bad idea. As humiliating as it would be to be turned down, at least she'd avoid getting any further into this terrible mess she was creating for herself.

'I don't have anything here.'

She pulled away and looked up at him. 'What do you mean?'

'Protection. I don't have any. I don't do much in the way of *entertaining*. There's been no one since—'

'Shh, I know, I know.' She ran a finger over his eyebrow. 'I'm infertile, Shay, and I told you – I was tested after, after what happened.'

'Hey, hey,' he soothed. 'You don't have to worry about that now. I won't let anyone hurt you ever again.' He stroked her hair so tenderly she thought she might cry. She closed her eyes and, seconds later, he was kissing her. Her hungry, searching lips were crushed under his soft, warm mouth. She could hardly breathe, but she didn't care, she just wanted more and more of him.

He continued to kiss her, his lips exploring not just her mouth, but her neck, her chest and beyond. He moved slowly, tentatively, as if allowing her to feel comfortable under his touch before he moved on to a previously undiscovered part of her body. By the time he reached her belly button, her body burned for him so fiercely that she reached between his legs as if it were the most natural thing in the world for her to do. The denim at his crotch was hot with his own need. No longer caring about her inexperience, she tugged at his fly, allowing him to take over when her efforts failed to free the hardness she could feel under her palm.

She didn't know how it happened, but moments later they were both naked. His skin, coarse and sprinkled with dark brown hair, felt incredible against her own. His movements, though still tender and courteous, became more urgent, as if he couldn't wait a second longer to experience more of her. This man made her feel sexy, beautiful, wanted. So this is how it's meant to be, she thought, as he slid himself into her.

She followed his rhythm, even as it became faster and more intense. The beautiful pressure he applied to her core, together with his groan which carried her name as he came, caused a heat to pulse between her legs, closely followed by the most out-of-this-world sensation. She tightened her grip on his arms as she let its powerful waves rush over her.

When the sensation subsided, she met his gaze. The look in his eyes was so raw, a surge of pleasure and uncertainty all at the same time swept through her. He didn't need to say or do anything for her to know the experience had meant as much to him as it had to her.

When his heart rate finally calmed down, he lay behind her, his arms around her waist, her plump, feminine bottom nestled in his lap. When he said he hadn't wanted to let her go, he meant it. It was a feeling he'd been sure would pass once their bodies met – a natural, protective male instinct toward the woman he was about to make love to. He hadn't expected the instinct to have grown in intensity after their physical needs were sated, and still be clawing at his insides.

He'd thought the need to possess her was a carnal one, borne out of his self-imposed chastity, and once they'd made love, the urge to hold her would die down, but he'd been wrong. Now, even more than before, the thought of his arms without Sarah in them left him cold.

'Are you okay?' Her ribcage vibrated under his arm as she spoke. It was nice, knowing he was so close to her he could feel her body working.

He buried his face in her hair. 'Better than I've been in a long time.' Was it wrong to open up to her like that? She'd been honest with him when he'd asked whether her desire to make love was due to a need to feel comforted. What if that's all it was to her, and now they'd done it, she didn't need him anymore?

She sighed and wriggled her body further into him and pulled his arm tighter around her. 'I'm glad. So am I.'

He kissed the back of her head and rested back on the sofa cushion. It must have been terrifying for her, watching him lose control over the fire, and yet she hadn't called him crazy or run off in a panic. She'd listened to him. Really listened.

She turned her head towards him. 'So, no regrets this time?' she murmured. 'Not like our first nearly kiss?'

'No regrets.'

She smiled, turned back around and resumed her position as the smaller spoon with her back against him.

What was it she'd said earlier? *We're the ones still alive, Shay, you and I. You owe it to Clodagh and Elsie to be the best you can be.* He turned those words over and over in his head until a hazy flicker of light appeared in the dark place his mind had become five years ago and remained until now. Perhaps she had a point. He stroked her arm and pondered why it had taken this woman, who'd only just arrived in his life, to make him see that.

Chapter Eleven

Shay stood at his kitchen sink, watching out of the window as Sarah walked down the hill back to her cottage. Clive, safely tucked in the cat box she held, peered out from behind the slatted door. To say Shay had been disappointed this morning, when he'd seen the snow had melted into a grey slush, was an understatement. He'd offered to give her a lift but she insisted the walk would do her good.

Stay. One more day at least. He recalled the words he'd murmured in her ear when they woke this morning, still on the sofa with her nestled into his lap. She'd rolled over and kissed him; a lazy, sleep-heavy kiss, which held so much promise his heart had practically burst out of his chest. Spending the night with her had shifted his universe. For the first time in longer than he could remember, he felt something akin to happiness. Or perhaps it was hope. It had been such a long time since he'd experienced either, he could barely distinguish one from another.

She hadn't wanted to go. That much was evident from the frown that creased her pale, freckled skin as she turned and waved on her way down the path, but she'd insisted on going home to make sure she was in for when the plumber arrived, and because her work was calling.

He understood, of course he did. Work – if that's what he could call the single thing that had got him out of bed since finding much-needed solace in Wetherstone – was important. It defined him, became the only thing that mattered when he had nothing else. But now, had he found something else ...?

He rubbed his eye sockets. 'What's wrong with me? I've not been anywhere near a woman for five years, not felt the need. The minute one comes along, I go completely gaga.'

He could tell himself that all day long, but the truth that

burned inside him was that Sarah Pickering was not just any woman, to whom making love had merely served as a comfort to his grief, or to scratch the itch of a sex-starved man. It would be a whole lot easier if that were the case. Instead, she was the one woman who had reached inside his hollow chest and stirred him. He hadn't ever felt that kind of connection with Clodagh.

He placed his arms on either side of the sink and bowed his head. Shame washed over him like a bucket of ice-cold water. How could he compare a woman he'd only just met with his dead wife – the mother of his child? He could feel himself starting to slide into the sludge of his old, familiar thoughts. Guilt. Shame. Self-loathing.

He kicked the hard wood of the under-sink cupboard with his bare foot. A millisecond delay, then the searing pain reached his brain. He welcomed it. It derailed his thoughts and brought him clarity. *We're the ones still alive, Shay, you and I.* Sarah's words danced around his heart.

If Elsie had lived, she'd be almost six years old. He pictured her looking down on him, all gappy-grinned and fine ginger hair like her mum's curling up at her shoulders. What would his little girl think of him, living like a recluse in the middle of nowhere? No friends, no relationships, no fun. Sarah was right. It was time he stopped feeling sorry for himself and started living again. Elsie deserved a daddy who was man enough to pick himself up and do just that.

He flung open the kitchen window. 'I'll call you tonight,' he shouted out of it. Sarah turned around, flashed a huge grin, then continued to walk with a more pronounced swing of her hips. He found himself grinning too, even though she was no longer looking. The realisation that his promise to call had put a swing in her step made his chest swell.

'Right, to business.' Standing around all day wishing she would reappear wasn't going to get his work done. He had a big contract to sign with a luxury international hotel chain, who wanted him as a supplier. 'Not our kind of place, eh, old girl?' he said as Bess came into the kitchen, searching for her breakfast. 'But it keeps the dog food on the table.' He tipped kibble into her bowl and gave her hind a pat. 'At least you've got your home back. No cat to contend with anymore.'

Rather than going straight to her food, Bess looked at him and whimpered.

'What? You're not missing him, are you?'

She licked her lips and bowed her head and began scoffing up the contents of her bowl.

Shay laughed. 'Well, if that was a yes, it's nothing a good breakfast can't cure then, I see.' He left Bess to her meal and began rifling through the envelopes on the table. What do we have here then?' He'd forgotten about the post Sarah had brought around two nights ago. In amongst the garish print of the junk mail and dull plain envelopes he assumed to be bills, was a slim envelope with a postal mark that sent his stomach plummeting southwards. 'Not again!'

He'd lived the last two days in a blissful bubble, barely thinking about the damned bypass. 'What do those city fat cats want from me now? I've already told them where they can shove their offer to buy me out.' He stabbed his thumb inside the envelope flap and ripped it open.

'COMPULSORY PURCHASE ORDER'. He read aloud the three underlined words at the top of the typed letter, and his blood ran cold. He tried to read the rest but his brain couldn't make sense of the text. The letters jumbled in front of his eyes. Over and over he skimmed the lines of print. *Notice is hereby given … under section 48 of the planning act … compulsory purchase of McGillen's Farm … to construct a section of the new bypass.*

The letter fell out of his hands and floated down to the table. Along with it went the spark of optimism that had flickered within him. When he'd told Sarah the farm was his saviour, he hadn't been exaggerating. He couldn't cope with losing his home, his business. The farm was the one place that kept him going. It was everything and all he had since the day he'd dragged himself out of Ireland, driven by grief and despair, to pick up the remnants of his life.

He strode over to the window, eyes burning, and saw his industrial greenhouses packed with the beautiful yellow flower he'd named after his daughter. A hot rush of fury and determination bolted through him. There was no way he was going to let an office full of city slickers chuck him away like a rag doll so they could bulldoze everything he'd worked for and everything he held dear to build a few miles of grey concrete. No way.

'Clive, that's really not helpful.'

Sarah lifted the meowing ginger mass off her laptop keyboard and set him on the floor. He looked up at her with narrowed eyes.

'You can give me evils all you want, but having a cat walk all over my keys and put his bum in my face is not conducive to me working.'

Clive twitched his whiskers and voiced his annoyance with a loud meow.

'Okay, okay, you win. A handful of treats in exchange for you leaving me to get on. I'd have thought playing with all those new toys I bought you would be preferable to learning to type with paws, but then who am I to judge?'

She headed to the kitchen cupboard in which she stored the cat treats, and pulled out a packet. Clive shot over as soon as he heard the crinkle of the foil.

'Here you go.' She bent down and opened up her palm. Clive wasted no time in gobbling the fishy-smelling biscuits down before trotting out of the room, head held high like an emperor on parade.

Sarah brushed her hands on her trousers and crossed the

room, back to the plastic white patio table, that acted as her kitchen furniture. She sat down and shivered, pulling her thick cardigan tighter around her shoulders. She could have cried earlier when she'd phoned the plumber and learned he wouldn't be able to come over to fix her heating today, due to having several emergencies to attend following the snowstorm. If having no heating or hot water for over a week in the middle of a Yorkshire winter wasn't an emergency, she didn't know what was. But she'd bitten her lip. There were a lot of elderly people in this area and clearly her needs shouldn't take precedence over theirs. Maybe she'd take a look at the boiler herself later; see if she could work it out.

She stared at the blank screen in front of her, struggling to recall her train of thought before she'd been rudely interrupted by her attention-seeking feline.

'There's something I've really got to do,' she muttered, as she opened up a new internet tab. All day she'd been desperate to search for news articles on the tragic accident Shay had told her about, not because she wanted to revel in his misfortune – far from it – just because … She wasn't even sure why. Part of her, a part she hated herself for, wanted to check the story's validity. It wasn't that she doubted him. No one in their right mind would make that kind of thing up; she just wanted to check out the reported version.

Shay blamed himself for the whole event, that much was clear. But was any of it really his fault? Was there something he was holding back? Although his recollection of that fateful night had made her heart bleed, she was pleased he'd chosen to tell her. Julie and Shareen had said how private a person Shay was, and she'd seen evidence of that herself. So, to confide in her, especially after such a short time, was in a strange way quite flattering.

That said, he'd only told her because he really had no other choice. The whole debacle with her starting the fire and him freaking out meant he had to give her some explanation.

His account of that terrible night had horrified her, and she could see the pain it caused him to relive it all. If she could just get a more objective review from the news stories, then she'd be able to see for herself if there was any validity in his guilt. Maybe the news presented a different angle, one she could use to persuade him he wasn't to blame. She typed into the search bar a few words she thought might bring up the story. The only information she had was that the accident had taken place somewhere in Ireland, the names of Shay's wife and daughter, and that he was a fireman.

As it turned out, that was all the information she needed. A few clicks and scrolls later, and a picture of a pretty young red-headed woman with a grinning baby perched on her lap filled the screen. Although the woman's hair was tied back, there was no mistaking her from the photo on the mantelpiece in Shay's house – the photo facing the wall. It was Clodagh McGillen, Shay's dead wife. Sarah gulped. Seeing Clodagh's image under the bold, black newspaper headline somehow made the story even more real. And tragic.

"WOMAN AND BABY DIE IN CAR FIREBALL AS HUSBAND LOOKS ON"

Her eyes brimming with tears, she began to read the article.

Yesterday, the joint funeral of Clodagh McGillen (34 of Blarney, County Cork) and her daughter, Elsie (6 months), took place at St Mary's Church, Lower Road, Cork. Hundreds of mourners attended the service to pay their respects to the mother and baby who lost their lives on Friday 7th June following a road traffic accident.

In a bizarre and cruel twist of fate, Shay McGillen, husband of Clodagh and father of Elsie, witnessed his family's tragic deaths. According to reports, McGillen, a highly experienced firefighter with Cork City Fire Brigade, was called to an incident on Hurst Road, unaware until he reached the scene that his loved ones were involved.

An onlooker said: "It was absolute carnage. There was a huge bang as one of the cars went up in flames. I could see him [McGillen] trying to barge his way through the other firefighters to get to it. I thought they were fighting at first, but then I realised they were trying to hold him back. Luckily, they managed it. Otherwise he would have been seriously hurt or worse. The fire was so fierce it was obvious no one in the car could have survived."

Shay McGillen is being hailed a hero as, just moments after his wife's car exploded, the quick-thinking firefighter freed the woman trapped in the second vehicle, seconds before it too caught fire.

The rescued driver, who escaped with only minor injuries, is believed to be an 18-year-old woman, who has not yet been named. The cause of the accident is currently unknown, and the Gardaí are appealing for witnesses. Reports that Leading Firefighter McGillen could have saved the life of the driver who caused the accident which led to the death of his wife and child, are yet to be confirmed. An inquiry is underway.

So, the girl had survived, and all thanks to Shay. He had omitted that part of the story, letting her believe the other driver had died. But why? He was a hero. Why would he prefer for Sarah to believe the girl had perished? Holding her breath, she read the final paragraph.

Tributes have been pouring in for the victims, with Clodagh McGillen being described by one mourner as "A kind and caring person, who would be forever remembered as being as beautiful on the inside as she was on the outside". One teddy bear tribute read: "To an angel and her mummy, who were taken much too soon. Take care of one another in Heaven. R.I.P."

The article ended with a phone number for people to call who may have information. She rolled her finger down the mouse wheel and paused when she came across a second article. The heading made her breath stick in her throat.

"HERO LEARNS WOMAN WHOSE LIFE HE SAVED WAS FAMILY'S KILLER"

Under the heading was a photo of Shay wearing a black suit that hung off bony shoulders. 'Oh my God, Shay.' He looked stones lighter than the man she knew. His gaunt face was sheet-white, providing a ghost-like backdrop for his sunken, soulless eyes. From the caption she learned the photo was taken outside Cork City Coroner's Court, as he arrived for the inquest.

She didn't need to read any more – the heading said it all. Shay had saved the life of the woman whose actions had caused the deaths of his wife and daughter. Desperate to get the image of his haunted face out of her head, she flipped down the lid of her laptop and stared at its silver surface. Question after question raced through her mind, but the one that bothered her the most was why Shay hadn't told her about rescuing the other driver. Maybe, on the grand scale of things, it didn't matter to him. After losing Clodagh and Elsie perhaps saving the life of someone he didn't even know was insignificant information. Or maybe he wished he never had.

She rested her head on her laptop lid. The cold, smooth plastic at least went some way to soothing her whirring thoughts. Shay McGillen, tragic widower and reluctant hero, had had his heart shattered to pieces, and she was here to smash it up all over again by taking away his beloved farm.

The sudden trill of her mobile phone on the table beside her head caused her to bolt back up to sitting. She saw whose name was on the display screen and groaned. She swiped the screen to accept the call, held the phone against her ear and issued a professional greeting.

'Sarah, the villagers are revolting, in more ways than one.'

The sound of Duncan's elongated vowels brought back to her – in an unpleasant rush – what she was in Wetherstone to do. 'What do you mean?' she said. 'Has there been a development in the project?'

'You could say that. The first batch of compulsory purchase orders have been issued. That got your country bumpkins in a tizz. Never have I known a group to be so up in arms. You'd think they live in paradise the way they've been whining about not wanting to move out of Weatherfield.'

'Wether*stone*,' she corrected. 'Wait a minute – you said the orders have gone out already?' She widened her eyes as she realised she may have inadvertently delivered Shay's to him when she'd taken his post. Had he seen it already? Her stomach turned over at the thought. 'I thought they weren't being issued for another three weeks at least. Wasn't that the whole point of me coming here – so I could explain in person the advantages of selling to us, offer the human touch, rather than sending a faceless demand through the post?'

'Yes, yes, but the shareholders are getting impatient. The longer it takes to get the first spade in the ground, the narrower our profit margin. Anyway, you've already been there over a week. I thought you'd have worked your magic by now and had all the hillbillies queuing up to sign on the dotted line.'

He gave a high-pitched chuckle, which had Sarah pulling the phone receiver inches away from her head. For the last two, wonderful, nights, Shay's deep Irish baritone had been like balm for her ears, making Duncan's faux highbrow accent all the more off-putting.

'They're not hillbillies,' she said through gritted teeth. 'They're perfectly nice people and they deserve to have a representative from LJ Networks visit them and talk them through their options.' Her voice rose with every word as her frustration grew. 'Hence my being here!'

'Not going soft now we've sent you to the country are you, Pickering? Maybe the decision to relocate you wasn't such a good one after all. Is it time to call it a day and bring you back to head office?'

'No!' Being away from the city where the nightmare happened was going some way to helping her shattered heart patch itself together. She couldn't go back now. Then there was the matter of Shay. It was completely out of character for her to sleep with a man she'd only just met, and she'd hate for him to think she'd only done it to get ahead in her career. She had to make it right with him first – have a chance to explain. 'I can't come back until I've spoken to the villagers one by one and answered any queries they have.'

Typical Duncan, not giving a damn about anyone. Truth was, in the comfort of head office, she hadn't realised the impact the firm's projects had on people's lives. The company always paid generously for the property they obtained. She assumed the money helped people, but now, face to face with people like Barb, Tim and Tom, Mrs Grey, George and, of course, Shay, she was starting to realise it wasn't quite so simple.

'Tell you what.' His drawl was really getting on her nerves now. 'I'm giving you the perfect chance to take to the stage tonight and tell those country folk you seem to love so much why we are offering them the chance of a lifetime.'

She narrowed her eyes. 'Take to the stage?'

'Yeah, coffee with soy milk. Two sweeteners.'

She rolled her eyes. Duncan clearly knew where his priorities lay, placing his drinks order ahead of telling her what the hell he was talking about.

'What did you say, Pickering?'

'You said something about me having the perfect chance to talk to the villagers tonight.'

'Oh yeah, that was it. I've called a meeting in the village hall at 7 p.m. Now that people have started to receive their letters, they'll no doubt have plenty of questions. Rather than waste time and money speaking to them all individually ...' There was a wet smacking sound as he took a sip of coffee. 'I thought it made sense to do it all in one go. You can say your piece, then take questions from the floor.' His voice rose at the end of the sentence, as if he expected a round of applause.

She mimed an expletive.

'Unless, of course, you're not up to the job.'

His statement was issued with a challenging tone, one that made Sarah feel sick. She had no choice but to take the meeting. Not only had she never spoken in public before, but it would also be the first time any of the villagers learned of her connection with LJ Networks. Including Shay. *He's going to hate me!*

'Are you up to it, or what, Pickering?'

'Yes.' She practically spat out the syllable. What choice did she have? Go home with her tail between her legs, proving to her colleagues and to herself she wasn't the independent woman she aspired to be – the independent woman she'd desperately wanted her mum to be to get her to finally believe she could do a sterling job of bringing up her daughter alone?

'I thought so. I knew you wouldn't let me down.' Duncan's voice was so thick with syrup she could practically taste it. 'Remember: village hall – 7 p.m. sharp.'

'I'll be there.' Sarah hung up, then ran upstairs to the bathroom. She leaned over the toilet bowl, unsure of whether she was going to throw up. When her nausea abated, she moved over to the sink and splashed her face with ice-cold water. She stared at her reflection in the mirror. Red-rimmed eyes peered back at her above dark circles, and her skin was even paler than usual. She looked how she felt – ugly, tired and hopeless. Totally hopeless. 'I'm so sorry, Shay,' she said to the ghost of a woman looking back. 'What will this do to you?'

The tap of Sarah's heels echoed throughout the village hall as she walked up the aisle towards the stage at the front.

Almost every one of the plastic chairs arranged in rows was occupied, and every occupant turned to look at her as she passed.

She kept her eyes forward, focused on the one remaining seat on the stage designated for her. The local councillor and head civil engineer on the project were already there, and had left the chair in between them vacant. In fewer than twenty seconds every one of the villagers present would realise who she was – that she, the new girl in Wetherstone, was a representative of the company responsible for changing their lives.

'Sarah, Sarah, we've saved you a chair. Come sit with us.'

Out of the corner of her eye she made out the unmistakable bright pink streaks of Barb's hair as the post mistress waved at her from halfway along one of the rows. She was sat next to an old lady with 1950s-style cat glasses and a purple rinse. *That must be Barb's mum.* Sarah couldn't just ignore them. She gave Barb an apologetic smile. *Come on. Keep walking. Prove you can do this. It doesn't matter what anyone else thinks. You're on your own now.*

Legs shaking, she ascended the three steps up to the stage and took her place in between the two men already seated behind the desk. The spotlights on the ceiling directly above swathed her in an unpleasant, sticky heat. Row upon row of wide-eyed and, in some cases, open-mouthed faces stared at her. Many were familiar: Tim, Tom, Shareen, George, Mrs Grey, and a few others she'd visited or passed the time of day with.

Although it was the last thing she should be doing if she had any hope of holding her nerve, she couldn't stop her eyes from dragging through the row of heads to scan for Shay's tousled mane and unshaven face. *He's not here.* She breathed a silent sigh of relief.

Her relief was short-lived when a chorus of gasps swept through the audience. The realisation had clearly sunk in that the new girl in the village, the one they'd made feel so welcome, was the enemy.

She gulped and a bead of sweat trickled from her armpit down to her bra strap. 'Good evening, ladies and gentlemen.'

There was an ear-piercing screech of feedback from the desk microphone. She pushed it back a few inches before continuing. 'My name is Sarah Pickering. I'm the Project Coordinator of the new Wetherstone bypass.'

More gasps and a harmony of *boos*.

'As a representative of LJ Networks, it's my job to ensure you all receive fair and swift payment for the sale of your properties, and adequate compensation should you be eligible.'

'You can't put a price on uprooting families!'

'Some of us have lived here all our lives. You can't just force us out!'

'How do you sleep at night, Missy? You should be ashamed of yourself.'

The villagers hurled their arguments at her. Some stood up to deliver their piece, faces scrunching, fingers pointing, spittle flying. Each complaint, each hackle, stung her heart more than the last and, the moment she caught sight of Julie, staring at her with disbelieving, wide eyes, she thought she was going to break down and cry. There was no two ways about it; she'd effectively lied to these people – been in many of their homes, accepted their hospitality – and hadn't once been honest about what she was in Wetherstone to do.

Thankfully, the councillor regained order and persuaded the crowd to calm down. Those in the audience who had stood up took their seats and a hush finally fell over the room.

She pushed her shoulders back and straightened her posture. *Come on now. You've got this*. 'As you all know. There is a real and urgent need for the build of this bypass in order to serve the new communities which will soon neighbour Wetherstone. That unfortunately means some of you living on the east side of the village will have to sacrifice your properties to enable its construction, but you have my word that LJ Networks will ensure you receive adequate compensation to allow you to relocate within the county.'

'That's a joke. My kids grew up here. How would you feel if you could never go back to the home you knew and loved?'

The comment was thrown at her by a faceless woman – someone in the crowd she couldn't see – but she didn't need to see her to feel the pain in the woman's voice. It was a pain she could relate to only too well. She too had loved the home she'd grown up in, the home she couldn't return to because her lasting memory of it was of her mother's lifeless body swinging from the banister.

Claps and cheers rang out in support of the woman's comments. The heat from the light overhead seemed to dissipate instantly from Sarah's body, leaving her freezing cold. A sourness rose in her throat and she thought she might actually throw up this time. She stood, about to make a dash for the exit when a voice, low and powerful, and with a familiar Irish lilt came from the back of the hall.

'Let the lady speak.'

Every head in the place turned around to look at the tall man who stepped out of the dark corner.

Shay! No wonder she hadn't spotted him – other than his chosen uniform of jeans and a T-shirt, he'd completely transformed. In place of the unruly mop of hair was a neat, close crop. His beard was gone, and yet clean shaven he looked more roguishly handsome than ever.

No one spoke.

With four words he'd silenced the entire room.

The sickly sensation in her gut gave way to a vacuum of shock at seeing him. As if she were a puppet whose strings had been cut, she plonked herself back down onto her chair. She heard her own voice before she realised she was speaking. 'Thank you. Before we proceed, I'd like to reassure you that over the next few weeks I'll be visiting each of you for a one-to-one meeting to help you through the whole process. Now, onto questions …'

'Wait right there!'

Despite his gruff command for her to stop, Sarah didn't turn around to face Shay. The village hall car park was dimly lit but she picked up her pace anyway. She couldn't face him tonight, not when she was already so exhausted from the relentless questions the villagers had thrown at her over the last ninety minutes. She'd underestimated how intense it would be, and just how strong people's emotions were about being forced to move out. Duncan told her people always objected to projects until they learned how much money was in it for them. *Everyone had their price*, he said. Tonight she'd learned that simply wasn't true.

Her heel scraped against the tarmac. 'I'm sorry, Shay. I'll explain everything, I promise, just please, not now, all right?'

A large hand closed around her upper arm and whipped her around.

'No, it's not all right. You lied to me. You lied to us all.'

She struggled to break free from his grip but he was too strong. 'Let go of me, will you? You're hurting me.'

He released her from his grasp as if she were made of molten iron.

She straightened her shirt and flicked her fringe out of her eyes. 'First of all, I didn't lie to you.'

'Withheld the truth then, call it what you want – it amounts to the same thing.'

'Okay, okay. I haven't been entirely honest, I'll admit that, but I did intend to tell you about my involvement in the project. I was just waiting for the right time.'

'The right time? When was that going to be? Obviously, you thought it right we sleep together first.' His dark blue eyes flashed like dancing flames. The memory of those same eyes looking at her with the purest tenderness manifested itself in a physical pain deep within her.

'I didn't mean for that to happen, honestly. I should never have let things get that far.'

He folded his arms across his wide chest and scowled down at her. He cast a menacing figure. But even though he stood so close to her that they were almost touching, she didn't fear him. Shay McGillen, for all his size and muscle, would never knowingly hurt anyone. That's what really crushed her – knowing she had kicked and stamped on this gentle giant where it hurt him most: his big, tender heart.

'How many times were you planning on sleeping with me before you confessed that you were only doing it to whip my land from under my feet?'

'Shay, it wasn't like—'

'How many times?' He boomed the question with so much force a vein down the centre of his forehead threatened to break through his skin.

Acid burned in her throat and her legs trembled. It wasn't true she'd used him to get what she wanted. But what good was the truth when all evidence pointed to her being a career-driven harlot?

'I'm not that kind of person,' she stuttered. 'I didn't sleep with you to persuade you to sell your farm. I would never do that.'

He clenched his jaw. 'Oh yeah? Why do it then? Felt sorry for me living all alone on the farm, did you? Made love to me out of pity? Or do you have a talent for weaselling your way into the lives of wealthy widowers?'

She took a sharp intake of breath, the icy air stinging her nostrils. 'How dare you!' Any sympathy she did have for him dissipated faster than her warm breath into the freezing night. The cold made her back ache, but the blast of anger that crashed over her head heated her entire body and forced her to stand poker straight and face him head-on.

She laughed mirthlessly. 'What an idiot I am. Those two nights at your house I told you *everything*, and I mean everything. I told you things about me, about my past, things I've never told anyone before. I literally opened my pathetic, broken heart up to you, because I thought you were different.'

He stared at her, his mouth turned downward. His chest rose and fell as he breathed.

'How do I know that wasn't all a lie too?'

She opened her mouth and released a strangulated squeal of frustration. 'What? You think I would lie about my mother committing suicide because I'd walked out and left her when she needed me? Do you think I'd concoct some story that I found her hanging in the home I grew up in?' She spread out her fingers and pressed her palms together. 'Do you really think I'd make all that up just to get in your good books?'

He shrugged, his face expressionless.

She screamed into the still night. 'Oh my God!'

Shay broke his composure. His shaking fists flew down to his sides. His face reddened. 'Do you blame me, Sarah? What do you expect me to think? You turn up at my door, you confide in me, you make love to me. Then the next thing I know – surprise! Turns out all along you've been working for the company who want to flatten my farm.'

She scratched under her fringe, where itchy red stress spots were beginning to form.

'For the record,' he continued, 'I thought *you* were different too. When I said there'd been no one for five years, that was the honest truth. I've never even entertained the idea of another woman. And then—' He gestured towards her. 'You're in front of me, beautiful, vulnerable, funny, open. Like a magic cure for an invalid. I wanted to resist you, believe me, it would have been easier that way, but if I wandered an inch from you, I craved you all the more.'

She choked on a ball of emotion, and reached forward to touch his arm. 'Shay.'

He didn't move away, but nor did he take her in his arms like she so desperately wanted.

'When we were together in my house, it was as if the world outside didn't exist. I could tell you the things that give me nightmares every single night, just as you confided in me. You inspired me to do that. I even did *this*, and *this*.' He pointed first to his hair, then to his smooth chin. 'Because finding you actually made me believe I deserved a new start – when really all I was doing was sleeping with the enemy.'

'Shay, please. I had every intention of telling you the truth of why I'd come to Wetherstone—'

'You told me you were here to escape from the memories.'

'I was. I *am*.'

'But it just so happens your company is building a new road here too. Convenient, wouldn't you say?'

'Yes. I mean, no. I—'

He held out a hand to silence her. 'Please. Don't insult me with your lies any more. When you told me you were here to run away from it all, I got it. Because that's what I did too. Here in Wetherstone I found some semblance of a normal life. But then it materialises you're here for this.' He looked pointedly at the village hall.

'I saw the project as an opportunity to get away from everything that had happened.'

'Save it, Sarah. You think *you're* an idiot?' He shook his head. 'Nah. That label belongs to me.'

He turned and walked away. 'Oh, and if you want a fight,' he called over his shoulder. 'You're on.' The single outdoor light mounted on the wall of the village hall wasn't powerful enough to illuminate him as the distance between them grew. She could barely make out his impossibly broad frame by the time he gave his parting shot, but his voice rang out loud and clear. 'That farm belongs to me, and it's staying that way.'

Chapter Twelve

Shay slouched back in his armchair, his feet on the footstool in front of him. A whole week had passed since the night in the village hall when he'd discovered who Sarah Pickering really was.

He ran a hand down the coarse stubble he'd let re-grow on his face, and snorted as he remembered how he felt watching her disappear from view the morning the snow thawed. After the intensity of their time trapped inside his house together, he'd almost had her down for some sort of divine creature, sent to free him from the torment his life had become. What a prize idiot he'd been to let himself be drawn in by her lies.

He didn't need to look at the table next to him to know Elsie's footprint tile was on it. He reached for it every evening and knew exactly where to place his hand. He grasped the cold tile, brought it in front of him and uncurled his fingers to reveal the varnished fossil of his baby's tiny foot.

Silent tears streamed down his face until he could no longer read the verse under the footprint. His mind turned over with the injustice of it all. His wife and daughter's tragic deaths and the part he had to play in them, Sarah's deceit, the prospect of losing his farm and livelihood.

He was through trying to find someone else to blame; Katie Draper for causing the accident; Sarah for playing her part in the bypass build. It was time to admit to himself that it was all his fault. He was the one who'd driven Clodagh away. Him. No one else. He was the one who'd taken the decision to pull Katie from the car. He was the one who'd been weak enough to let his guard down and allow a woman he'd barely met to enter his life and claim a big, pathetic piece of his heart. What he was going through now was just experiencing the fallout from that hat-trick of mistakes. And he'd had the power and opportunity to prevent every last one of them.

A hot surge of rage pulsed through him – dirty raw frustration at himself for constantly making the wrong call in a spectacular fashion. He roared, a beast-like sound, which released a tirade of anger, grief and sorrow. For a split second he wasn't in control of his body or mind. He saw his arm stretch into the air as if it belonged to someone else, and throw Elsie's footprint tile across the room with brute force. Eyes wide, all he could do was watch as the tile spun through the air, hit the wall on the opposite side of the room and smash into pieces.

'No, no, no!' He drove his fingers hard into his hair. *The only thing I have to remind me of my beautiful baby, and it's gone. Broken. Like me.*

Bess, knowing something was very wrong, trotted over from her position on the rug and lay her soft head on his lap. His teardrops, big and fat, fell onto the dog's head, but she still didn't move from her master.

He leaned forward and buried his face into Bess's long hair. For a long time, he sobbed against her warmth, his shaking shoulders threatening to dislodge her from her position on his knees. Yet still, his faithful hound didn't budge.

'What the hell am I doing, Bess?' he said, once he was void even of the energy to cry. 'I must be going insane, trusting someone I've only just met after keeping it together for so long. What in God's name was I thinking, imagining I could actually turn my life around and start again?'

Bess whimpered.

'I know, I know. The quicker I accept that's just a crazy pipe dream, the better off I'll be.'

He swiped his arm across his face and rested his head back against the chair. 'I said I'll fight her and I will. I'll fight her till my last breath if I have to.'

Despite his strong words, the brick that sat in the pit of his stomach warned him that his reserves of strength were fast depleting and the fighting spirit he used to have in droves as a younger man was an ever-fading memory.

He wouldn't admit to anyone, even his trusty dog, that some days just dragging himself out of bed to live out his day took every ounce of willpower he had. *I'm a fireman frightened of fire, for goodness' sake. How can I think I have the strength to win this thing?*

Sarah sighed and thumped her pillow. She'd gone to bed early, emotionally exhausted after a week of meetings with the villagers, but all she could think of whenever she closed her eyes was the heartbreak etched on the faces of every single one of them. The way Barb had looked at her as she'd left the hall – not with anger, but more with disappointment and as if she'd been betrayed – she'd never forget that look.

She couldn't believe she'd come into this project so naive, believing all the propaganda the managers at LJ Networks fed the ground staff. The corporate mantra, *We help people turn their lives around*, was emblazoned on the walls of their swish city head office, and she'd always been proud to be part of a team which she believed did just that.

Now, still tossing and turning hours after she'd come to bed, she felt like a complete fool for taking it all in.

Mr and Mrs Palmer, the sweet old couple who'd lived in the same cottage in Wetherstone their entire lives, had begged her to reconsider building the road. If only she had that kind of influence.

Single mum of three, Fiona Drew, who hadn't lived in the village very long but whose eldest, Connor, had autism and thrived in tranquil Wetherstone, had told her that for the first time since she broke up with her husband, her family had started to feel settled. The bypass was going to ruin so many lives, and no amount of compensation money could make up for that.

Over the last seven days, Sarah had come to realise that, to the people who lived here, Wetherstone wasn't just a postcode that could easily be replaced; it was a special village, where these people had chosen to plant their roots. And their hearts. Yet that was all in serious jeopardy because the area had been earmarked for new housing and therefore the building of a new bypass was deemed necessary. But why here when there was plenty of space elsewhere in the country, where new homes and roads wouldn't ruin people's lives? She already knew the answer: because the housing company and organisations like the one she worked for would make more money building in such a desirable location.

'I've let you down, Mum,' she whispered into the darkness. 'I thought I could do this, show you how much we women could achieve on our own, but all I've managed to prove is how I'm not cut out for all this.' When a restless sleep finally consumed her, broken fragments of her mother's voice played over and over, punctuating her dreams like a scratched record.

When she jolted awake, she didn't know whether she'd been asleep for hours or merely minutes. She knew instinctively something was wrong, but her sleep-fogged head couldn't make sense of what that was. She tried to breathe, but her lungs refused to fill with air. Her heart thumped, as if reminding her she needed to feed it with oxygen to keep it beating. However much she tried to breathe, she felt as if a heavy slab lay on her chest, keeping her lungs from inflating.

She blinked several times to try and demist her eyes, but she still couldn't bring her bedroom into focus. With a panic-inducing thud to her belly, she realised her eyes weren't the problem – the room was filled with a thick, acrid smoke.

Fire!

Coughing so much her throat grew raw, she clambered

over the bed and sank on her knees to the carpet. *Keep low.* She ransacked her mind for any more knowledge she might possess for what to do in a fire, but her incessant coughing prevented her brain from working.

It must be the heating system. She'd pressed a few buttons, turned a few dials, thought she'd got it working. But it was an antiquated system and she didn't really know what she was doing. *Is that what caused this?*

She crawled to the window and tried to stand up to reach it, but her body, depleted of oxygen, refused to comply and wouldn't keep her legs steady enough to bear her own weight. She collapsed into a heap. *I'm dying. I'm dying and I spent my last week on this earth breaking good people's hearts.*

Her eyes closed and she felt herself slipping, slipping. She swirled downwards, oscillating between torture and euphoria.

Then, the huge arms of a divine being closed around her. She was floating upwards now, higher and higher, still held in the being's protective embrace. *This is it. This is what my mum went through. This is what it's like to die.*

'Stay with me, Sarah. I'm getting you out of here.'

What? Her mind was a muddle. She hadn't expected the presence to talk. She opened her eyes. 'Sh-Shay?' she spluttered his name with the last ounce of air she had inside her.

He didn't answer, just pulled her close to his firm chest and made for the door, which he forced open with one hard kick.

In her semi-conscious state, she wasn't sure what was real and what was her imagination. But the flames that licked the walls and furniture of her house – they were real. The acute intensity of the heat pierced her skin. Every inch of her body was so hot she thought her skin must be melting. How Shay ran through her house with her in his arms, dodging the vicious flames and falling debris, she had no idea.

And then, as if they'd been shrouded in a blanket, there was cool, black sky overhead. She could still feel heat spewing out from the cottage behind them. It spiked her head, making her want to claw at her hair.

She was vaguely aware of being gently placed on the floor. As soon as the cold from the ground seeped through her skin, she rolled onto her side. Her lungs kicked into action, fighting for breath with heaves and coughs. She tried to suck air into her body, although her chest still felt as if it were clamped in a huge vice, stopping the vital oxygen from reaching her organs.

'Oh my Lord. Will she be all right?'

She couldn't open her eyes. The tears created by the smoke had glued her eyelids together, but she recognised Barb's voice.

'Hold on there, lass. The ambulance is on its way.'

'Where's Clive?' she spluttered.

Barb frowned. 'Clive?'

'My cat.'

Barb stroked her fringe back. 'Your cat's fine, love,' she soothed. 'Shay made sure of it.'

The relief her pet was all right went some way to helping her breathe easier.

Mrs Palmer, whom earlier that day she'd reduced to tears by telling her she had three months to move out, was stroking her hand. Sarah strained her eyelids open to see the woman's grey hair and kind, wrinkled face. She wanted so much to say sorry, but she didn't have enough air inside her to utter a sound.

'Don't try and talk, lovey. You'll be fine. You were lucky, though. The cottage is a furnace. Shay's a brave lad. I don't know how he got you out of there.'

Shay. Where is he? Is he all right?

As if reading her mind, Mrs Palmer's velvety hand closed over her own. 'He's fine, lovey.'

In-between the barks raging from her throat, she saw a tall figure looming over her. With his blackened, bearded face and bloodshot eyes, Shay looked like he'd fought his way out of the pits of Hell.

What happened next was a jumble of flashing blue lights, the thud of vehicle doors being flung shut and strangers in green uniforms with reassuring tones. As the ambulance bumped over the uneven roads of Wetherstone towards the city hospital, the hand of the man who had saved her life caressed her hair.

It wasn't just the smoke she'd inhaled that knocked the air out of her – it was the realisation that Shay had faced his biggest fear to save the life of the woman whose job it was to ruin his.

With a bunch of flowers he'd grown at the farm cradled in his arm, Shay reached out to pull aside the green hospital curtain, when the sound of a man's voice coming from behind it stopped him.

As far as he knew, Sarah's mum had been her only family. He breathed in sharply through his nose. So who was this man – a boyfriend? The thought made him feel nauseous, although he didn't know why. It was no business of his who visited Sarah. Ever since he'd discovered her involvement with LJ Networks, he'd come to the conclusion their night together was purely an attempt on her part to win him over.

He didn't even know why he'd decided to visit her in hospital. To check she really was okay, he told himself. Although she'd lied to him, he didn't wish her harm.

The man's voice increased in volume. 'I knew you weren't cut out for this, Pickering. I should never have promoted you. You'll only ever be good enough to be a secretary. As soon as they discharge you, I want you back in the office pushing that pen of yours.'

Sarah responded, but her softer voice was dampened by the curtain and he couldn't make out what she said.

'What the hell are you talking about, you stupid woman?' The man spoke again, his over-the-top fake posh accent sliced through the air like glass. 'I'll ignore that, and put it down to the smoke having affected your tiny brain. I stick my neck out to further your career and this is how you repay me? Women like you are no good for anything but the typing pool.'

Shay curled his hand into a fist so tight his fingernails dug into his palm. He hated men who spoke to women like that.

From behind the curtain, Sarah responded. To Shay's frustration, she spoke too quietly for him to hear the words she was saying.

The man laughed in response to whatever she said. 'Oh, you think you'll get away with that, do you? Well, if you're going to leave me in the lurch at this important stage in the project, then it's only fair to tell you now that as an *ex*-employee you'll be liable for the insurance claim excess.'

Shay heard the shuffle of papers and the squeak of leather shoes.

'The company's insurance covers it, of course, since it's our property, but the excess payment is somewhat hefty to say the least. If you're not a representative of the company any more, we're within our rights to make you pay it. Bet you wished you'd have thought of that first, don't you? Trouble is, silly little girls like you don't appear to have the brains to do something as challenging as think.'

A spear of anger pierced Shay in the stomach at the man's bullish tone. He swiped the curtain to the side, causing the metal loops to rattle on the pole.

Two sets of wide eyes met his. One pair, swollen and bloodshot, belonged to Sarah, who was sat up in bed. Her usually silky hair was matted and scraped back into a messy ponytail, and her once round face looked thinner and drawn.

The other pair of eyes, green and close together, belonged to a man Shay had never seen before. He was dressed in a sharp navy-blue suit and had dark hair slicked back with too much gel.

'Who the hell are you?' The smarmy-looking man took a step back as he spoke, pulling his sheaf of papers close to his chest as if he was prepared to protect them with his life.

Shay lay the flowers on a trolley, which stood against the wall. 'Someone who doesn't like the way you're speaking to Sarah.'

The man's lip curled up into a self-satisfied smirk. 'What's it got to do with you, Goliath? Come to save the damsel in distress have you, because let me tell you, this one's more trouble than she's worth.'

'I think you'd better leave,' Shay growled. He stretched out his fingers, then clenched his fist. He ached to wipe the fiendish smile off the man's face. The only thing that stopped him was his hatred for violence and knowledge that Sarah had been through enough stress already.

The smug-faced stranger adjusted the knot in his tie and strolled towards Shay. 'She's all yours, big guy, but here's a word of advice – you might want to watch yourself, because if she's anything like her mother, she'll be desperate to get her claws into you.'

Sarah's face creased and she bowed her head.

At seeing Sarah's pain caused by this chauvinist in front of him, the anger inside Shay's belly expanded like a bomb, filling his veins with searing heat. He shoved the man's shoulder, forcing him backwards. 'I said GET OUT!'

The man regained his balance and laughed. 'Wow. You've got it bad. She's obviously got you wrapped around her finger. Like I said, she's all yours, big man.' He cast a sideways glance at Sarah. 'Our legal wing will be in touch with you about the excess. I suggest you might want to start saving.'

Shay took a step forward and raised his fist. He'd never hit anyone before, but this suited bigot was pushing all his buttons.

The man held up his palms. 'Chill out, buddy. I'm outta here.' He darted through the gap in the curtain, leaving Shay and Sarah alone, staring at each other.

Shay's chest rose and fell heavily, accommodating the furious pumping of his heart. His reaction had surprised him. He hardly ever lost his temper. 'Are you okay?'

She sniffed and nodded, then did a double take at him. 'Oh my goodness, you're hurt!'

He put his fingers to the gauze bandage on his cheek. 'Nothing serious. Just a surface burn. It'll heal.' He cocked his head to the curtain. 'Who was that imbecile?'

'Duncan, my boss. Well, ex-boss. I just told him I'm not going back to work for LJ Networks.'

'Why not?'

She bit her bottom lip. 'I can't do it anymore, Shay. I'm done pretending to myself the bypass is a good thing. This last week I've seen the pain it's causing people and I don't want to be part of that.'

He took the few steps over to her bed and gestured to the end corner. 'May I?'

She nodded and he sat down, then ran a hand through his wind-dishevelled hair. 'I see.'

An awkward silence descended between them. The potent stench of hospital bleach travelled up his nose and stuck at the back of his throat. If he uttered the words playing on his lips, he worried he might gag.

'Why did you—?'

'Is it true—?'

They both began talking at the same time.

'Go ahead,' he said.

She paused before speaking. 'I was just going to ask how you knew the cottage was on fire.'

'I'm not a great sleeper.' His voice was gruff. 'I was taking a walk around the village, trying to burn off some energy when I smelt the smoke. I smelt it before I saw it. It's been a while since I was faced with a burning building but you never forget the stench ...'

'Why did you do it? Run into the cottage to save me, I mean. You freaked at the fire in your living room. I can't believe you ran straight into a burning building putting your own life at risk like that.'

He shrugged. 'To prove I still could, I guess.'

'Oh, I see.' She looked down briefly, then lifted her head back up again and gave a small smile. 'Well, you obviously *can*, so thank you. You saved my life.'

'You're welcome.' He cursed himself. He could see his flippant response had made her feel that saving her life had come second to massaging his own ego. It wasn't true of course, but it felt wildly inappropriate to articulate the real reason he'd run into a blazing Ouseside Cottage.

'Of course, mine and Clive's aren't the only lives you've saved, are they?'

He looked up, met her eyes and tried to read them. *Does she know?* She couldn't. When he'd told her about the accident, he'd deliberately left that part out of the story because he hated going there, even in his own head. He shook the thought away and realised she must have been talking generally.

'That was my job,' he said. 'It's what the Brigade does.'

She held his gaze, her eyes now void of any hurt or pain. 'I mean one life specifically.'

His heart plummeted. So, she *did* know.

'I'm talking about the woman in the car,' she continued. 'The other driver who was in the accident when Clodagh and Elsie were ...'

She was trying to find a euphemism for *killed*. He winced inside. He didn't want to hear the word any more than she wanted to say it. To save her from any further awkwardness, he resigned himself to the conversation he hoped he'd never have with anyone – especially her. God knows what she'd think of him when she found out how he really felt about pulling that woman from the wreckage.

'There was an investigation after the accident. The girl. Katie Draper was her name—' He swallowed. That name would never be erased from his memory, even though he wished it would be. Elsie hadn't lived long enough for many memories to be created but he'd never forget the name of the woman who killed her.

Sarah lowered her head and looked up at him. A look which said *go on, it's okay*.

'She was found guilty of dangerous driving, sentenced to fourteen months in prison and a five-year driving ban. Fourteen months for taking the lives of my two girls.' He rubbed his rough hands against his throat, hoping to ease the lump that had formed inside it. 'She was out in six. Give it a few months and she'll be driving around again, possibly posing a danger to others, and all because *I* pulled her out of the wreckage before her car blew.'

Disgusted at himself for feeling the way he did about saving the young woman's life, he screwed up his face.

'Shay, you surely can't regret saving her? You didn't know at the time she was responsible, and even if you had you would have done the same thing, wouldn't you?'

And there it was, just as he knew it would be. Revulsion. She was appalled he regretted saving another human being's life, not that he could blame her. His regret appalled him too.

'I can't tell you how many times I've asked myself the same question, Sarah. And I'm still not sure of the answer. All I can tell you is I'm glad I didn't know then that she was responsible, because I'm not sure what I would have done if I had.'

'You would have done the same thing. I know it.'

'Do you?'

'Of course. They called you a hero.'

'Who did?' He spoke slowly, cautiously. Should he be asking a question he was damn sure he already knew the answer to?

Her eyes widened, just a fraction, but enough for him to notice. He knew very well what that look meant. It confirmed all his fears.

'I saw the news reports on the internet,' she said quietly, avoiding his gaze. 'I'm sorry. I guess I just wanted to show you, prove to you, you weren't the one to blame.'

He bit down on his tongue so hard he tasted the bitterness of blood inside his mouth. His instant reaction was to blow up, walk out, do whatever to let her know how much he really didn't appreciate her looking into his past behind his back. He counted to ten and focused on his breathing, telling himself she'd only done it for the right reasons. That much was obvious by the guilt painted across her sallow, but still beautiful, face.

Finally he lifted his shoulders in a heavy shrug. There was nothing more he wanted to say on the matter. He didn't even want to think about blasted Katie Draper and his part in helping her walk free, and he sure as hell didn't want to think about Sarah being disgusted at him for wondering if pulling a woman – whatever her crime – from a burning car was the right thing to do.

'I'm sorry I couldn't save the photo of your mum.'

'What?' She wrinkled her brow, clearly confused at his sudden change of subject.

'You said you had a picture of your mum, that you found too painful to look at, kept it in a drawer in your living room. I tried to look but the flames were too—'

'Shay, I wouldn't have expected you to go searching through drawers in the middle of a burning building.'

'I just knew how important it was to you.' He thought back to Elsie's footprint tile, and the lengths he'd go through to get that back. The pieces were too small to glue back together, but he couldn't bear to throw them away, so he'd kept them in a box on his bedside table.

'Please don't even think about that,' she said. 'There are plenty more back at the house in York. As soon as I work up the courage to go back, I'll …' She trailed off, as if the thought was too horrendous to consider.

'What did Duncan mean?' he asked. 'When he said about your mum?'

She sighed and tipped her head back to look at the ceiling. 'He'd been on a few dates with her a few years ago. I first met him when he came by our house to pick her up. He seemed really nice at first. We got chatting and he told me I'd be perfect for a job going at the company he worked for: LJ Networks. It seemed like such a good opportunity – a massive step up from the call centre where I was working at the time. He said he'd put a good word in for me, so I applied and was hired.

'He and Mum's *relationship*, if you can call it that, fizzled out after about six weeks. After that he started coming on to me at work but I wasn't about to get involved with one of Mum's exes, especially when he was my boss. He seemed to get the message eventually, although he'd still flirt outrageously when there was no one else around.'

'Why didn't you tell someone? You could have complained to his superior.'

She smiled wryly and brought her head back level. 'Oh, Shay. Firefighting and farming might work like that but the corporate world definitely does not. Besides, I loved my job. I didn't want to do anything to sabotage my position there. Plus, I was grateful to him for getting me the job in the first place. Believe it or not, I actually thought I was playing a part in helping people improve their lives.'

He raised an eyebrow.

'I know, I know,' she said. 'I realise now us office staff were protected from the harsh reality. I learned that the hard way.'

He pressed his lips into a smile. 'A harsh lesson.'

She nodded. 'I guess. But an important one. And in some ways, it's done me good. When Mum died I was so desperate to get away – to escape, you know?' She looked at him, pointedly, as if hoping he understood.

Of course I understand. I'm the master of running away.

'Where will you go now?'

She shrugged. 'There's only one place I can go. Back to my mum's house. I don't have a choice. Until I find a new job, I'll have no money for rent. And I don't care how long I have to save to pay the insurance excess, I'm not going back to my old job even if it takes me the rest of my life to pay for it.'

'You can stay with me.' The words were out of his mouth before he had a chance to think them through.

She raised her eyebrows. 'What?'

'No agenda on my part, obviously,' he said quickly. 'We've both got enough issues of our own without adding a relationship to our problems. And, despite everything, I'm sure we can manage to be civil to each other.'

He thought he detected a flicker of a shadow dart past her eyes, but her expression quickly brightened and she spoke before he could be sure.

'That's so kind of you. Do you really not mind? I'd hate to put you out.'

'You haven't had a great experience of men so far what with the animal your mum went out with and that idiot of a boss. One of us male species needs to convince you we're not all bad.'

Her mouth fell open and she stuttered her response. 'Why would you do that for me, Shay? After everything I've done – working with the opposition to buy the farm you love?'

He puffed out his cheeks. 'Because I know what it's like to need an escape. You can't go back home before you're ready. You need room to heal.'

'Like you did, you mean?'

He gave a single nod. 'Exactly like me. I'm not saying I'm healed, far from it, but I'm still breathing, which I probably wouldn't be if I'd stayed in Ireland, surrounded by everything that reminded me of what I'd lost.'

She reached her arm forward and laid her hand on his. 'Thank you. Thank you from the bottom of my heart. I promise I'll be out of your hair as soon as I find work.'

His gaze fell to her hand, which against his outdoor-roughened fingers, appeared fragile and china-white.

He looked back up at her and smiled. 'Sure.'

She grinned back, and the sadness in her eyes gave way to a faint shine. 'So, tell me, how's Clive doing? Barb visited me this morning and told me you'd taken him in. Thank you for doing that.'

'He's fine. He's ruling the roost, showing Bess who's boss.'

She laughed and Shay's heart flipped at that beautiful, tinkling sound.

'Making himself at home then?'

'You could say that. Spends most of his time chasing mice around the farm. It's like heaven for cats around there.'

'He nearly *did* end up in cat heaven. Lucky he got out of the cottage when he did. Just a shame he didn't think to alert me to the fire first.'

'That's the difference between cats and dogs,' he said. 'A dog will risk his life for his owner, while it's every cat for himself.'

She laughed again.

Silently, and in vain, he begged his body not to react.

'I'm glad he's okay. I'd never forgive myself if he came to any harm because of me.'

He knitted his brow. 'Because of you?'

'The fire. It was my fault. It was going to be ages before the plumber could come out and fix the heating. I ended up fiddling with it myself. It was a stupid thing to do, I know, but it was bloody freezing in the cottage.'

'Why didn't you make it LJ Networks' problem? I heard that dopey boss of yours say it was their property. If the fire investigation report proves it was a faulty boiler and they'd done nothing to fix—'

'I didn't report it to them.'

'Sarah! Why on earth not?'

She sighed. 'I know I should have, but I didn't want to be a pain. I already felt they'd done enough for me by agreeing to station me out in the field. I just thought I could handle it all myself.'

'You should have called me. You could have come back to the farm and stayed longer.'

She blinked slowly. 'I didn't want to bother you any more than I already had.'

'You wouldn't have been bothering me.' He sighed. 'Concentrate on getting yourself better for now. We'll sort all that out when you're home.' *Home*. For years it had been just him and Bess rattling around in the farmhouse. Now it was going to be home to Sarah too. For a short time at least.

He hadn't meant to leave her as hastily as he had. The need to get out of that room, out of that hospital, and into the fresh air was so intense it had him almost running for the door. She must have thought he'd lost his mind. One minute he was offering her a room in his house, the next he was running for the hills. In his urgency to escape, he couldn't even remember if he'd managed a goodbye.' He needed to go home, calm himself down, and come back to see her tomorrow with a clear head. He'd have to make an excuse about why he'd bolted quicker than a sprinter out of the starting block, but he'd think of something. For now, he just needed to get his head together.

It wasn't that he wanted to get away from Sarah. Quite the opposite. Being with her gave him a sense of reassurance he'd never experienced in his life before. The feeling was so strong it scared the hell out of him. So, had he done the sensible thing of wishing her well and walking away? No, he'd invited her to live with him. *Nice move. Just peachy.*

Reality dawned and hit him like a blow to the gut. For a reason he couldn't fathom, he'd offered his spare room to the only woman who, despite all her baggage and complexities, had the ability to take a hold of his heart and milk it of all its resistance, leaving him in danger of doing exactly what he didn't want – falling hopelessly in love with her.

The hospital's automatic exit doors slid open so painfully slowly he had to summon all his willpower to stop himself using his brute strength to force them apart. Once outside, he gulped in fresh air as if he'd just surfaced from holding his breath underwater. The stench of cigarette smoke from the dressing gown clad patient beside him made him want to gag. He bent over, with his hands on his knees, and coughed until he thought his lungs would burst. When the queasiness subsided, he hauled himself back to standing and leaned against the brick wall of the hospital for support.

'These buggers got you too, did they, mate?'

Dressing gown man nodded towards the cigarette clenched between two of his fingers, exhaled a breath full of smoke and dropped the tab end to the ground, where he crushed it under a slippered foot.

'Something's got me, but it's not fags,' Shay muttered.

'Well, whatever it is, pal, my advice would be to give it up while you can. It's obviously not doing you any good.' He laughed, then wheezed.

Shay slapped him on the shoulder. 'Great advice, mate. But I'm afraid I might already be too far in to get out.'

Chapter Thirteen

Sarah pressed the red button on her phone to end the call. That was it. Done. The childhood home she'd loved so dearly was officially for sale. She sighed. *What a failure I am.* She always thought in time she'd overcome the sheer terror that gripped her whenever she stepped through the door into the hallway, expecting to once again see her mother's body hanging like a rag doll over the stairs.

Being able to walk into the house and be surrounded by happy memories of the times she and her mum had spent together was her ultimate dream. Now that she'd given the estate agent the go-ahead to put the house on the market, she'd never find out whether she had the strength to realise that dream. She'd hoped – believed – that one day, with time, the happy memories would reign, and she'd love the house again. But time was a luxury she no longer had. It was either put the house on the market or be completely broke.

If it weren't for Shay's generosity, letting her stay at the farm rent-free, she didn't know where she'd be. Her paltry savings were at dangerously low levels and with no source of income she had no choice but to sell.

She let out a deep sigh. Her finances weren't the only thing she'd made a mess of. She'd ruined things completely with Shay when she made the decision not to tell him straightaway that she worked for LJ Networks – something she'd never forgive herself for. It was incredibly decent of him to let her stay with him while she sorted herself out. She didn't know many people who, given the circumstances, would be quite so accommodating.

'He'll never trust me again,' she said to herself. Of course he wouldn't. Why should he? She'd thought about trying to explain that she'd truly believed she was helping him and the other villagers get the best deals for their properties. But now she'd learned how special Wetherstone was to them – that this place meant more than bricks and mortar – it seemed like such a naïve argument.

She folded her arms across her chest and squinted at the glaring screen of her laptop. The black text fuzzed before her eyes as yet another wave of tiredness swept through her. Recently she'd been plagued with constant exhaustion. A lasting effect of all the smoke she'd inhaled in the fire, no doubt.

She rubbed her eyes and groaned. Three weeks of applying for countless positions and still not so much as a sniff of an interview. She might not be decorated with a fancy degree but she was hardworking and loyal, and was applying for jobs well within her abilities. It might be her imagination running away with her, but she was starting to suspect someone – such as a former boss with a grudge to bear – was using his influence to discredit her.

She rested her chin on her hand. *Maybe I was too hasty handing in my notice if this is the consequence. What was I thinking? I should have known that people like me don't stand a chance against the big boys.*

It wasn't that she feared going hungry. Shay would never let that happen, even though after the way she treated him, she probably deserved it. No, he was far too good a human being to let that happen to her. What worried her more was the way her independence was diminishing by the day. With the help of her counsellor she'd got herself into a good place when it came to handling her grief. And with her job she had been financially sound. *Look at me now*, she thought. *Living off the generosity of a man who feels sorry for the state I'm in.*

They couldn't go on like this for much longer. It wasn't healthy for either of them. She was entirely dependent on him for a roof over her head, while he worked all hours to avoid her. She blew out her cheeks. No job, no money and with Shay doing his best to dodge her, things had to change. Perhaps a brand new start was what she needed. A new town? Somewhere no one knew her.

Getting up from her chair and with shoulders slumped, she walked over to the kettle and flicked it on. Out of the kitchen window she saw Shay inside one of the greenhouses. Her shoulders sank another inch. 'Working at this time again? I know you're trying to avoid me, Mr McGillen.'

Spying the fruit bowl on the kitchen counter she picked up a satsuma and peeled away its waxy skin. Her mouth watered as soon as the sweet citrusy smell invaded her nostrils. She closed her eyes and relished the sensation of the orange's flesh popping in her mouth and the resulting explosion of juice. Before she knew it, she'd eaten another four and still had an appetite for more. *You've got to stop eating him out of house and home, Sarah, or you'll be sleeping in your car before you know it.*

In her reverie she hadn't noticed Shay leave the greenhouse until the kitchen door opened and he appeared in the doorway. With his windswept hair and streaks of dirt on his face he looked wild and rugged.

To her dismay, her stomach performed a double somersault. She thought back to their conversation at the hospital and put her hand to her middle to try and calm her disobedient insides. *Come on now. There's no point going all gooey over a guy who has made it perfectly clear that a relationship with you would be only adding to his problems. Your future isn't with this man. Face it, you need to move on.*

'Oh, hi,' he said.

He hadn't expected – or wanted to see her today. He'd deliberately worked late every day since she moved in, hoping to minimise his time with her. He'd worked out that if he left the farmhouse before seven in the morning he could get out before she awoke, and if he didn't return until late afternoon he often didn't see her at all as she tended to take a nap around that time. If he went to bed early, he could avoid seeing her all together.

Although he figured avoidance was the best coping method, it wasn't working particularly well. He hoped it would be a case of *out of sight, out of mind*. Whoever invented that inaccurate saying clearly hadn't shared a house with a woman who had got firmly under his skin – even if she didn't know it.

She turned to face him, leaning against the edge of the sink. 'Can I ask you something?'

He shrugged. 'Sure.'

'I've been here for three weeks now and I've hardly seen you in all that time.'

'I'm busy, Sarah. Got a business to run.'

She pressed her lips into a thin line and regarded him so intently he felt under scrutiny.

'It's hard,' he said. 'At this time of year. We're finally coming into spring now but this is North Yorkshire, not the Med. Growing flowers in these temperatures takes a lot of care and attention, especially when you prefer to work alone.'

'Are you deliberately staying out of my way, Shay? Because if you are, I can move out now. I'm sure I'll find somewhere to stay for a few days before I decide where to settle more permanently. The last thing I want is to make you feel like a stranger in your own home.'

'You're not,' he insisted, but his tone sounded flat, even to his ears.

'I've been mulling things over,' she said. 'I think it would be best if I move away. Out of Yorkshire completely. I'm not having any luck getting a job around here and, well, it might be better all around if I make myself scarce.'

'What's brought this on all of a sudden?' His heart tightened inside his chest at her suggestion she move away. She'd been right about him trying to avoid her, but the thought of never seeing her again wasn't a notion that sat easily with him.

'Actually, I've been thinking about it for a while. I would have mentioned it earlier but even though we're living under the same roof we hardly seem to see each other.'

Yes. Because seeing you and forcing myself to believe I don't want you is killing me.

'It's not fair on either of us living like this. You've been very kind, but I hate being a burden. And you need your home back.'

He walked over to her, picked up a glass from the draining board and filled it with water from the tap. He took a long glug, using the time to consider how he should best respond. He fought with the urge to pull her into his arms and tell her never to leave, but deep down he knew she was right – not about her being a burden, she'd never be that – but about him needing his home back. The temptation to give in to his feelings for her intensified with every day she lived with him. If she wasn't here with him anymore, perhaps the feeling would subside and his normality would be restored. At the same time, he couldn't bear for her to leave yet. He wasn't ready to let her go. He needed a few days to pull himself together first.

'It's not you.' He wiped a bare forearm across his moist lips, hoping it would disguise the half-truth. 'I've got a lot on my plate at the moment. I'm negotiating a big contract with a hotel in Dubai but don't know if I'll still have the farm by the time it's due to kick off.'

She looked down and shuffled her feet. 'Have LJ Networks been in touch again?'

He nodded. 'Got another letter through this morning. It said if I don't comply with the compulsory sale, they'll forcefully evict me.'

'Oh God, no.' She rubbed her forehead, causing her heavy fringe to flick up and expose the smooth skin beneath.

He felt an urge to reach out and run a finger over the freckles which covered her nose and cheeks and extended all the way to her hairline. He restrained himself by taking another swig of water. 'Unfortunately, just because you're off the project, it doesn't mean they've eased off the pressure. Quite the opposite in fact. They seem to have put the accelerator on since you quit.'

She swore under her breath. 'We need to act now before it's too late. If we get all the villagers together and collect signatures, stage a protest, drum up some media support – we might stand a chance, or at least delay them.'

'You're dreaming, Sarah. You know how these corporations work. If a project's set to be lucrative enough, they'll find a way of making it happen. A few residents holding up placards won't stop them.'

'What happened to your fighting spirit? You said at the village hall you'd oppose the order till your last breath.'

'Yeah well—' He leaned across her to wash up his glass. 'Maybe I've had enough fighting for a lifetime. I've spent the last five years battling flashbacks, nightmares and my own stupid fears.' He shook his head. 'As much as saying it makes me hate my own guts, I'm not sure I'm capable of fighting another day.'

She grabbed his arm. 'Don't say that, Shay. You're the strongest and bravest person I've ever met. You can't give up now. The villagers need you to stand up for them and oppose this road build. So do I.'

He was about to answer back, to tell her relying on him would be a mistake given his track record, when a streak of ginger and white dashed through the door.

'Clive, what have you got there?' Sarah let go of Shay's arm and darted over to her cat, who was busy chasing a small creature around the table. 'Stop it, Clive!' She bent down and expertly swooped up the feline before he could pounce on his intended victim. 'I know you think you're bringing me presents, but we really don't want mice in the house, thank you very much.'

Shay peered at the pursued creature, which had taken refuge behind one of the table legs. Black and lizard-like with spikes along its back and a long tail, it looked more like a miniature dinosaur than a rodent. 'That's no mouse.'

Sarah peered under the table and gasped. 'No, it most certainly isn't.' She looked at him with wide eyes. 'Do you know what that is?'

He laughed at her obvious excitement and held up his palms. 'Hey, I'm a botanical man, not an animal man. Why don't you fill me in?'

Holding Clive tightly, she sank down to her knees to get a better look at the mini beast. 'If that's what I think it is, then this farm could remain your property for as long as you want. And the same would go for everyone else in the village with their properties.'

'What are you talking about?'

She stood up, her arms wrapped around a squirming Clive. 'I could be wrong, but it looks to me to be a Great Crested Newt.'

He raised his eyebrows. 'So?'

'So ...' She gestured excitedly towards the creature, which took its opportunity to scamper across the kitchen and out of the door. 'If I'm right, then that little guy is a highly endangered and protected species. If he and his fellow newts are using your pond as a breeding habitat it means all plans to work on the road will have to stop immediately.'

'Wouldn't they just move them?'

She went over to the door, shut it with her bottom, and let a meowing Clive jump out of her arms. 'They can, but it's not that simple. They'll have to call in ecologists who'll need to take water samples and test for Great Crested Newt DNA—'

He frowned. 'Great Crested Newt DNA?'

'—and if environmental activists get wind of it, they'll have a field day.'

'You've got to be joking. Are you saying they could cancel the whole build for a few newts?'

She smiled and nodded. 'It happened once before, on a project down South. The company was put under so much pressure from animal activists and the media it cost them a fortune in PR to manage the crisis. Not that it helped much. The whole thing was handled really poorly and their reputation was damaged due to all the bad press. They even lost out on a couple of future contracts as a result.

'I overheard Duncan saying that if they so much as suspected this species of newt to be on the land of a build again, they'd rather find an alternative than proceed. I know that at the beginning they were looking at a different route for a much longer access road, which didn't go through Wetherstone and didn't involve uprooting a village community. They didn't go for it in the end because the Wetherstone option was cheaper, even when you take into consideration buying up all the houses. But if there really is Great Crested Newts on the land, they might not have a choice.'

Shay took hold of both her arms and looked at her square on. 'Are you saying that tiny creature might scupper the whole bypass build?'

She bit her lip. 'Yes. But only if I'm right about that being a Great Crested Newt. I remember seeing the pictures from the project they had to draw to a halt, and I could've sworn it looked just like that. It was a while ago though, so we'd need to get it checked out before we say anything to anyone in the village. Don't want to get people's hopes up if I'm wrong.'

He gestured for the door. 'Should we have let it go like that?'

'Don't worry,' she said. 'I'll send an email to the environment department. They'll be able to do tests to see if the Great Crested Newt really is present on the land.'

His mind raced, full of the implications of what she was saying. He should be delighted, and he was, to a point, but he couldn't give himself over fully to any sort of joy when moments ago she'd been talking about moving away. A thought struck him. It was crazy, but once it had lodged in his brain, he couldn't shake it off.

'Let's go out. Tonight. Now. We should celebrate.'

'Oh, well, maybe we should wait until—'

'I know just the place as long as we can get a table. It's stupidly swanky. It's where all the celebs go.'

She looked taken aback. 'That doesn't sound like your kind of thing.'

'It isn't, normally, but this is news worth celebrating.'

'*Could be* worth celebrating,' she said. 'But like I said – I might be wrong.'

He took hold of her hand. Her warm, soft skin was like balsam beneath his rough fingers. 'It doesn't matter if you are. Tonight, we're celebrating hope. Not certainty.' *And because the revelation you're thinking of moving away has made me realise I can't let you go that easily*, he added silently to himself.

'Right.' He dropped her hand and turned towards the hall. 'I'm going to get ready. See you back down here in half an hour?'

He bolted up the stairs before she even had time to reply, pulled his mobile phone from his jeans pocket and dialled the number. After two minutes on the phone, he'd secured them the best table in the house. He pulled off his clothes and headed for the shower. As the rushing water cascaded over him, the realisation of his actions dawned. What had he done? Why had he insisted they go out together? Was spending an evening with Sarah really the best way to deal with her imminent exit from his life ... or was he about to make the situation far worse?

Chapter Fourteen

'Oh no.' Shay pulled on the handbrake of his Land Rover and looked over at her, frown lines slashing his brow.

'What's the matter?'

He rubbed his forehead, then let his hand fall heavily onto the leather steering wheel. 'I didn't think. I can't believe I brought you into York City centre without asking you first. I realise it must bring back bad memories for you.'

She looked out of the windscreen up to her favourite York landmark, Clifford Tower. William the Conqueror's magnificent castle stood, majestically lit against the darkness, aloft its grassy mound. She reached over to him and laid her hand on his thigh. His muscle tightened beneath his suit trousers in response. 'It's fine,' she said. 'My counsellor said a good way to deal with my demons is to face them.'

He sighed despite her reassurance.

'Honestly, Shay, it *is* fine. How could anyone see that view and not be happy?' She gestured towards the Tower, and he followed her gaze.

He nodded. 'I might not be a city guy, but I do appreciate the history of this place.'

She snapped her seatbelt open. 'I can't wait to see where you're taking me tonight.'

He waggled his eyebrows, making her laugh. 'I've never actually eaten there myself, but one of my customers owns the place so I've been there plenty of times. If appearances are anything to go by, we should be in for a treat.'

He climbed out of the car, then came around to her side and opened the door.

'Thank you.' She stepped out and he helped her into her coat.

'I thought we'd go for a walk before dinner to work up an appetite.'

She took the arm he offered and moved in step with him. 'Perfect.' And it was. No man had ever treated her this way before. It made her feel like a movie star. She read about it in books, saw it in romantic films, but hadn't thought it existed in real life.

'So,' he said. 'What's it like being back?'

She caught a waft of his cologne – warm and spicy – and felt instantly at ease. 'Not like I thought it would be.'

'Which is?'

She tipped her head to look up at him. Even in her heels, he towered above her. His firm bulk of a body gave her a reassuring sense of being protected. 'I know it sounds corny, but I think it's because you're here with me. I feel—I don't know … safer, somehow.'

He squeezed her hand which hooked around his arm. 'Good.'

She didn't quite know how to interpret his monosyllable. His dark, normally brooding eyes twinkled when he'd said it. Was he happy his presence made her feel safe, or reassured that she was regaining her independence and would soon be out of his way?

'How about we go down here?' Shay nodded towards The Shambles, the quaint old street lined with overhanging timber-framed buildings, all leaning forwards slightly as if whispering into each other's roof eaves. 'I know a great little wine bar about halfway down.'

The Shambles was Sarah's favourite street in York – where she often used to treat herself to the odd purchase after she'd been paid or at least a coffee in one of the quintessentially English cafés. Tonight, however, she didn't think venturing down the ancient street was such a good idea.

'Um.' She looked down at her heels. 'I'm not sure

159

I'm wearing the appropriate footwear to navigate those pavements and cobbles.'

'That's easily solved.' Without warning, he swept her up into his arms.

She let out a yelp and flung her arms around his neck, where his hair was starting to curl up at his jacket collar.

'I'm far too heavy for this,' she yelped.

'Trust me,' he said. 'You're as light as a feather compared to Mrs Grey.'

'What?'

'Never mind.'

'I don't know what you're talking about, you crazy man.' She laughed, as he strode down the middle of the cobbled roads much to the amused glances of everyone they passed. She'd never seen him like this before – jolly and carefree. It was a version of him she liked. Very much. She rested her head in the crook of his neck, enjoying his warmth and the strength of him pressing against her. If only she could lose herself to the happiness of this moment. Instead, confusion whirled inside her. Since leaving hospital and moving in with Shay, he'd been distant – aloof with her even, but tonight something about him was different. Was it because she'd mentioned moving away? Was he in high spirits because he knew they wouldn't have to dance around each other for much longer?

'Here we go, my lady.' He set her down outside a tiny, cosy-looking wine bar with fairy lights crisscrossed in its dark windows. The swirly silver writing on the door told her it was *Romans*. She'd never been inside before but had heard from her colleagues in the office it was the most romantic bar in the whole of the city.

His big hand closed around hers. She looked up at him and was met with such warmth in his eyes that something inside her lower belly flipped. He led the way inside the bar, where table candles in small red holders illuminated the intimate room with an atmospheric glow.

A well-stocked bar, groaning with extravagant-looking bottles spread across the whole of one side of the room, while the remaining space was taken up with round tables and plush red velvet chairs. All but one of the tables were occupied with loved-up couples holding hands and gazing at each other over artisan wine and cocktail glasses.

Shay let go of her hand and placed it on the small of her back, sending an unexpected surge of lust shooting up her spine.

'Why don't you sit down?' he said. 'I'll fetch the drinks. What would you like?'

Panic fluttered in her chest. 'Um, I don't know. I, er, I've never been anywhere like this before.'

She half expected him to laugh at how pathetic that must sound, but he didn't. 'No worries,' he said, treating her to another gorgeous smile together with devastatingly handsome eye crinkles. 'How about I surprise you?'

She smiled back. 'That would be great, thanks.' She could have kissed him in relief. The last thing she wanted was to be presented with a drinks menu that might as well be in Greek. The idea of sipping on a brightly coloured cocktail from a beautiful glass had always appealed to her, but it had been something she wasn't well schooled in. While some of the other women her age at work had been on lavish nights out with their boyfriends, she'd spent most weekends at home waiting for her mum's safe return from her dates.

Sarah sat down at the free table and watched Shay walk over to the bar and order their drinks. His back and shoulders looked even more muscular than usual in the suit he was wearing. She'd never seen him wear anything other than jeans, casual T-shirts and jumpers and work boots before. In his tailored charcoal grey blazer and trousers and leather brogues, he looked so natural and comfortable, it was like he'd been born to wear the finest Italian suits.

'Have you been here before then?' she asked when he

returned with two tall glasses. An uncomfortable niggle stirred within her as she thought of Shay being in this very bar with another woman. She reached out to take hold of her glass and brought it to her lips, hoping he wouldn't sense her jealousy. *Don't be a silly little girl. He's only invited you to live with him because he feels sorry for you. He's not your man and never will be. You blew that chance!*

Shay took a sip of the dark purple liquid from the ice-filled glass, placed it back on the table and nodded. 'Just once, with Keith.'

She raised her eyebrows. 'Keith?'

'He's the guy who owns the hotel we're eating at tonight.'

'Pardon me for saying so, but bit cosy in here for two guys on a business meeting, isn't it?'

He laughed, a big hearty laugh that brought pure joy to her ears.

'It was a lunchtime. It's a completely different atmosphere during the day. And they serve the best sandwiches in the whole of York. Keith brought me here as a thank you for pushing through a last-minute order when he had an important function to cater for.'

'Ooh, this is gorgeous,' she said, as spicy sparkles of deliciousness from her cocktail fizzed on her tongue. 'What kind of function?'

'It was a few months ago, when the Duke and Duchess of Cambridge came to York.'

She almost choked on a mouthful of her drink. 'Wh-what? You mean Will and Kate? They ate at the restaurant we're going to tonight?'

'That's right,' he said, as if dining in the same places royalty frequented was normal. 'Although,' he added, leaning towards her so close she could see the twinkle in his eye. 'I don't think there's much chance of them being there this evening.'

She slapped his bicep playfully. 'I *know* that. I'm just

starting to worry whether I'm dressed appropriately. I didn't realise it was going to be *that* posh. Is what I'm wearing all right, do you think?' She pointed to the silk champagne-coloured blouse and black pencil skirt she was wearing. The fire had destroyed everything she owned and she'd had to buy a few pieces from the charity shop ready for when – *if* – she was ever invited to a job interview. The only thing she'd bought new was a pair of black, patent Mary Jane's. While she thought they were a little old-fashioned, at least they were versatile. The ensemble she had on was more office wear than night out, but her wardrobe was so limited, it was the best she could do at short notice.

'You look beautiful.' His eyes were no longer crinkling at the corners and his smile had disappeared, leaving her in no doubt his every word was earnest.

'Thank you.' She felt suddenly shy and looked down into her glass. Why was he being so complimentary and saying things like this? It didn't make sense and wasn't doing her head any good. Earlier today, when she'd decided the best course of action was to move away, she'd felt sick to her stomach at the thought of never seeing him again, but at least there had been some sort of clarity in what the future held. Now, she was just confused. It must be the discovery of the newt, she told herself. That's what it is. He's so happy that it might end all his woes, that he's acting like this. It's got nothing to do with the way he feels about me.

Did I give him too much hope? Do I want so badly to believe it is an endangered species that I acted too sure of myself? If it turns out I'm wrong, I'll be letting him down all over again. Her stomach twisted at the thought and she forced it away.

'What is this by the way?' she asked quickly, changing the subject. 'It's delicious.'

'Dark and Stormy. It's rum and ginger beer mainly.'

'Mmm, I could get used to it.' No sooner had the words

escaped her lips that she wished they hadn't. She didn't want him to think she was trying to worm her way into his life when he couldn't have made it clearer their arrangement was a temporary one.

'Shay, I can't tell you how grateful I am to you for letting me stay at the farmhouse. I will be out of your way as soon as I can, I promise. I've applied for loads of jobs. I guess the market is a bit slow at the moment. I'll do anything though,' she added quickly, not wanting him to think she was snobby about what kind of position she took. 'I'd rather clean toilets than survive on handouts. But I've even been turned down for cleaning jobs. I'm starting to wonder what's wrong with me.'

His fingers found hers, sending a shot of electricity zipping up her arm. 'There's nothing wrong with you, Sarah. You're smart and hard-working. Maybe employers are suspicious as to why you're applying for jobs you're overqualified for. There are loads of businesses in York. Just give yourself time and you'll find the right opportunity, I'm sure of it. Upping sticks might not be the answer you think it is.'

She paused before she answered, computing what he was saying. Was he trying to convince her not to move away and, if so, was it really for the reason he was suggesting – her job prospects – or was there something more at play. Didn't he want her to leave? She flicked her hair off her shoulders as if it would help her flick away any empty hope that he might actually want her to stay. No. He was just being kind. She had to accept there was nothing more to it. 'You could be right, but I'm just getting no joy at all from any of the big employers in York. I'm starting to wonder whether Duncan might have something to do with that. Do you think he's so bitter about me leaving that he'd go out of his way to make my life difficult?'

'I wouldn't put it past him,' he said. A guy with an ego as big as his must feel serious pain if it gets dented, and you well and truly dented his by pulling out of the project.'

'Wow. You only met him once and yet you seem to have got an excellent grasp of his character.'

He averted his gaze and she instantly knew by the shift in his eyes there was something he wasn't telling her.

'Shay. What is it? Do you know something I don't?'

'Duncan and some of his smarmy cronies came to the farm looking for you the other day while you were napping.'

She widened her eyes. 'What? Why didn't you tell me? How did they know I was staying with you?'

'They must have heard on the grapevine.'

She breathed in sharply.

He ran his fingers down the back of her hand, soothing her tension. 'Don't worry. I told them you weren't there.'

'But they'll come back. Honestly, they will. I know what Duncan's like.'

His dark eyes bore into her. 'They won't be back. I promise.'

'How can you be so sure?'

'They were there demanding money for the insurance excess.'

'Oh God.' She placed her free hand to her forehead. 'I can't possibly pay that.'

'It's dealt with,' he said, taking a swig of his drink and wiping an arm across his mouth as tough, outdoorsy Shay was back, replacing the civilised gentleman he'd been a moment ago.

'What did you do?'

Silence.

'Shay!'

'I gave them the money.'

'Oh Shay, you didn't?' Despite the relief that washed over her at knowing at least she wouldn't be chased for money she didn't have, he'd just proved what she already knew – that she was far too reliant on this man.

'It wasn't a lot on the grand scale of things, Sarah.

165

Certainly not enough for you to have the worry hanging over your head. I checked it out first, of course. They had all the paperwork with them that you'd signed when you'd taken the job. They were right – there was an excess to be paid on the insurance that they can hold you liable for if you cease to be employed by them.'

'I know,' she said, her stomach turning. 'I read it in the small print. I should never have touched the bloody boiler, but it was so cold, and with the storm and all, it was going to be ages before the plumber could come around. I'll pay you back, though. As soon as I get myself a job. It might have to be in instalments, but I'll repay every penny. I promise.'

'No you won't.' He said it so matter-of-factly she didn't dare argue. She *would* pay him back, but now wasn't the time to labour the point.

'Thank you.' Her words were barely audible even above the low level of vintage swing music playing in the bar. It felt wrong exchanging two lame words for the money he'd shelled out to spare her worry. She didn't even know how much – hundreds, thousands? Yes, perhaps it was small change to him, but he still hadn't needed to do it all the same. *Why did you do that for me, Shay, when I lied to you so badly?* She desperately wanted to ask the question but didn't want to risk ruining their night out, by dragging up the past.

'I wish you'd have asked me to come around and see if I could help with a temporary fix,' he said. 'Even if you didn't want to stay at the farmhouse, I could have come and taken a look. I'm no plumber any more than you are, but I had to teach myself how to operate the greenhouse irrigation system. I might have been able to offer some help.'

She met his gaze. 'Too stubborn, I suppose. It was important to me to be as independent as I could. After years of living with a mother who didn't seem to believe her life could be complete without a man, I wanted to prove to myself – and I suppose to her memory – that all I needed was myself.'

He tapped the back of her hand. 'A very admirable aim.'

'Yeah, and one that's still really important to me. It makes me so uncomfortable knowing how much I'm relying on your hospitality and that you had to pay off LJ Networks for me. I'm absolutely determined to get back on my own two feet. Even if it kills me – which, I hate to say – a few weeks ago, it very nearly did.'

'Just promise me the next time you move house, you'll get an expert to sort out the heating.' A smile tugged at the corners of his lips.

'I promise,' she said, returning his smile.

'Not that there's any rush for you to move out. I'd prefer for you to wait and get a job you like rather than take something you wouldn't be happy with.'

'But surely you want your own space back?'

'Well, yes, at some point. Like I said though, no rush.'

She dropped her shoulders, resigned to reigniting their conversation from earlier that day. 'I meant what I said earlier. I don't want you not to feel at home in your own house.'

He frowned. 'What do you mean?'

'It's just you seem to be doing your best to stay out of my way.'

'I told you, Sarah. My work is labour intensive. I'm out of the house tending to the flowers a lot.'

'Yeah, I know that, but, well, I can't help thinking you're avoiding me.'

He twitched his nose. Was he finally going to drop the facade and tell her the truth?

'You're very astute. I said you were smart, didn't I?'

'So I'm right? You have been avoiding me?'

He shrugged. 'Not avoiding, exactly, more mitigating the risk.'

She caught her breath at his confession. 'What risk?'

'The risk that things between us could get complicated again.' He stared so deeply into her that she couldn't fail but understand what he was saying. There was a chemistry between them that neither of them could deny, and by staying out of her way, he was attempting to quell it.

He raised his glass. 'Here's to a good evening.'

They clinked glasses and she noticed his gaze lingered on her for longer than it needed to. The skin along her arms prickled as she dared to hope that maybe, just maybe, she was more to him than someone who needed a roof over her head for a few weeks.

Sarah and Shay made their way across the marble floor of the lobby towards the dining room. Thankful for the slow pace, she gazed upwards and stifled a gasp when she saw a huge chandelier gracing the high ceiling. Its thousands of crystals dusted the five-star hotel's lobby with tiny sprinkles of dazzling light.

Everywhere she looked there were beautiful people. Stunning women with designer dresses and expertly coiffed hair, perched on bar stools next to perfectly groomed, dashing men; businessmen and women in expensive suits sat at tables, poring over important-looking documents; and a perfectly polished couple she recognised from the latest TV drama breezed past them arm in arm.

'Oh my goodness, that's Anita and Del Gabori,' she hissed to Shay as she caught a whiff of the actress's heady perfume.

'Who?' he hissed back, in a comedy stage whisper.

She nudged him and giggled. 'Don't tell me you haven't heard of them? They're TV's darlings. Plus they're on the front cover of just about every glossy magazine at the moment.'

'I thought I recognised him. Assumed I'd seen him down the flower market.'

She let out a snort of laughter, and shot a hand over her mouth. 'I don't think Del Gabori is the type to go down the flower market at dawn. I can't imagine he goes out of the house before he's been manicured, pedicured and had his personal hairdresser tend to his tresses.'

Shay wrinkled his nose. 'He'll miss out on all the good deals then. The freshest cuts are gone by 5 a.m.'

She laughed, careful not to snort this time. 'Why do *you* even go to the flower market? I thought you did big deals with international restaurants and hotels.'

'It's not about *needing* to go,' he said. 'I like going. It's good to see and smell what's out there; makes me feel alive.'

She reached for his hand and gave it a squeeze. 'That sounds better than any big hotel contract.'

He squeezed her hand back. 'It is.'

They entered the most beautiful dining room Sarah had ever seen. While Shay announced their arrival to the maître d', she took in the elegant yet cosy restaurant area. It was dimly lit with tall candles on each table, and much smaller than she imagined, creating an incredibly exclusive feel. She tried not to look too much like a fish out of water as they were led to their table.

The maître d' was just pulling out a chair when a smiley man in his forties, wearing a smart white shirt and chinos, came bounding over to their table. 'Shay! Great to see you, mate!' He slapped Shay heartily on the back and grinned. 'I thought you'd never take me up on my invitation to come to dinner at *Divine*. You need to get out more.'

Shay flicked a wayward lock of hair out of his eye. 'Yeah, buddy, tell me about it.'

'Well, better late than never,' said the man, who looked over at Sarah and gave her a big, friendly smile.

Shay took his friend's hint to make the introductions. 'Keith, meet Sarah. Sarah, Keith.'

She held out her hand for him to shake. 'Pleased to meet you.'

'The pleasure's all mine. Are you sure you want to be out with this renegade?' Keith said, nudging Shay. 'I think he's punching well above his weight there.'

Shay laughed. 'Don't listen to him, Sarah. Keith likes to think he's a comedian, but he's actually the owner of this incredible place. And one of my best customers.'

Keith patted Shay playfully on the shoulder. 'Hey, steady, big guy. What's all this *one of* business? I buy thousands of those flowers of yours. Cost me a small fortune.'

'And worth every penny,' said Shay, his eyes shining with good humour.

'Too true. In all seriousness, it's what got this place off the ground when we opened last year.' Keith looked at Sarah. 'He might look like a country farmer, but this awesome fellow of yours is one hell of a talented botanist. A famous local blogger came for dinner and wrote a glowing review. Even though our head chef is one of the best in the business, she talked more about the edible flowers than anything else. After that, we were inundated with bookings and have been ever since.'

He turned to look at Shay. 'I can honestly say without you, mate, I don't think we would have had this level of success so quickly.'

'Oh, I don't know about that,' said Shay, looking around. 'What you've done with this place is fantastic. I didn't think we'd get in the restaurant tonight at such short notice.'

Keith winked at Sarah. 'Ah, I might have overheard the maître d' say your name when you called earlier, and made sure we found you a table.'

Shay placed a hand on his friend's shoulder. 'Thanks Keith, appreciate it.'

'No worries. It's the least I could do. Please, sit down, both of you.' He waved over a waiter. 'These are my very special guests. Give them whatever they want. Everything's on the house.'

Shay took the menu. 'No, no. Don't do that. We'll pay like everyone else.'

'Oh no, you won't, my friend. I won't hear of it. And you'll start with a bottle of our finest champagne.'

'Just the one glass, please,' Shay said to the waiter. 'I'm driving.'

'No you're not.' Keith took the napkin from Sarah's glass, flicked it expertly in the air, and laid it on her lap. 'I took the liberty to book you a suite – complimentary of course. That way you can relax and enjoy yourselves, and even take breakfast in bed tomorrow.'

'Actually—' Shay began.

'Thank you, Keith,' said Sarah, cutting him off quickly. 'That would be lovely.'

'Super. Well, I'll leave you two lovebirds to it. Enjoy your evening. Catch you later.' He clasped Shay's hand once more before leaving them alone.

'Sorry, Sarah. I really didn't know he was going to book us in to the hotel. I don't want you to think I engineered that somehow.'

She rested her chin on her hand. 'I didn't think for a moment you did.'

His shoulders dropped, and she couldn't help but smile at his obvious relief.

At that moment the waiter returned to their table to pour two glasses of champagne. Once he'd left with a nod, Shay picked up his glass. 'Why did you accept the room?'

She could be mistaken, but she thought she detected a hint of hope in his voice. She took his lead and took a sip from her glass. She'd never tried champagne before, but now she understood why it was so highly rated. The delicate sparkles danced on her tongue, then slipped like sweet nectar down her throat. 'He obviously thinks a lot of you and wants you to have the room. I thought it would be rude to refuse.'

'Ah, I see.' If there had been hope in his tone, it had disappeared now. 'That's very perceptive of you. And it is a suite, so there should be plenty of space. It's not like we have to …'

'Oh no, of course not,' she said, saving him the embarrassment of saying the words, *It's not like we have to sleep together.* A lead weight sank down to the pit of her stomach, and only then did she realise how much she wanted him. Not just the physical side of him, but his acceptance, his love, his whole heart. It had been so good to hear those words he'd said to her when they'd spent time together during the storm – that being with her made him feel content for the first time in years. She'd ruined everything and she had no one to blame but herself.

Unable to look at him through fear of giving away her emotions, she lowered her head to scan the menu. She could have fed herself for more than a month for the price of dinner at Divine. Shay had chosen to bring her to York's most exclusive dining venue not knowing the owner wouldn't hear of them paying. She straightened her back. For the first time in her life someone thought her special enough to bring her to a place where princesses dined. Even if there was no chance of a future for her and Shay, she wouldn't let it spoil the evening. He deserved that much from her at least.

She made her selection, opting for the chicken as at least she understood the description of the sauce on that dish, closed the menu and looked around the restaurant. More gorgeous people in more gorgeous outfits. A few caught her eye and seemed to be scrutinising her hair and her clothes. A familiar wave of self-doubt washed over her, leaving her numb. She was so out of place here it hurt. Who did she think she was? Sarah Pickering, child of a single parent, unemployed and of no fixed address, did not belong in a place like this.

'Everything all right?' Shay asked, the concern in his voice audible.

'I feel a little out of place.'

He closed his menu and wrinkled his brow. 'Why?'

'I don't think I'm wearing quite the right clothes for a place like this. People are looking at me funny.'

He turned his head to the left, then the right to span the room. 'Trust me, the men are wishing you were their dinner companion. The women are wishing they looked like you. You look ravishing, Sarah.'

'Oh, um, wow.' She stuttered at his huge compliment. No one had ever called her *ravishing* before. She tipped her head to the side and studied his face. His full lips weren't turned up into a smirk, and his eyes weren't crinkled with humour. His sentiment was genuine, even if it was meant platonically. 'Thank you, Shay. That's a very kind thing to say.'

He shook his head. 'It's not kind. It's the truth.'

Suddenly her body was bathed in warmth, almost as if a big bubble had closed around them at their table and no one else mattered or existed. Even the thought that this level of intimacy between them wasn't set to continue didn't dent her mood. If this is as much as she could hope for from Shay, then she was going to damn well enjoy every second.

The beautiful feeling intensified as they ate, drank, talked and laughed together. When she licked the last remnant of ice cream from her spoon, she wished the meal had consisted of ten courses rather than five; not just so they could share more of the delectable dishes Keith's team had triumphed in preparing, but so the night could go on and on. She detested the thought it had to come to an end. Once they got to their suite they'd go to their separate rooms and the bubble would inevitably burst.

'Sarah. Sarah Pickering, is that you? I almost didn't recognise you!'

Sarah turned to the woman who appeared at their table. It took her a few seconds to place the polished blonde in a leopard-print blouse, pointed heels and slim leather trousers. 'Melanie, hi.' She stood up and gave her ex-colleague a quick hug, then turned to Shay. 'Shay, this is Melanie, PA to Ray Stevens, Managing Director at LJ Networks.'

As Shay rose to his full height and shook Melanie's hand, her heavily made-up eyes raked hungrily over him.

'Hello there,' she purred, eyeing him through a veil of fake lashes.

Shay smiled, then, unlike Sarah, sat down again, and although he was perfectly polite, his expression suggested he was immune to the allure of Melanie. More than can be said for most men, thought Sarah. In fact, only because she'd been treated to so many of Shay's gorgeous, sincere smiles this evening did she realise the one he gave Melanie was far blander. If she didn't know him better, she'd go as far as to say he seemed mildly irritated that their evening was being interrupted.

'I wouldn't have expected to see you here of all places,' Melanie said.

Sarah smiled sweetly, despite catching the underlying tone that said staid and boring Sarah Pickering did not dine at *Divine*. 'Oh, I've never been here before. Shay very kindly brought me here for dinner tonight. The food was incredible.'

'Mmm.' Melanie took her opportunity to take in as much of Shay as she could without appearing to ogle him. 'Me and some girls from the office came in for a few drinks after work. We've wanted to eat here for ages, but—' She paused and pressed her tongue to a perfectly glossed upper lip as if choosing her words carefully. 'It's so difficult to get a reservation.'

Yeah, right. Expensive, you mean.

'Oh my God, Sarah!' Melanie shot her hand to her mouth as if she'd just remembered something. 'You poor thing. I heard about that awful fire and that you're not working for us anymore.' Melanie batted her eyelids, giving the appearance of perfect innocence, but Sarah was well aware of Melanie's reputation to make everything her business, even when it wasn't. There was no way she wasn't fully aware of every last detail of the fire – including how it started.

'That's right.'

'How *are* you, darling? It must have been *awful*.'

'It was,' she agreed. 'But I was lucky that someone very brave rescued me.'

'Oh?' Melanie raised an eyebrow, but Sarah didn't elaborate. Knowing how modest Shay had been about the whole thing, she didn't think he'd appreciate being made a fuss of.

Melanie flicked her shiny hair over one shoulder. 'Well, between me and you, I think you jumped a sinking ship if today's development is anything to go by. Looks like Duncan and his team could soon be ancient history.'

'Oh?' Sarah shot a look at Shay before returning her focus to Melanie and mirroring her eyebrow raise.

Melanie looked from side to side as if one of the bosses from LJ Networks might happen to walk through the restaurant at that very moment. She leaned forward in a dramatic swoop and said in a conspiratorial tone, 'This afternoon we received an anonymous email saying some endangered animal or another might have been discovered on the land earmarked for the bypass.'

'Really?'

'Yes. And if it turns out to be true, you know what that means, don't you?'

Unsure what Melanie was getting at, she waited for her to go on.

'It means,' said Melanie, obviously desperate to be the one who broke the news. 'Not only is there a real big chance that the plans for the bypass have to be shelved, but also Duncan Saunders will be exposed for not doing his homework.'

'I see,' said Sarah, pleased her email was being taken seriously.

'If you ask me'—there was a distinct hint of glee in Melanie's voice—'he'll get sacked over this.'

Sarah felt something shift in her stomach. 'Do you think the whole team would be sacked? All of them? I mean it's one thing to hold Duncan responsible, but it's not the team's fault.'

'Oh, well, I don't know.' Melanie waved an arm as if that particular detail was inconsequential. 'I suppose Ray would do his best to find them positions elsewhere in the company. You know what he's like – such a softie.'

Melanie's coarse laugh rang in Sarah's ears making her want to clamp her hands over them. Ray Stevens could only be described as a *softie* where his pretty PA was concerned. With everyone else, including herself, he was a shark only with sharper teeth.

'I hope so,' she said, realising for the first time some of the possible implications of the email she'd been so happy to send earlier that day.

'Anyway …' Melanie pulled away. 'I'd better leave you to your *date*?' She raised her voice at the end of her sentence to phrase it more like a question, clearly fishing for information as to who Sarah's handsome, rich dinner companion was. Office gossip fodder, no doubt.

Sarah didn't indulge Melanie with the answer she was hoping for. Instead, she bid her goodbye, which even to her sounded half-hearted as she was still caught up with the thought she could have inadvertently caused her ex-colleagues to lose their jobs.

Melanie waved a hand. 'Don't worry about Duncan,' she

said, misinterpreting Sarah's concerned expression. 'You know what they say about silly men with a lot of power – give them enough rope and they'll hang themselves.'

In those few words, the bubble that had protected her and Shay throughout their dinner burst in one huge, sickening pop. It couldn't just be the reference to hanging – with her counsellor's help she'd been able to stop words like that triggering a physical reaction in her. It must be something else that brought on the intense wave of nausea that flooded over her whole body and left her swaying and clutching the edge of the table to support herself.

'Oh, Sarah, I'm so sorry. I didn't realise you and Duncan were that close.'

'We weren't. It's not—' The room spun around her. Her vision began to cloud over, and she had an overwhelming urge to close her eyes.

Big arms encased her and the familiar scent of Shay's cologne surrounded her as he pulled her to his chest.

'It's okay, Melanie. I've got this. It was nice to meet you, but I think Sarah needs to go somewhere quiet for a moment. Please excuse us.'

With her head pressed against Shay's firm torso, she couldn't make out Melanie's reply. All she could hear was the pounding of her own heart and the clack of Melanie's heels against the hard floor as she left. She didn't recall collecting their room key from reception or going up in the elevator, only that as they walked along the corridor towards their suite, Shay's strong arm was around her waist, holding her up.

By the time they reached their suite, she was beginning to feel normal again, although the dizzy spell had left her exhausted.

'I'm so sorry. I don't know what happened,' she said, as he eased her gently down onto the bed and propped pillows up for her to lean against.

'No need to apologise,' he said. 'After what you went through with your mum, it's not surprising that an ill-considered comment can leave your head spinning.'

'Hmmm.' She allowed herself to concur, but inside she knew it wasn't Melanie's reference to hanging that had brought on her nausea. Come to think of it, she'd been having a few light-headed moments recently, although that was the worst yet.

'Why don't you give the counsellor a call tomorrow?' he said, pulling off her shoes so she could lay more comfortably. 'At least let them know what happened.'

'Yes,' she said, absentmindedly, silently thinking that a visit to her GP might be more in order. She expected it was just stress. All that worry about her finances and the guilt she carried for her part in trying to move people out of their homes had no doubt built up. Perhaps finding the newt earlier had sent her loaded mind into overdrive and things had just culminated in her having a strange episode.

Shay made no attempt to take off any further items of her clothing. Instead, he tugged the duvet from under her and lay it on top of her body.

Even in her post-dizzy state, every one of her limbs ached for him. *I need you Shay McGillen. I need you.*

'Get some rest now,' he said and made for the door.

'Where are you going?' she croaked.

He paused in the doorway, his hand on the frame. His body was a faceless silhouette against the single light from the suite's drawing room.

'To sleep in one of the other bedrooms.'

She reached a hand out towards him. 'Please stay. I—I don't want to be alone. Not tonight.'

'You'll feel better after a good sleep.'

'Please, Shay. I need you.'

She couldn't see his face in the darkness, but could sense the anguish emanating from him. *He wants to stay. I know it.*

He let his hand fall from the doorframe and undid his tie, hanging it across the door handle. He removed his shoes, then his jacket, which he draped over a chair in the corner of the room.

The mattress dipped as he mounted the bed, on top of the duvet, and the bubble she'd felt earlier at dinner re-formed around them. *With him, I'll always be safe.* Still wearing his trousers and now untucked shirt, he remained on top of the duvet. The perfect gentleman.

Inside their bubble, warm lips and soft bristles pressed against her forehead. A heavy, muscular arm closed around her. A deep voice breathed words so insanely beautiful that tears welled beneath her closed eyelids. 'Let's just sleep for now', he said. 'You need to rest.'

The last thing she wanted with him in her bed was to sleep, but, enveloped in his warm embrace, she resigned herself to the fact that resisting each other was most likely for the best.

Oh no. As sleep gave way to consciousness, memories from the previous evening flooded back to her. Not only had she made a complete fool of herself in front of Melanie – which would no doubt translate into the latest water cooler conversation topic, she'd then begged Shay to sleep with her. *And* he'd refused. Shame and humiliation manifested itself as a dull throb at her temples. She pressed her fingers to the aching spot and winced.

'Everything okay?'

She snapped her eyes open and searched the dark for the source of the voice. Shay. Where was he? She stretched out her arm across the bed to reach for him, but rather than a warm, muscular body, all she felt was a cold sheet.

As her vision grew accustomed to the dusky light, she made out his outline, sitting in a chair in the corner of the room. He was still dressed in his shirt and trousers.

'Wh-what are you doing?'

'You looked so weak last night I thought I'd better keep an eye on you, make sure you were all right.'

'What time is it?'

At that moment a bird's trill pierced the air, providing all the answer she needed: it was daybreak.

'Did you manage to sleep?'

'Not much. Couldn't relax.'

Guilt stabbed at her chest. She'd got herself in such a state that he was worried enough about her to forgo sleep for her sake. 'You look exhausted.'

He shrugged again. 'I'm fine.'

He didn't look fine. Even in the hazy morning light barely allowed in by the thick curtains, she could see his eyes looked baggier than usual.

'I'm fine, honestly.'

She pulled back the duvet beside her, exposing the unslept-on sheet. 'Why don't you get some sleep now? You can get a few hours in at least, before breakfast.'

He scowled at the empty side of the bed as if it were shark-infested waters and she was suggesting he take a leisurely dip.

'It's fine, Shay.' She heard the irritation in her own voice. How repulsive did he think she was that, even as exhausted as he was, he couldn't bear the thought of getting under the duvet with her?

His brow still creased in a frown, he slowly stood up and crossed the room to the bed. Without taking off his clothes, he slid in next to her.

For several moments they both lay on their backs, side by side, fully clothed. The connection that had buzzed between them last night was severed. There couldn't have been more than a foot between them, but it might as well have been an enormous gulf. But even though their bodies weren't touching, the heat from his penetrated into her, making the fine hairs on her arm stand on end. *Reach over and take me in those big arms of yours again, Shay*, she silently willed. The need she felt for him to touch her burned so deep, she could have cried. The only thing stopping her was fear of him thinking she'd completely lost it. As far as embarrassing herself went, she'd surpassed herself last night.

With tears threatening to spill, she turned over, her back to him, and begged her mind to switch off to let sleep's sweet oblivion take her again. Was it relief from giving in to unconsciousness that pulsed through her, or was the pleasure surging over her a result of something else? After a few fuzzy seconds, it all became clear. She became aware of the weight of his arm across her body, his gentle pull rocking her onto her back, her moan being stifled by his lips on hers.

It took them a while to undress, so reluctant they were to tear their lips apart from each other to allow the space to do it. But when they finally were naked, skin on skin, it was worth every sacrifice. Like their first time together, their bodies somehow entwined, effortlessly, together. Their movements, moans and even their breathing were in synch. *They* were in synch. The fire inside her burned hotter for him as his mouth explored her every curve – his hands, big and calloused as they were, held and stroked her with an intensity so passionate, it sent her nerve endings into overdrive. Every cell in her body cried out for him.

He moved his hand toward her breast, then hesitated, regarding her straight on. His eyes flashed with a heady mix of desire and uncertainty. 'Is this really what you want, Sarah?'

She nodded furiously. 'You'd better not get all chivalrous on me now.'

His expression remained serious and for a moment she was sure he was going to pull away from her. She could have cried with relief when, instead of pulling away, he wrapped her legs around his back and tilted her hips upwards until her soft centre met his hardness.

'Are you sure?' he rasped.

'For God's sake, Shay, yes I'm sure. Just promise me you won't hold back.'

He sucked in his breath, and his excitement at her answer was evident by the way his fingers pressed into the soft skin of her buttocks. He filled her and she gasped with pleasure. The more noise she made, and the more she rocked her pelvis against his, the more primal beast and less perfect gentleman Shay became.

Unlike the first time they slept together, which had been slow and sensual, this time was very different. It was faster, more passionate and with an undercurrent of energy so strong, the need she had inside her for him was almost desperate.

His hard body slammed against the most sensitive part of her core over and over until the spark he'd ignited in her blew into a full-blown firework, exploding inside her and flooding her veins with intense, hedonistic pleasure. She grasped his wrists, holding him still until the fire began to simmer.

After giving her time to recover, he smiled down at her, a slow, sexy smile, and began to rock in and out of her again, gently at first, before picking up speed and power. With a final, forceful push, he came inside her. His fingertips pressed into her clammy skin and he closed his eyes. His face was a picture of pure bliss, that turned her on all over again.

He pulled himself out of her, and lay beside her, his arm slung over her sweat-damp stomach. She liked the weight of it on top of her. It said she was his. His breathing grew heavy as he gave into sleep, and a smile of contentment spread across her face, quickly to fade as her heart come down to earth with a heavy thump. There was no use denying it anymore. She was in love with this crazy, damaged and beautiful man. And there was nothing she could do about it.

Chapter Fifteen

Sarah stepped into the house, still in a daze following what she'd learned at the GP surgery in the nearby town of Stoneyfields three hours earlier. She hadn't come straight back to the farmhouse after her doctor had broken the news; she'd needed time to digest everything, so had walked aimlessly around town trying to make sense of it all.

Three times she'd asked the doctor whether she was sure and three times she'd told her the test was conclusive. It wasn't stress that had caused her sudden bouts of nausea and dizziness. It was pregnancy. Now, standing in the kitchen, shoes and coat still on and handbag still over her shoulder, a cry of apprehension and delight, escaped her. The thrill of it all made her heart pound. She pressed a hand against her chest, willing herself to remain calm. She didn't want to do anything to harm her baby.

Her baby.

Was she really going to be a mum, after all these years of believing she never would? And Shay a father? A wave of panic washed over her, just as it had every other minute from the moment she'd found out she was carrying Shay's child. How would he take the news? Was she about to make him the happiest man alive or ruin their relationship all over again just as things were so wonderful?

And it really had been wonderful. Even with the embarrassing near-fainting episode, their night together at *Divine* had been nothing short of, well, divine. The bubble that had surrounded them as they lay wrapped in each other's arms on the bed, still hadn't burst. In the last two weeks, the time she waited to get her appointment at the doctor's, they'd talked, laughed and cooked together, and made love every night – plus most mornings. It had been like a romantic fantasy playing out in real life. There had been no more talk of her moving away. She hadn't even thought about it. She was still relying on him for a roof over her head, yes, but it felt now more like they were equals; that they had something to offer each other.

She still craved financial independence, although now, with things between them being as they were, she was feeling a lot more positive about the future and was certain it was just a matter of time before the right job came along.

She was glad she'd noticed on her way back to the farmhouse that the tractor was down by the greenhouses. It meant Shay was still busy working. She needed to gather herself together – think things through before she told him the news. Would he be delighted? Disappointed? Would he feel anything at all? Their love for each other was so real, so palpable that she felt it every time his eyes fell on her. But the comment he'd made previously, about never being able to face being a father again, had he really meant it, or would the reality of his child being inside her make everything different?

She had to tell him, as soon as possible. Maybe she should test the water before she came out with it – somehow try to find out whether his opinion on having a family had changed? Oh God, her head was a complete mess – a mush of delirious happiness, bewilderment and apprehension at what Shay would make of it all.

Shay smiled at her sexily, lazily, as he watched her undress. His smile faded when she couldn't manage a return smile. 'Are you okay?' You've been a million miles away all evening. Was it something the doctor said? Was it really just tiredness that's causing your light-headedness?' He propped himself up on his elbow as she slid into bed, naked, beside him. 'There isn't something you're not telling me, is there?'

She snuggled her back against him and he wrapped an

arm around her. Was this it? Her perfect opportunity to tell him about the baby? She opened her mouth to do so but found she couldn't find the words. Her unspoken confession came out in a rush of air that she fashioned into a yawn so as not to arouse his suspicion. 'Don't be silly,' she said. 'I'm just tired, that's all.'

He dropped a kiss onto her shoulder and stroked his hand lightly over her arm. 'I noticed you haven't been sleeping well lately. If anything's bothering you, you would tell me, wouldn't you?'

I wish it were that easy. She turned her head towards him. 'Course,' she said, forcing a smile. 'I'm probably just worried about what the results of the environment department's test will show. I've got everything crossed that that thing we saw was a Great Crested Newt. I just wish I could be sure.'

He lay his head down on the pillow and hugged her to him. 'Time will tell. Try not to let it bother you.'

'Shay,' she said after a few moments of laying with her eyes still wide open.

'Yeah?' His response was groggy, as if she'd pulled him from the precipice of sleep.

'Could you ever ... could you ever see yourself being a dad again?'

His silence made her regret her words instantly. How insensitive of her to ask such a question given everything he'd been through with Elsie. She hated herself for phrasing it like that, but she needed to know. For both their sake.

'What?' he said, eventually and still sleep-drunk. 'No, no, sweetheart. I couldn't go through that again, you know that. It'd be more than I could take.'

Her stomach turned over. There she had it. All the proof she needed that having another baby would as good as kill him. She couldn't do it to him, not after the tragedy that had befallen him and how he'd somehow managed to drag himself from rock bottom. Who knows – perhaps telling him her news would send him on a downward spiral and this time it might be one he couldn't get out of. That wouldn't help him, her or their baby.

His breathing slowed and grew heavy, indicating he was asleep. His arm slipped from her waist to her lower belly. Unbeknown to him, his unborn baby was snuggled beneath his embrace. She sniffed as quietly as she could as tears leaked from her eyes and soaked into her pillow. Despite it being the last thing she wanted, she couldn't burden him with the prospect of another child and the responsibility that would bring and there was no way she wasn't having this baby. She had no choice but to go and leave him be. She'd make her move tomorrow. She had to. For all of them.

Shay was hot and sticky when he finally came into the farmhouse after a day in the greenhouses. The weather was warming up now and The Elsie flowers were thriving. He could have worked another couple of hours, there was so much to do, but he promised himself he'd finish early so he could make a special meal for him and Sarah. She'd been looking so tired and bothered recently that she needed a treat – an evening of complete relaxation. He'd give her a massage after dinner to help take her mind off that blasted newt. They should find out soon whether it really was a Great Crested Newt they'd seen that day and whether that meant the bypass couldn't go ahead. He sincerely hoped so. Not only would that mean he and the other villagers whose homes were in jeopardy could breathe again, it also meant he could spread the word about how Sarah had saved the day. He knew how bad she felt about her involvement with LJ Networks. Winning the villagers' approval and forgiveness would mean the world to her.

Funny to think how so much hung on one tiny creature. There was the future of the village of course, but also the effect the anticipation was having on Sarah. He could hardly believe the change in her, and it had come almost overnight, probably because they'd know for sure any day soon. Even if the outcome wasn't what they were hoping for, at least it would offer Sarah some closure.

And she had been acting strangely last night, he thought. Worry niggled him. He hadn't expected the question she'd posed out of the blue about whether he could see himself being a father again. She'd asked it when he'd been half asleep and when he woke up in the morning, he thought at first he'd dreamt it, but once his brain de-fogged he'd realised he hadn't.

He'd been so groggy, he couldn't quite remember how he'd responded – something like he didn't want to go through that again. And that was true. He had no intention of becoming a father again. How could he, anyway? Sarah couldn't have children and he was resolute that she was the woman he wanted, so it was academic. If he'd been more alert, he would have explained more eloquently that she was all he needed to make him happy.

It had struck him as strange at first that she'd even asked. He knew she couldn't have children, so why ask it? When he'd been watering the plants this morning he'd toyed it over in his mind, and come to the conclusion that she'd asked because she was concerned he wanted more than she could give him. He'd clarify tonight over dinner that he had everything he needed in her, and just her.

'Sarah!' he called loudly enough for her to hear him wherever she happened to be in the house. 'I'm back in. Fancy a glass of wine?'

When there was no answer he called again.

Hmm, that's odd, he thought. She normally came to greet him with a lovely, welcoming hug every day after work, unless she happened to be out at an interview. She hadn't mentioned having any lined up today, so he'd assumed she would be in.

He was about to kick off his boots and head upstairs to see if he could find her when he noticed a piece of paper folded up on the otherwise clear kitchen table. That definitely hadn't been there this morning.

For no reason, other than pure gut instinct, he knew the words on that paper were destined to bring pain. He snatched it up and his eyes raced over the neat handwriting.

Dear Shay,

I am so sorry to tell you like this. I hope you forgive me and can understand why it's for the best. I am pregnant. I know it must come as a huge shock. It did to me too. I didn't believe I could ever have children, but the doctor says the test is 100% positive.

You have always been honest with me about the fact you don't want to have any more children. Do you know something – I don't blame you. I know what you went through was horrendous and I can see – I really can – why you've made that choice, and I respect you for it.

The thing is though, Shay, I do want to have this baby. I want it with all my heart. Having been told I'd never be a mum, I can hardly believe how blessed I am.

I wish, my goodness, I really do, that I could have it all – you and our baby, but I realise that cannot happen. I couldn't face having this conversation with you. It would be far too upsetting for both of us, which is why I've written this note. I'm sure you'll understand why I want to give our baby the best life possible and, although it's been the hardest decision I've ever had to make, that means a life with a single mother who really wants him or her, over a life with both of us, when having another child would cause you a distress you don't deserve and never asked for.

To save you from the heartache of having to ask me to leave, I've taken the decision out of your hands, and taken it upon myself to go. I love you so much, Shay, and I'll always miss you. I just hope in time you can see why I've taken this option.

Please don't worry about me. I've found somewhere to stay where the baby and I will be comfortable. And please don't try to find me. It would just make things worse. It's taken all the strength I've got to pack a bag and go, hopefully causing you minimum disruption. I know you'll hate me when you read this note, for not telling you in person and taking the coward's way out, but I hope that in time you'll see it was the best and only way for all of us.

With love always,
Sarah xxx

He paced the length of the kitchen over and over, raking his hand through his hair as he tried to take in what he'd just read. Did she really believe he'd turn her away when he found out she was pregnant? Did she actually believe their baby was better off without him in his or her life? And the biggest question of all – was she right?

Feeling as if the bottom had just fallen out of his world, he dropped himself down onto one of the kitchen chairs with a thud and stared at her note still clutched in his hand. Was it true that she believed her leaving would protect him from feelings of distress, as she put it? Because if so, she couldn't be more wrong. Knowing she was gone, with their tiny baby growing inside her, tore his heart to shreds. Or, was the real reason that she didn't think him fit to be a father? After what he'd let happen to precious, innocent Elsie, why would she trust him with her own child?

He recalled he had once shot his mouth off and said something to her about never wanting to be a dad again. No wonder therefore that she'd been too scared to tell him about the baby. But that was then and this is now. Knowing there actually was a baby changed everything entirely.

He scrunched the letter up and held it tightly in his fist, a dilemma of the most sickening kind racing through his head. Should he find her, convince her she was wrong about him wanting the baby – because she *was* wrong – he wanted them both. More than anything. Or should he respect her decision and do what she asked by not trying to find her? He wasn't a good father, he'd already proved that in his monumental error. Wouldn't it in that case be better for Sarah and the baby to leave them be, and not risk screwing things up for another woman and child he loved?

Chapter Sixteen

Shay snapped on his living room wall light and practically fell down onto this old armchair, exhausted through thinking. In the hour since he'd learned that Sarah had walked out of his life, his mind had been plagued with nothing else other than what he ought to do – or not do – for the benefit of Sarah and the baby.

He stared at the light on the wall until his eyes burned. He squeezed them shut, but a bright orange blob still bobbed inside his lids. *You can't just shut out the world and expect everything that makes you uncomfortable to disappear.*

He flicked his eyes open. The light still glowed. Nothing had changed. Sarah was still gone.

With a loud groan of frustration he sprang up, walked across the room and thumped the light switch off. He pushed his fingers through his tangled hair and hung his head. That's when he caught a glint of something white on the floor, highlighted by the light shining into the room from the sinking sun outside.

He bent down to pick it up, and ran his thumb over its smooth surface. It took him just a second to work out it was a piece of the ceramic tile on which Elsie's footprint had been. His throat dried as his mind flashed back to the night he'd flung it against the wall and it had shattered into tiny pieces. The only reminder he'd had of his little girl.

He turned the piece of tile over in his hand. *Daddy.* That one word on the single surviving fragment was perfectly intact. He recalled the message that had been on the tile. It was a message he'd never forget.

To the best daddy in the world
I love you

Best daddy in the world? Nothing could be further from the truth. The woman he loved couldn't even tell him in person she was carrying his baby. Now she was God knows where, growing their baby in her body without any support from him; pondering the prospect of giving birth alone and planning to bring up another human being without him playing a part. And here he was, sat wondering what to do for the best.

As if a light switched in his brain, he realised the impact of what he'd done, and what he had to do. If it wasn't already too late.

He tipped his head back, looked up at the ceiling and clutched the tiny piece of tile to his chest. 'Thank you, Elsie, sweetheart,' he said through tear-blurred eyes. 'Thank you for giving me the one message that I really, really needed right now.'

He ran to the kitchen and snatched his Land Rover key from the table. Just as he reached the front door, he realised he didn't know where Sarah was. He knew better than to call her. She wouldn't pick up. She'd been adamant she didn't want to be found. Well, to hell with that. He'd find her if it was the last thing he did. He racked his brain. Where to even start looking?

'Julie!' He shouted into thin air. Sarah had mentioned on a few occasions before it had come out she worked for LJ Networks that she'd met Julie Flynn for a coffee. They seemed quite friendly, at least until Julie, like the rest of the village, realised what Sarah was really doing in Wetherstone. He didn't know if Julie was even still talking to Sarah after that, but there was only one way to find out. Three calls to three different villagers later he found someone who had Julie's number.

It took some serious persuading to convince Julie to reveal any details about Sarah's whereabouts, and only when he was on the brink of either yelling at her down the phone or breaking into tears did she finally relent. She must have heard the desperation in his voice. After scribbling the details down, he thanked her and ended the call. It wasn't a specific home address. Other than knowing Sarah was staying somewhere north of the city, Julie didn't have that, but at least she knew a key nugget of information that would give Shay a window of opportunity to find her – that tomorrow Sarah had a job interview in the city at 9 a.m.

There wasn't anything he could do now other than wait and pray that when he found her, she'd listen.

Chapter Seventeen

Sarah pushed the bowl of pasta away. She'd only had a few mouthfuls of the spaghetti bolognese, her go-to comfort food, but even that tasted no better than cardboard.

'Don't worry, little one,' she said, hugging her tummy. 'I'll get my appetite back soon, I'm sure.' Would she, though? Since walking out on Shay earlier that day, she hadn't touched a morsel of food. Pregnancy-related nausea, perhaps, or was it another kind of sickness?

She glanced over at Clive, laying on the window ledge. With squinted eyes and drooping whiskers, he looked as miserable as she felt. 'Come over here, you,' she said, patting her lap. Clive stretched out his front legs and yawned before jumping down from the ledge and strolling over to her.

'You and I need to stick together,' she said as he jumped up into her lap. She looked around at the bijou living room of the flat. All her furniture had been lost in the fire so she had been lucky to find a flat, last minute, that was furnished, even though right now she felt like a stranger in it.

'Plenty of time to make it feel like home, Clive,' she said. 'But it'll have to do for now. Once I've managed to save up for a few months, I'll make it nicer for us, just you wait and see.'

The cat, who still hadn't settled down on her lap, stood on her thighs, his paws digging into her flesh, and stared at her with glassy green eyes.

'I know,' she said, stroking his head. 'You miss Bess, don't you? I thought you hated each other, but you haven't been yourself since we left the farm. Can't live with her, can't live without her? I know that feeling.'

Clive licked his lips, lay down on her lap and closed his eyes.

'Tell me I did the right thing today ... leaving Shay,' she said, absentmindedly stroking Clive's back.

He didn't respond. Not even a purr.

She'd hesitated so many times when packing her bags this morning. She'd even turned her Mini around twice and started heading back to Wetherstone before thinking better of it and driving out of the village. Being without Shay hurt now, it hurt so much, but it would get more bearable with time, she told herself. And even if it didn't, what mattered most was that this was the right thing for her baby.

But was it the right thing? The worm of doubt burrowed into her skull, wriggling away until her head throbbed. Had she made the decision for the right reason, or in some warped way was she trying to prove to herself – and to the spirit of her mother – that she could do this on her own?

'Oh, God, I don't know!' she wailed, covering her face with her palms.

She imagined Shay's face as he read the note she'd left him, and she began to cry. 'I did it to protect you, Shay,' she sobbed, even though only Clive could hear. 'Please understand, I did it to protect you.'

As much as she tried to tell herself it was for the best, she couldn't help but question whether she might just have made the biggest mistake of her life in ripping Shay's heart out all over again – the one thing she wanted to avoid.

She sniffed, holding back any more tears. She had an interview to be at first thing tomorrow. Turning up with a puffy, red face wouldn't help her chances and she needed this job more than ever now she'd soon have two mouths to feed. On top of rent to pay. 'It's too late, anyway,' she told a now purring Clive. 'It's too late to turn back.'

Sarah saw the row of red brake lights ahead, ground her car to a halt and sighed. 'Great,' she said to herself, praying she wouldn't be late for her interview. 'Not the start to my day I was hoping for.'

When the queue of traffic didn't budge for over five minutes, horns began to sound, and some drivers got out of their cars, craning their necks to try to see what was causing the hold-up. A crowd of them gathered by the car in front of hers. There were a lot of hands on hips, pointing and confused faces.

One of the drivers, a man in a suit and tie, left the group, shaking his head. As he walked past Sarah's car, she wound down her window. 'Excuse me,' she said. 'Do you know what the problem is?'

'Yeah. It's some moron in a tractor refusing to budge.'

'What? What's he doing out in the middle of rush hour?'

'Search me. A nut job probably. Someone's called the police, apparently.'

'Oh good, okay. Thanks.'

The man nodded and continued to walk to his car.

She was winding her window back up ... when the sudden pang of hope hit her in the chest. *No. It couldn't be, could it?*

She unclipped her seatbelt, fumbled for her car door handle, flung the door open and leaned out. 'Sorry, one more thing.'

The man turned around.

'Did you happen to see what he looks like? The man in the tractor, I mean.'

'Big bloke. Stubbly. Looks like he's slept in a field all night.'

Oh God. 'Oh right. Thanks.'

She turned her head to look in the direction of the hold-up. She couldn't see a tractor from where she was, but did see something else that made her catch her breath. There, just yards away, walking towards her, practically eclipsing the low morning sun, was a tall, broad-shouldered man in long beige shorts and a white T-shirt. Typically, he was wearing far too few clothes for the chilly spring morning.

'Shay,' she whispered, and leaned against her car to stop herself from falling over.

He strode past the perplexed commuters, ignoring their stares, and only stopped when he was directly in front of her.

'Sarah. I know I let you down so very, very badly. You *and* our baby. And I don't blame you for leaving.'

'Let us down?' Her voice shook. 'How?'

'By letting you think I wouldn't want to be a father again.'

She opened her mouth to speak, but he held up his hand. 'Please. Just hear me out. When you said I blamed myself for what happened to Clodagh and Elsie, you were right. I've decided it's time to take your advice and get some help.'

'I'm pleased.'

'But that doesn't mean I don't want to be a father to our child. There's nothing I want more. I love you, Sarah. I love you more than anything on earth.' He took her hands in his.

'Shay—'

'Sarah. Every part of me loves every part of you. I want you and I want our baby in my life. I want to look after you both; protect you in every way I can. And I want more babies if we're lucky enough to have them. I'll even put up with your annoying, tree-climbing, dog-hating cat if it means you'll move back in with me.'

She smiled through her tear-filled eyes. 'I'm so sorry. I really, really wish I'd have talked to you about it. I just didn't want to make things hard for you. You'd already suffered so much and I couldn't bear to make things worse.'

'Just tell me you'll reconsider – that you'll come back.' His face crumpled into the most desperate expression of torment she had ever seen, and her heart reached out to him. Now she knew how he really felt, she couldn't believe she'd thought otherwise.

'Of course I'll come back,' she said, tears running freely down her cheeks. 'I love you too.'

He covered his face with his palms and made a noise, somewhere between a shout of joy and a sob.

She joined in with him, laughing and crying at the same time, and pulled his hands away from his face to reveal tears streaking down his tanned skin.

He wrapped his arms around her, squeezed her close to him, and buried his head in her hair. 'You don't know how much it means to me to hear you say that.'

His voice was muffled, but she savoured every word. 'Oh, I think I do.'

He lifted his head back up and stroked a tear from her cheek. 'I'll never let you down, you know, Sarah. Not you or our baby. I promise.'

Our baby. The way he said those words was so beautiful it made her womb contract. He brushed a loose hair out of her face and looked at her so tenderly she thought she might melt in his arms. 'I know you won't. Because you're going to be the best daddy in the world.'

A smile stretched across his face. A smile so wide she thought his cheeks would split. 'Do you think so?'

'I know so.'

He leaned against her car, the smile still glued to his face. The sight of such a big man against her Mini was so comical, she couldn't help but laugh.

'Have you finished yet, or what, mate?'

She spun around to see the driver of the car behind hers hanging out of his window. She let out a laugh. She'd almost forgotten Shay had stopped traffic.

'No, mate,' Shay shouted back. 'I haven't finished.' He stood up straight, wrapped her in his arms and pressed his mouth against hers. The salty taste of tears mingled in their kiss as drops of them – a mix of his and hers – fell to their lips. 'I love you so much,' he said when he finally released her. The love in his eyes seeped through her every pore and warmed her insides.

Her mum's greatest wish was for her to be part of a family. *'Imagine how wonderful life will be then,'* she used to say.

While Cherrie Pickering had been the only parent Sarah had ever needed, she was right about one thing – being part of this family, her own family – was wonderful. And no longer did she just have to imagine.

Chapter Eighteen

Sarah bumped her Mini up the lane towards McGillen's Farm. Her first day as receptionist at a firm of city accountants had gone well. Not just in terms of work and getting along with her new colleagues, but also how being back in the city had barely phased her at all. It was her first trip back to the centre of York since her night at *Divine* with Shay last month and she was relieved at how being back within the city walls had actually offered her comfort rather than leaving her feeling vulnerable. Despite that, it was still a joy to return to the country. She was starting to feel more like she belonged there than she'd ever thought possible when she'd first arrived. She laughed when she thought back to her grossly inadequate footwear and how she'd jumped in fright at the sound of wild animals. How quickly things changed.

The beautiful old farmhouse came into view with its white frontage and crisscrossed windows, and her fingers started to tingle with the same buzz she'd experienced every time she returned home. *Home*. Her heart filled with joy as she thought about McGillen's Farm in those terms. No longer was it just a building in which a kind man had offered her refuge. It was where their love for each other blossomed by the day, and where they'd soon be bringing up their child.

She tapped her fingers on the steering wheel to the beat of the tinny music from the car radio, enjoying the sense of contentment. She parked up, silenced the ignition and gathered her handbag from the passenger seat, noticing how the wonderful tingle spread up her arms and into her chest.

She smiled at the thought that in a moment, when she opened the door into the warm, welcoming kitchen, Shay would be there as he'd promised he would be, pouring her a chilled glass of wine while he prepared one of his delicious home-made dinners, this time in celebration of her first day at work.

But when she opened the door there was only silence. No mouth-watering smells of frying garlic or herbs. No frosted glass of wine. No Shay.

'Hello?' she called out, expecting at least to hear the thumping of Bess's paws as she thundered down the stairs, or even the lighter steps of Clive if he could be bothered to trouble himself. Nothing. She called again, but the only sound was the faint hum of the fridge.

Odd. It was gone six and although the spring evening was still light, she would have expected Shay to have come in from the farm by now to find out how she got on. An uneasy sense of foreboding struck her. Had something happened? Was it all too good to be true? Had he changed his mind about them being a family?

Her heart drummed in her chest as she looked across the kitchen to the window. She hoped to see the figure of Shay in one of the greenhouses, but what she saw made her gasp. 'What the—?' Blocking the view of the greenhouse was a huge white marquee. 'What's going on?' she muttered to herself. 'That wasn't there this morning.'

She stepped back outside and went over to the marquee. There wasn't a sound coming from the huge tent. Walking as best she could on tiptoes to avoid her heels sinking into the grass, she reached the canvas flap of the door and peered inside.

'*SURPRISE!*'

The burst of a welcome almost made her fall backwards. One by one, she started recognising individuals in the crowd of beaming faces. Julie, Shareen, Barb, George, Tim, Tom, and Mrs Grey and her grandson, plus tens of others she'd visited, and who had looked at her in a very different way that evening in the village hall to how they were looking at her now.

'Oh my goodness. What's going on?' she sputtered as the crowd made its way over to her and she was kissed, hugged and congratulated like a celebrity.

'Shay invited everyone in the village up here tonight for a little party,' Barb said in-between kissing both her cheeks. 'He's even checked Bess and Clive into a pet hotel for the night so they didn't get scared by all the noise.'

As soon as Barb said it, music began to boom out over huge speakers in the corners of the marquee.

'Wh-why?'

Barb grabbed her elbows and smiled a big, pink-lipsticked smile. 'Don't you know?'

Sarah shook her head.

Barb threw her head back and laughed, her huge dangly earrings swinging wildly. 'Because you saved the village, love. You saved our homes, businesses and families from that stupid road. You deserve a fuss!'

Before Sarah could respond, the next person was hugging her.

'Clever girl.' George's voice was doddery, but his embrace surprisingly firm.

'Am I?'

'Aye, of course. Spotting the Great Crested Newt and telling those suited city idiots to sling their hook. Genius.'

'So it was a Great Crested Newt? And they confirmed the bypass can't be built?'

'Absolutely, my dear. We all got the news in the post today that they're building an alternative road that doesn't affect Wetherstone or any other village for that matter, and it's all thanks to you.'

'Oh no, not really. I don't actually know much at all about wildlife. It was more of a lucky gue—'

George cut her off. 'Well, let me tell you, the Great Crested Newt, otherwise known as the Warty Newt, is a fascinating species of amphibian. Its favoured habitat for—'

'Oh George, do stop boring the poor girl. She's here to enjoy herself.'

George's eyes lit up as Mrs Grey barged in front of him. 'Sarah, I must say how delighted we were to hear the plans for the bypass have been cancelled, and all because of your remarkable bravery.'

Mrs Grey pulled Sarah to her ample bosom for a bear hug.

'We're so glad you're not working for that horrid company anymore, aren't we, Jude?'

Once released from the suffocating embrace, Sarah smiled at the lank, spotty youth by Mrs Grey's side. At his grandmother's mention of his name, Jude instantly turned a shade of beetroot. 'Yeah. We're well pleased.'

Sarah smiled. Despite his obvious embarrassment, she could tell Jude meant it. And getting more than a grunt out of a seventeen-year-old boy felt like very high praise indeed.

'See.' Mrs Grey gave a single, resolute nod as if her grandson's agreement meant the world. 'I said, Jude, didn't I? I said, when Sarah came to see us that day, she seemed far too nice a woman to have been working on such an unethical project. I knew you'd soon see sense, and I was right, wasn't I? I was right.'

'A-hem.' George, who had remained close to Mrs Grey, coughed and offered the old lady his arm. 'Might I say, you're looking particularly radiant this evening, Doris. Would you do me the honour of allowing me to get you a drink?'

Mrs Grey turned her attention to George and smiled. 'Well, don't mind if I do, George. Come along now, Jude.'

The youngster dutifully followed his grandmother and George to a table at one end of the marquee on top of which bottles of wine, spirits and beer sat along with towers of stacked paper cups.

'Am I forgiven?'

Sarah turned to the direction of the familiar voice to see Julie had sidled up beside her. 'Whatever for?' she asked.

'For breaking a tiny weeny part of my promise and giving Shay a clue as to how to find you.'

Sarah laughed. 'Technically, you didn't break it. You didn't give him my address even though you knew it. It was thanks to you and your lettings agent contact I got that flat as soon as I did. Thanks for helping me out, Julie. I didn't exactly deserve your help, not after lying to you like I did. I'm so sorry.'

'Stop apologising,' insisted Julie. 'You've done enough of that already – and from your hospital bed. I can't believe your first thought after nearly burning to a crisp was to ring around all the villagers to say you were sorry. You had nothing to be sorry about. You were just doing your job. Anyway,' she grinned. 'It's important us girls stick together.' Her grin faltered. 'Seriously, though, *do* you forgive me?'

'Forgive you?' Sarah almost spat out her drink. 'If you hadn't given Shay some sort of clue as to where I was staying and the fact I'd be travelling into the city first thing, I might not be standing here now. If anything, I owe you one.'

Julie's eyes sparkled. 'In that case, the mother-in-law's due to come round next week and has put in a special request for your mum's sausage casserole. I'm sure I'd make a total mess of it. Fancy coming round to help me out? Bring Shay this time and stay for dinner. I'll even confess that you did the cooking.'

'It's a deal,' Sarah said.

A half hour later, Sarah was still being greeted by a constant stream of villagers, all full of praise for her actions.

'Excuse me one moment.' The deep, Irish lilt directed at the latest well-wisher came from behind her.

She spun around and looked up at him, catching her breath as she took him in. He wore his hair in an uncharacteristically neat style, with the front swept back for a modern look. For only the second time since she'd first met him, he was clean shaven. The neat, fresh look suited him, showing off even more of his natural tan and angular jaw, and making him appear much younger.

'Wow, look at you!' she said, wrapping her arms around his firm waist and hugging him.

'Hi.' He planted a kiss on her forehead, causing her insides to perform a happy little jig. 'How did your first day go?'

She laughed. 'Perfectly well. I'll tell you all about it later. What's all this?' She gestured to their surroundings.

He grinned. 'A little celebration in your honour to show you how much you mean to all of us. Especially me.'

She rested her chin on his chest and looked up at him. 'I can't believe you organised all this for me. And without me knowing. You sure kept that quiet.'

'I was worried if I told you I'd invited everyone up here to celebrate how amazing you are, you might turn straight back to the city and never come back.'

Her heart bloomed. He'd done all this for her.

'I know you hated thinking you'd upset everyone in the village,' he continued. 'But just look around. They love you, Sarah. And so they should. They've got you to thank for them being able to stay in the area they love.'

'I'm not sure about that. I was the one who caused the problem in the first place, if you remember.'

His gorgeous dark blue eyes bore into her, scorching holes into her soul. 'Not you, Sarah.'

God, she loved the way he said her name, making it sound like the most beautiful word on the planet.

'You were only doing your job. You didn't know the impact your work had until you came here.'

She tipped her head to the side as if contemplating his point. 'True. But it's not me everyone should be thanking.'

He frowned.

'It's the Great Crested Newt. Otherwise known as the Warty Newt, apparently.'

He pulled a face.

'George told me that interesting fact earlier on.'

'Right. On that subject, I've got something to show you.' He released her from their embrace and took her by the hand, leading her through the partygoers.

'Urgh, it's not your warts is it, because that's something I really don't want to see.'

'No, it's not my warts. Not that I have any. Here. Let me just do this—' He went behind her and put his hands gently over her eyes.

'Oh, what's going on now?'

'You'll see.' He pressed his body against her back and guided her forwards. 'Here we go. You can open your eyes now.' He removed his hands from in front of her eyes and wrapped them around her shoulders.

A huge cake in the shape of a newt lay on the table in front of them. Whoever had made it had gone to a lot of trouble creating each of its spines individually out of coloured icing and its black beady eyes from dark chocolate-covered sweets.

She clapped her hands to her mouth.

Some of the guests must have noticed Shay guiding her to the cake, as a huddle of them had gathered around, and they were laughing and cheering at her reaction.

She spun around to face Shay, whose eyes shone as they met hers. 'I can't believe you've organised all this for me.' Joyful tears slid down her cheeks. She couldn't remember ever feeling this happy before.

'I can't take credit for everything. That chocolate sponge creation, for example.' He held his hands up. 'That definitely wasn't me. My cake-making skills leave a lot to be desired. You've got Jake from Jake's Cakes to thank for that one.'

'I'll be sure to thank him before he goes home tonight. Even so, it must have taken you ages and cost a small fortune to put all this on.'

'You're worth it.' He pulled her in for a long, deep kiss.

There were a few whistles and claps from the crowd before they started chattering between themselves again.

'Shay,' she said, when he finally released her. 'Everyone's going to know that we're, well, you know, together. Does that mean we're making it official?'

He smiled a lopsided smile that was very, very sexy. 'Too right we are. They all know anyway. I've practically been shouting it from the rooftops all night. Haven't told them about the baby, though,' he added, quieter. 'That's our news to share not just mine.'

'Oh, Shay.' She reached up and placed her hand on the side of his face, touched at his thoughtfulness. She stood on tiptoes and pressed her lips onto his.

'How can I ever thank you for doing all this for me?' she whispered. 'You've helped me so much, Shay. You've been so forgiving, so understanding. You've even saved my life. I don't know what I could ever do to repay you for all that.'

He took her hand in his. 'Actually, there is one thing.'

He led her out of the marquee to where a pile of wood was stacked up on the grass.

'Our guests don't look like they'll be ready to go home anytime soon. They're here to party. I figured we'll need some warmth later when the temperature drops.'

He took a lighter out of his pocket, threw it up in the air and caught it again. Then, he bent over the wood, reached his hand inside a gap in the pile and stepped back to stand beside her. Smoke began billowing from the stack.

He reached for her hand. 'You *have* helped me, Sarah. More than you could ever know. A few months ago I'd fly into panic mode if someone so much as lit a candle anywhere near me. With you—' He turned to face her and wrapped his arms around her shoulders, pulling her against him. 'I feel like I can take on the world and win.'

She clung to him and heard the strong, steady beat of

his pulse against her ear. The heat from the bonfire grew in intensity, just like the love pouring from her heart.

'I told you he was into you.'

Sarah grinned at the dark-haired woman who joined her as she piled even more food from the buffet table onto her paper plate – being happy did wonders for the appetite.

'What can I say, Shareen? You were right all along.'

'It's all in the body language.' Shareen tapped the side of her nose. 'It never lies.' She took a swig from her cup. 'I have to say, you make a very attractive couple.'

Sarah blushed.

'Don't be embarrassed, darling,' said Shareen. 'I'm pleased for you. You're both lovely people who are long overdue some happiness.'

'Thanks Shareen. That's sweet of you to say.'

'And do I sense that two will soon be three?'

'What?' Sarah stopped chewing and looked at the brunette.

Shareen gestured towards Sarah's stomach. 'It's obvious. Your posture says it all.'

'Does it?' Sarah, blown away at Shareen's perceptions, looked down at her tummy.

Shareen broke into a smile. 'Not really,' she said. 'I made that rubbish up about posture. It's more to do with the fact you've been stuffing your face full of strips of pepper all night. Either Shay's been starving you or you've got yourself a little craving there.'

'Oh. I guess I must have,' said Sarah, looking down at her plate, which was predominantly a pile of yellow and red strips of raw pepper.

Shareen patted her arm. 'Don't worry, darling. Your secret's safe with me.' She gave Sarah a wink and disappeared off into the crowd.

Sarah smiled at Shareen's retreating back. Didn't miss a

trick, that woman. Her gaze fell onto Shay, who was deep in conversation with the couple who owned the antique shop. He caught her eye and waved. She waved back and grinned. Their baby might be a secret for now, but not for long. And she couldn't wait to tell the world that she was having her hero's child.

Epilogue

Sarah launched at the kitten darting along the mantelpiece, and managed to pick her up just as she reached the photo frames. She peered into the tabby's adorable face. 'Hey you, I've told you before – that's a no-go zone.' She kissed the tiny wet nose and placed the furry bundle on the floor. 'Go and see Clive. He'll teach you how to behave.'

At the mention of the older cat's name, the kitten sprang up to the window ledge and pounced on a sleeping Clive, who opened one eye in complete disinterest at her attempts to play.

Sarah chuckled and picked up the silver photograph frame that had landed face down on the mantel's ledge. 'That was close, Mum. You nearly ended up on the rug again.' She pulled her cardigan sleeve over the heel of her hand, and dusted the glass, then smiled. She hadn't even known the photo existed, not until, thanks to Shay's gentle persuasion, she'd finally worked up the courage to return to the home in York she'd shared with her mum.

With Shay's support, she hadn't had to sell the house, but was happy to rent it out so others could enjoy it, even if that had meant walking back through those doors and cleaning out her belongings. The first step over the threshold had been the hardest, but with Shay holding her hand, she'd done it. It got easier after that, especially when she found some of her mum's possessions that brought back so many happy memories.

Finding the photo had been the highlight of the day. It showed her mum, her head flung back mid-laugh, with shining eyes and an expression of pure joy on her face. She didn't remember the photo being taken, or even who had taken it, but she remembered the very moment. She'd been a young teenager at the time. She and her mum had been guests at a neighbour's wedding and the people they'd been sat with had made them laugh throughout the reception. Her mother, the social creature she was, had cried with laughter at the jokes being told around the table. Sarah's guess was that someone had taken the snap just at the right moment, recognised what a lovely picture it was, and sent it to her mum to treasure.

'Did you ever realise how beautiful you were?' Sarah asked the woman inside the frame.

'Do you realise how beautiful *you* are?'

The deep voice behind Sarah made her jump. She grinned as Shay came up behind her and closed his big arms around her middle. 'Oh, I might be a lot of things, but I'm not sure beautiful's one of them.'

He buried his head into her neck and nuzzled her. 'You're beautiful to me. Every bit of you. Especially this bit.' He kissed the top of her ear, and she laughed. 'And this bit.' He kissed her cheek. 'And did I mention this bit?' He pecked the top of her shoulder.

She slapped his arm gently and giggled. 'Okay, I get it. Now stop, you're tickling me!'

He squeezed her tighter, rested his head on her shoulder and peered at the photo in her hand. 'You have her eyes.'

'Do you think?'

He nodded, and she reached forward to stand the frame back on the mantelpiece next to the photo of Clodagh hugging an excited-looking Elsie in her arms. The mutual love between mother and baby in the photo was clear.

'Now we've had Clodagh and Elsie's photo up here a couple of weeks, how are you finding it?'

She could almost hear his mind whirring as he searched for an answer. 'A comfort,' he said at last.

She smiled and leaned back into him. 'I'm glad.'

'Thank you.'

'What for?' she said in surprise, and turned around within his arms until she was facing him.

'For convincing me that we should go and visit Clodagh's parents.'

She wrapped her arms around his neck. 'You did the hard work. All I did was make the suggestion.'

'You came with me to Ireland. I wouldn't have gone of my own accord. I was worried how they'd react when they heard I'd met someone. It meant the world when they were so accepting of you and little Cherrie. They fell in love with you both straight away, I could see that.'

'And they gave you this gorgeous picture of Clodagh and Elsie.'

He nodded. 'Thank God. I left Ireland so quickly after the accident that I didn't stop to gather any photos of the two of them together. The only thing I had to remember Elsie by was her footprint tile.'

His voice faltered, and she rubbed his upper arms. 'Don't feel bad about breaking it. You have a beautiful photo of your little girl now, and if you hadn't smashed the tile – well, who knows, maybe you wouldn't have come to your senses that you'd let a good thing go.' She batted her eyelashes with comic effect and grinned up at him. 'I know,' he said with a watery smile. 'As much as I hated myself for breaking it, it brought us together.'

'Elsie brought us together.'

'You, me, and Cherrie. I couldn't imagine life without you. I love you both so much.'

'And we love you. More than you could ever know.'

He leaned down to kiss her, just as the jolly and insistent call of *Mummy! Daddy!* came from the floor above.

Shay rested his forehead against hers and laughed. 'I think someone's woken up from her afternoon nap. 'I'll go get her.'

'Okay. Don't take too long. There's something I've been meaning to talk to you about.'

He raised an eyebrow. 'The last time you said that, you were planning to flatten half the village and build a road. It's not that again is it?'

She tutted and gave him another joke slap on the arm. 'No, of course not. You'll find out when you come back down.'

'Oh? Sounds ominous.'

'Not at all. I could do you a favour actually.'

'O-kay. Well, how about I cook dinner, then you can tell me all about it?'

'Sure.'

He turned to leave the room, but just before he reached the door, she blurted it out, unable to keep the secret she'd been dying to tell him any longer. 'I'm pregnant!'

He spun around, his expression serious. For a heart-stopping second, she was transported back two years ago when she'd run away, leaving him with nothing but a note explaining why. Now they were so happy together it seemed such a ridiculous thing to have done, but at the time she'd felt she'd had no other choice to protect the man she loved.

Shay took one single step towards her, then stopped. 'Pregnant?'

She nodded.

'Are you sure?'

'Very sure,' she whispered through dry lips. She thought he'd be pleased but perhaps adding another child to their family, and giving him even more responsibility, was pressing too hard on this man who had experienced so much and still come out fighting. The joy she'd felt since learning Cherrie would soon have a baby brother or sister shattered inside her and lay like lead at the pit of her stomach.

A slow, wide grin spread across his face. He ran to her, picked her up, and spun her around as she squealed, half through delight and half through dizziness.

'That's brilliant news!' He pressed a hard, loud kiss on her lips, then, holding her shoulders he stood at arm's length from her and gazed at her, his eyes shining. 'Do you know how happy you make me?'

Relief washed over her. How could she ever have doubted him? 'If it's as happy as you make me, then I think I've got a pretty good idea.'

'*Mu-mmy! Da-addy!*' came the sing-song voice from upstairs.

She raised her eyes to the ceiling. 'You'd better go get Cherrie-pie. Then we can tell her the good news too.'

Shay didn't move, just stood, holding her, looking into her eyes, the huge smile still fixed on his face.

'Shay ...' She laughed. 'Go get your daughter before she decides she's not in such a good mood, after all.'

He blinked, snapping out of his reverie. 'Right, yes.' He turned, walked to the door, then bounded back to her.

She threw her head back and laughed. 'What are you doing, you crazy man?'

He drew her into a hug and rested his head on top of hers. 'Thank you again,' he said, his expression much more serious.

She circled her arms around his back. 'Whatever for?'

'For giving me my life back. I never thought—I never thought ...'

'It's okay, I know.' She gave him a squeeze.

'You and I have a lot to be grateful for, Mrs McGillen.'

She pulled her head away and looked up at him. 'But I'm not Mrs Mc—' She stopped talking as she realised what he meant.

'Not yet,' he said. 'But you should be.'

'Shay, are you proposing?'

'No, just checking you didn't run a mile when I suggested it.'

She let out a shocked laugh.

'I will be proposing, very soon, but I want to do it properly. Ring, romantic setting, the works.'

A burst of happiness exploded inside her. 'I don't need the works. Just you, Cherrie and …' She placed a hand on her stomach. 'This little one. And for the record – I'd be delighted to be Mrs McGillen.'

'MUMMY! DADDY!'

At Cherrie's insistent shout, Shay darted for the door, then paused and looked back at her. 'I can't wait to marry you, Sarah.'

She didn't have time to respond before he left the room, and she heard his feet thudding up the stairs. Seconds later, he reappeared at the door, with a ruffle-haired two-year old. She'd been through the mill to get to this point in her life, but the sight of her gorgeous man with their daughter in his arms, and the thought of the tiny new life growing inside her, made her realise, not for the first time, just how lucky she was.

Thank You

Dear Reader

I really do hope you enjoyed reading about Sarah and Shay, their romance and adventures. If so, please do hop onto Amazon, or wherever you bought the book, and leave a review. It means so much to us authors (like you wouldn't believe!)

Like most writers, I love to read, especially when there's a happy ending involved. The world isn't always as bright a place as it could be, so there's nothing quite like escaping into a story where they may be ups and downs, but the end is guaranteed to warm your heart.

If you'd like to keep up to date with me and my books, you can find me at facebook.com/ginahollands and tweeting at @ginaholls.

And if you love all things books and writing, you might like to take a look at my blog, www.ginahollands.com.

Take care and thanks for reading.

Gina x

About the Author

Originally from Yorkshire, Gina now lives by the sea in West Sussex with her husband and son. When she's not working in her job in marketing and PR, or writing her latest book, Gina can be found dancing everything from lindy hop to salsa, shopping (she loves clothes far too much for her own good), eating out (she hates cooking far too much for her own good), or relaxing, which generally involves reading a book someone else has written or indulging in her new hobby of learning to play the piano. She has a sneaky suspicion she may be a musical genius in the making, but isn't about to give up the day job just yet.

To find out more about Gina,
follow her on social media:
Twitter: @ginaholls
Facebook: https://www.facebook.com/ginahollands
Blog: www.ginahollands.com

Introducing Choc Lit

We're an independent publisher creating
a delicious selection of fiction.
Where heroes are like chocolate – irresistible!
Quality stories with a romance at the heart.

See our selection here:
www.choc-lit.com

We'd love to hear how you enjoyed *Little Village of Second
Chances*. Please visit **www.choc-lit.com** and give your
feedback or leave a review where you purchased this novel.

Choc Lit novels are selected by genuine readers like yourself.
We only publish stories our Choc Lit Tasting Panel want to
see in print. Our reviews and awards speak for themselves.

Could you be a Star Selector and join our Tasting Panel?
Would you like to play a role in choosing which novels
we decide to publish? Do you enjoy reading women's
fiction? Then you could be perfect for our Tasting Panel.

Visit here for more details…
www.choc-lit.com/join-the-choc-lit-tasting-panel

Keep in touch:
Sign up for our monthly newsletter Spread for all the latest
news and offers: www.spread.choc-lit.com. Follow us
on Twitter: @ChocLituk and Facebook: Choc Lit.

Where heroes are like chocolate – irresistible!